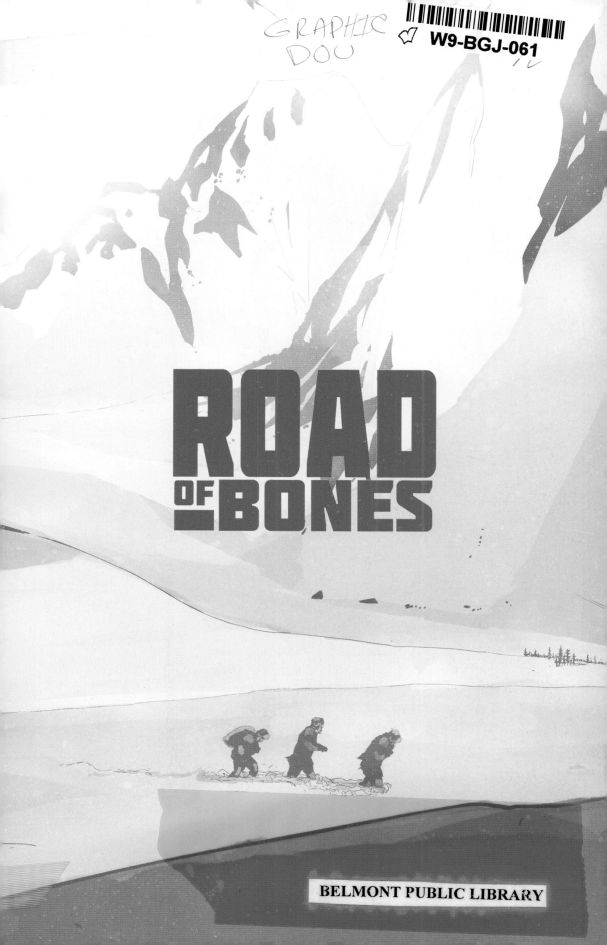

ROAD OF BONES

Facebook: **facebook.com/idwpublishing**
Twitter: **@idwpublishing**
YouTube: **youtube.com/idwpublishing**
Tumblr: **tumblr.idwpublishing.com**
Instagram: **instagram.com/idwpublishing**

ISBN: 978-1-68405-598-2   23 22 21 20   1 2 3 4

Cover Artist
Alex Cormack

Series Edits by
Bobby Curnow

Collection Edits by
**Justin Eisinger &
Alonzo Simon**

Collection Design by
Ron Estevez

Originally published as *Road of Bones* issues #1–4.

Chris Ryall, President, Publisher, & CCO
John Barber, Editor-In-Chief
Cara Morrison, Chief Financial Officer
Matt Ruzicka, Chief Accounting Officer
David Hedgecock, Associate Publisher
Jerry Bennington, VP of New Product Development
Lorelei Bunjes, VP of Digital Services
Justin Eisinger, Editorial Director, Graphic Novels & Collections
Eric Moss, Senior Director, Licensing and Business Development

Ted Adams and Robbie Robbins, IDW Founders

WRITTEN BY **RICH DOUEK**

ART & COLORS BY **ALEX CORMACK**

LETTERS BY **JUSTIN BIRCH**

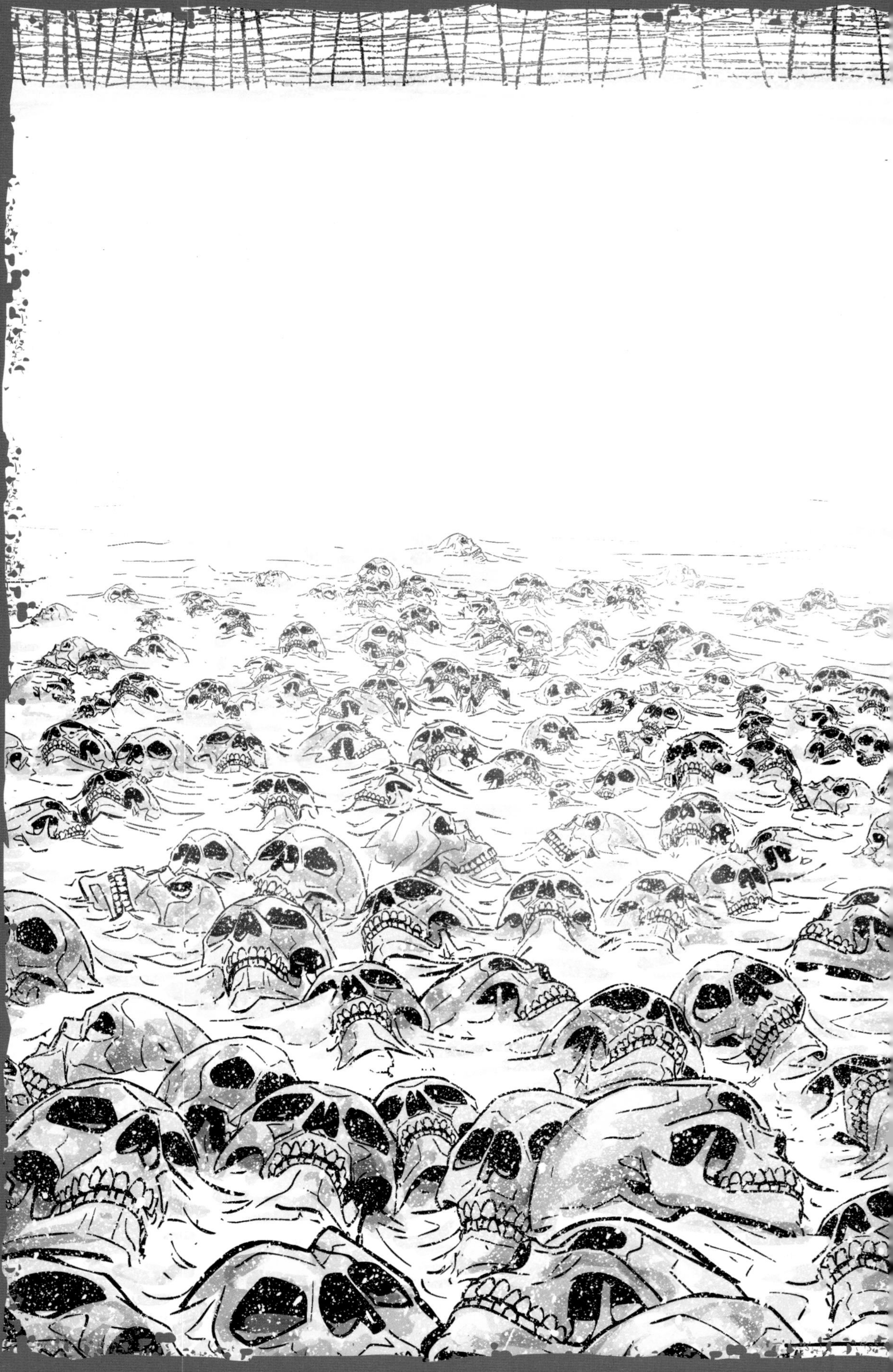

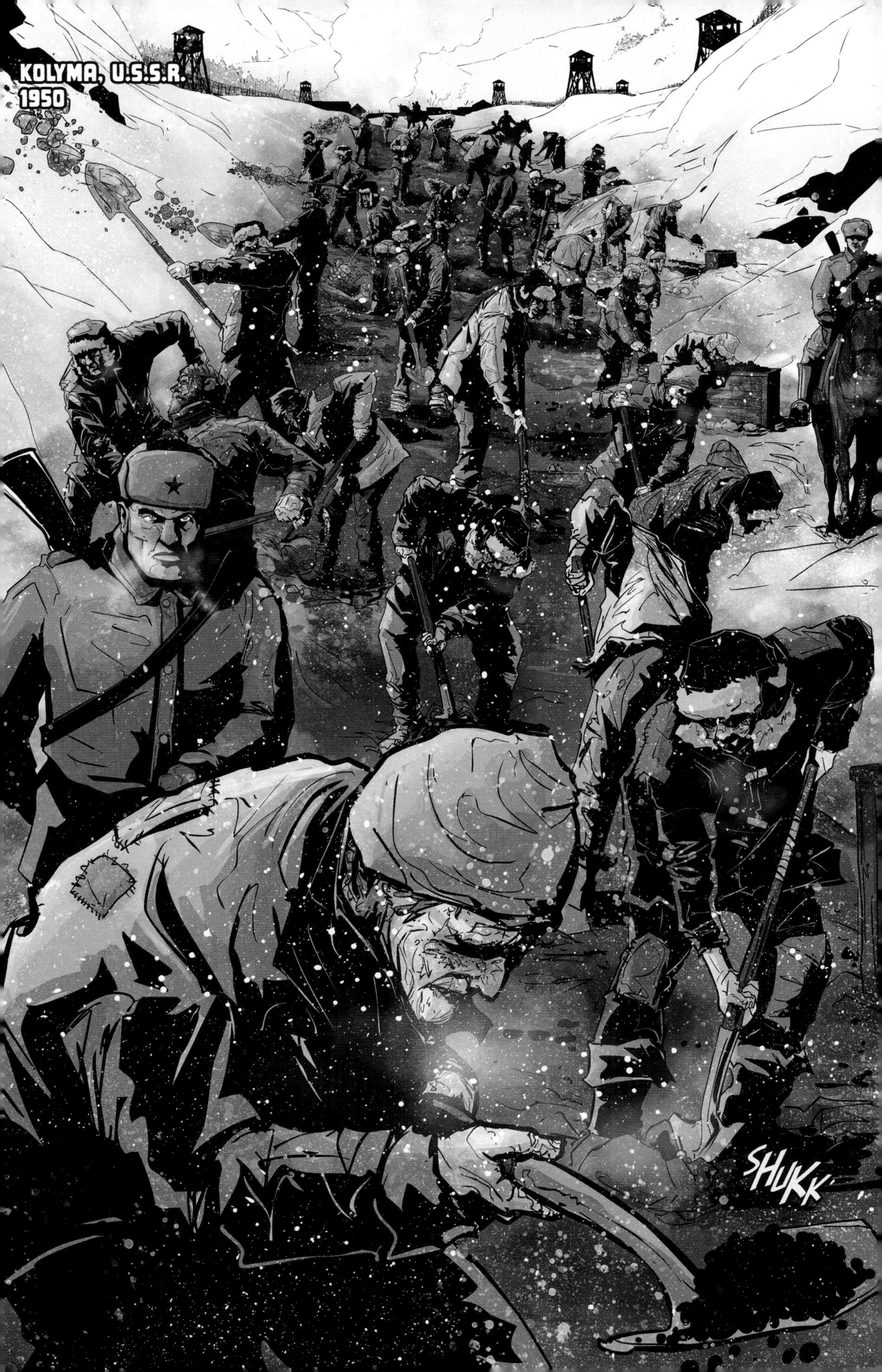
KOLYMA, U.S.S.R.
1950
SHUKK

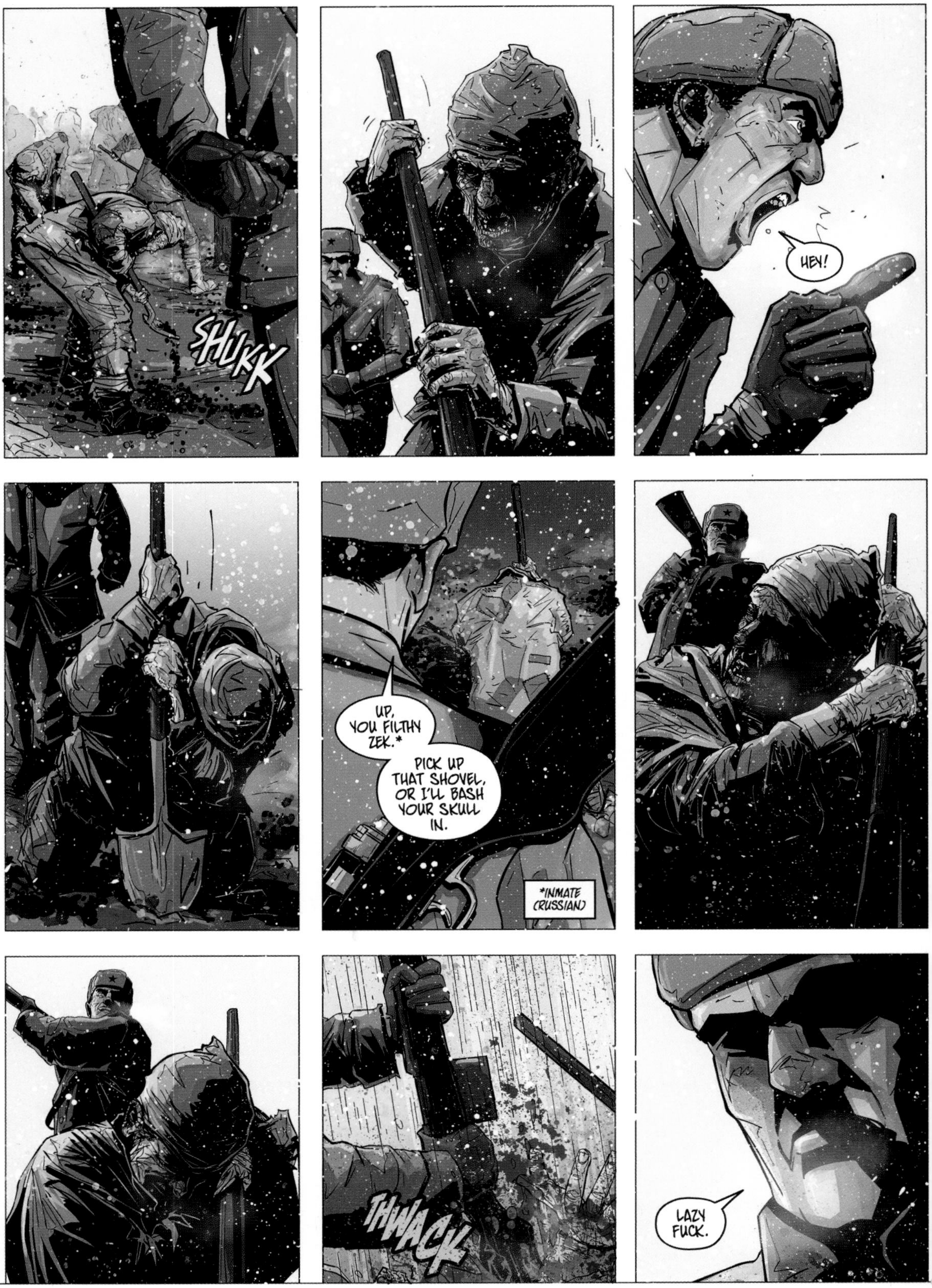
SHUKK
HEY!
UP, YOU FILTHY ZEK.*
PICK UP THAT SHOVEL, OR I'LL BASH YOUR SKULL IN.
*INMATE (RUSSIAN)
THWACK
LAZY FUCK.

WRITER: RICH DOUEK ARTIST: ALEX CORMACK LETTERER: JUSTIN BIRCH

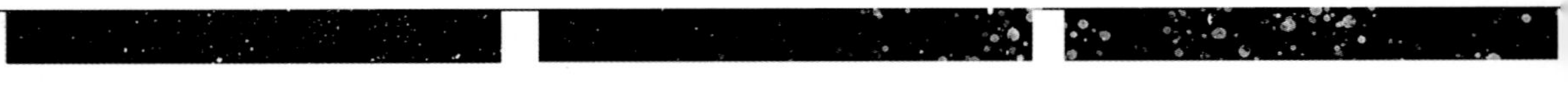

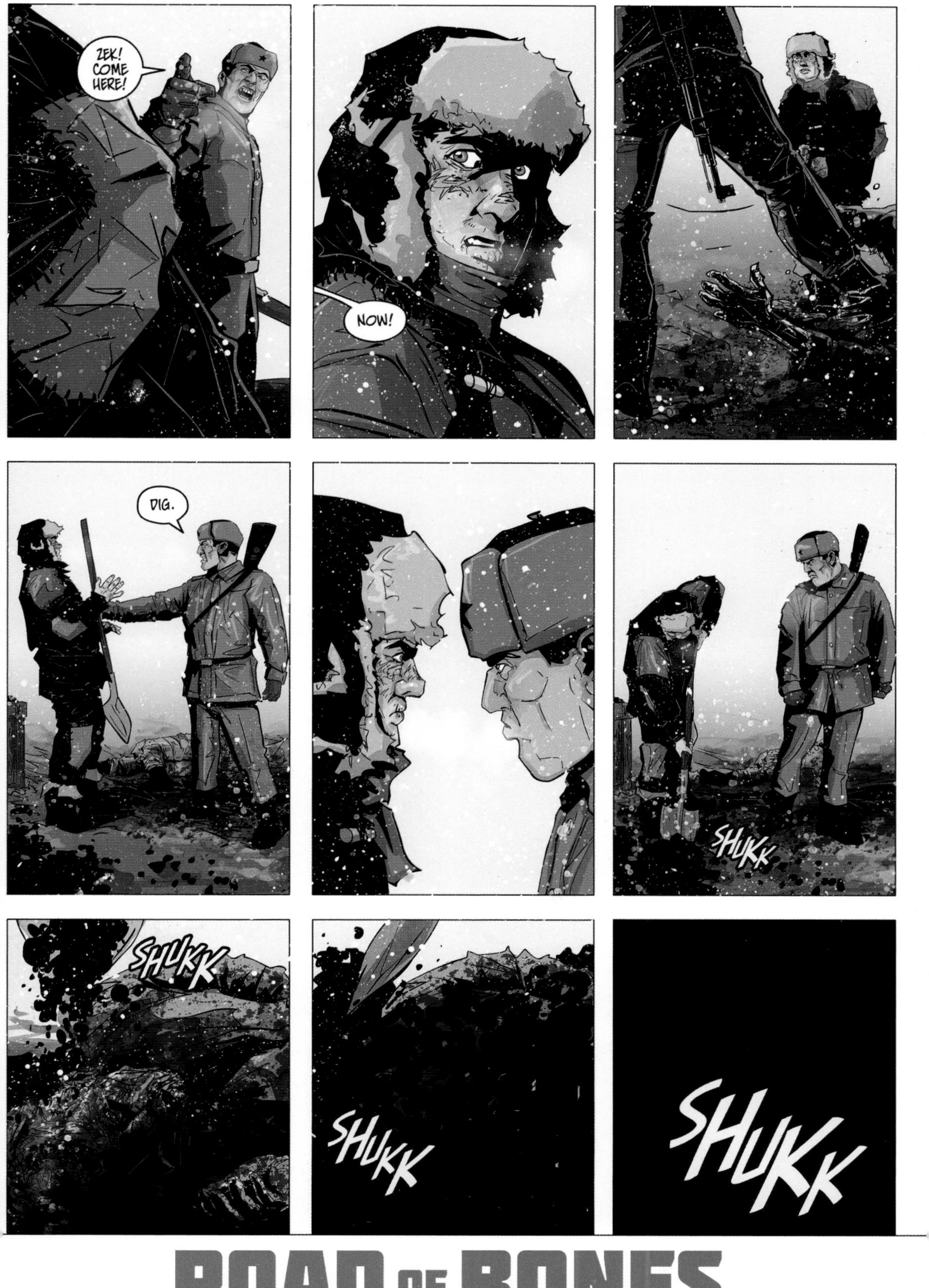
ZEK! COME HERE!
NOW!
DIG.
SHUKK
SHUKK
SHUKK
SHUKK

ROAD OF BONES

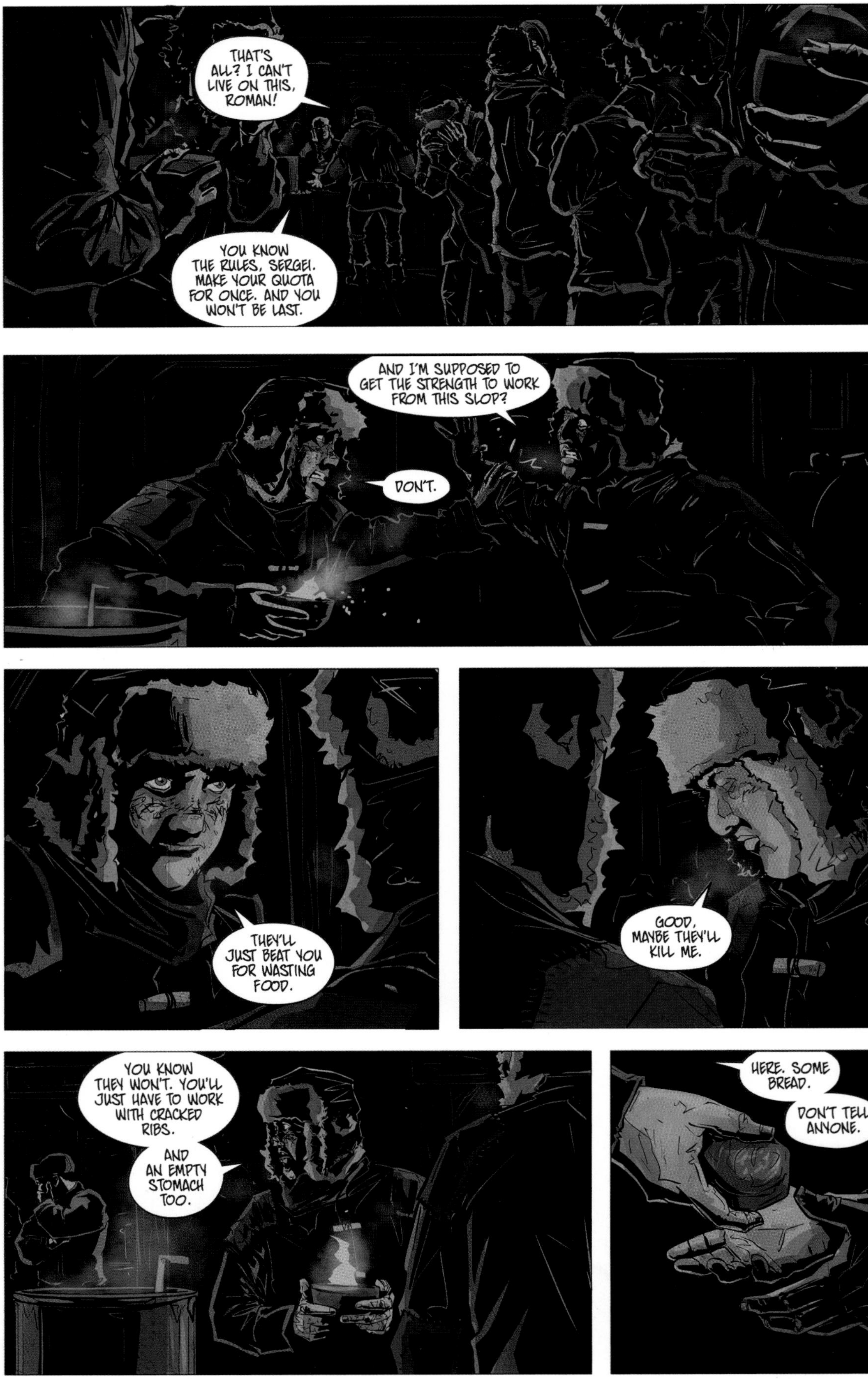
THAT'S ALL? I CAN'T LIVE ON THIS, ROMAN!
YOU KNOW THE RULES, SERGEI. MAKE YOUR QUOTA FOR ONCE. AND YOU WON'T BE LAST.
AND I'M SUPPOSED TO GET THE STRENGTH TO WORK FROM THIS SLOP?
DON'T.
THEY'LL JUST BEAT YOU FOR WASTING FOOD.
GOOD, MAYBE THEY'LL KILL ME.
YOU KNOW THEY WON'T. YOU'LL JUST HAVE TO WORK WITH CRACKED RIBS.
AND AN EMPTY STOMACH TOO.
HERE. SOME BREAD.
DON'T TELL ANYONE.

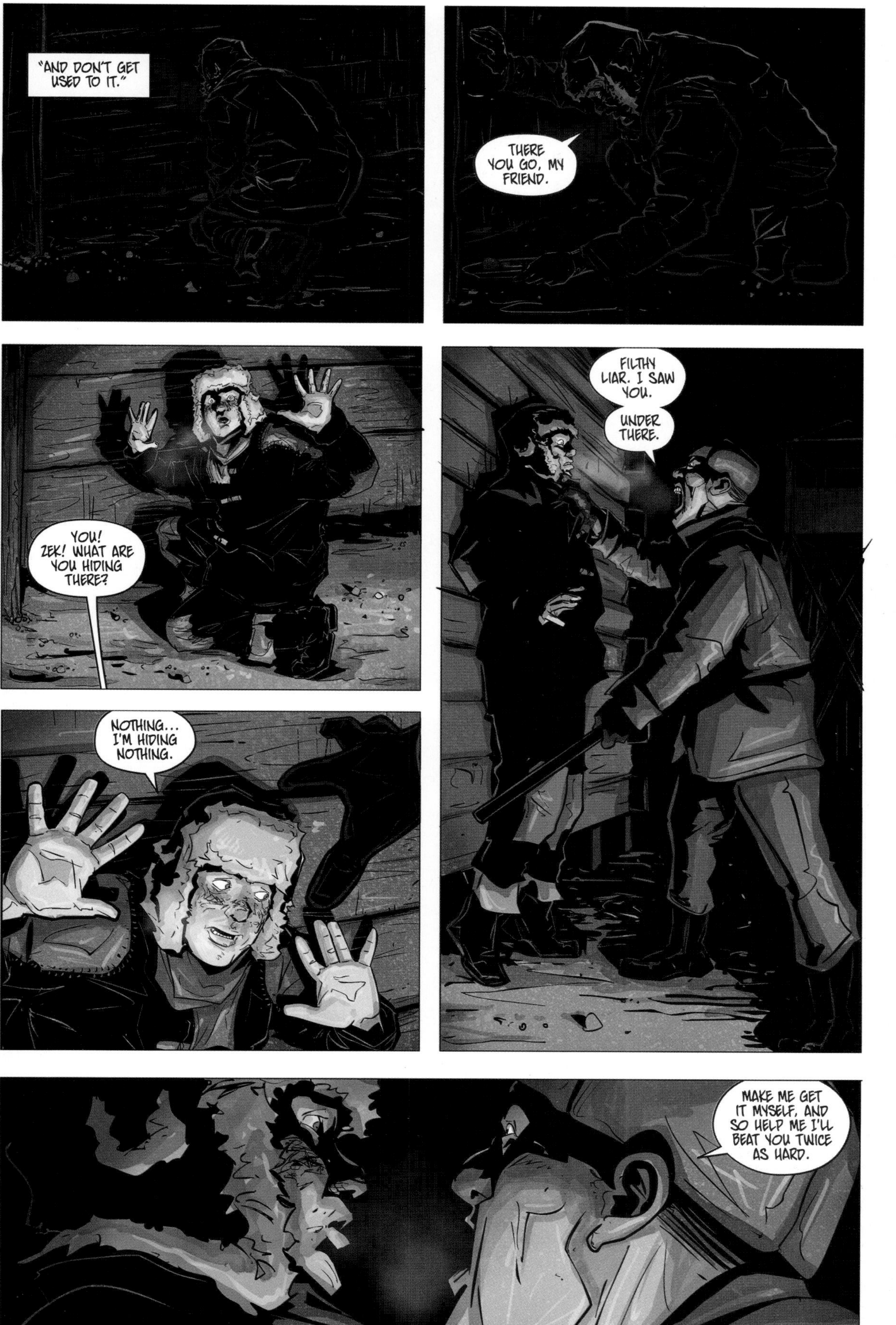
"AND DON'T GET USED TO IT."
THERE YOU GO, MY FRIEND.
YOU! ZEK! WHAT ARE YOU HIDING THERE?
NOTHING... I'M HIDING NOTHING.
FILTHY LIAR. I SAW YOU.
UNDER THERE.
MAKE ME GET IT MYSELF, AND SO HELP ME I'LL BEAT YOU TWICE AS HARD.

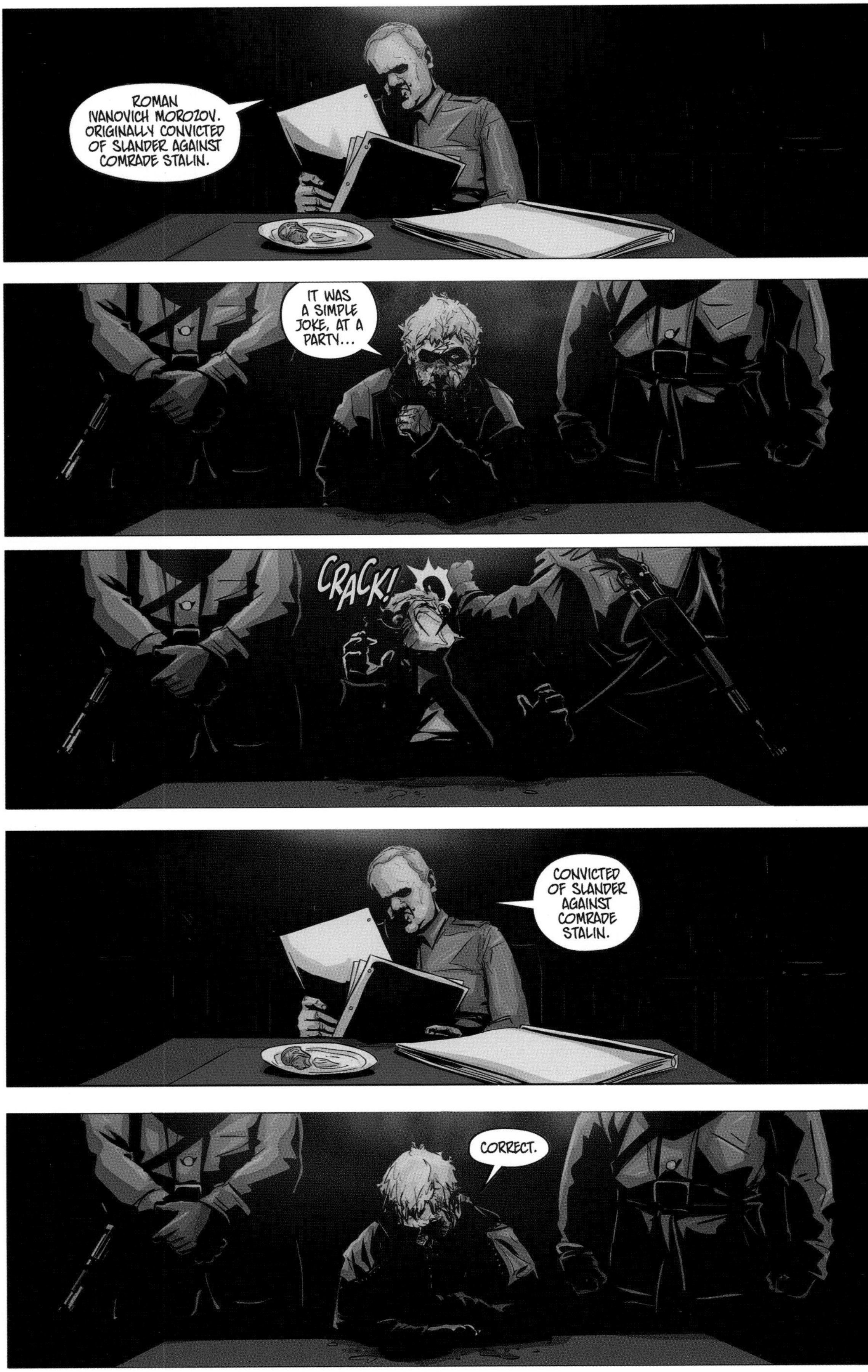
ROMAN IVANOVICH MOROZOV. ORIGINALLY CONVICTED OF SLANDER AGAINST COMRADE STALIN.
IT WAS A SIMPLE JOKE, AT A PARTY...
CRACK!
CONVICTED OF SLANDER AGAINST COMRADE STALIN.
CORRECT.

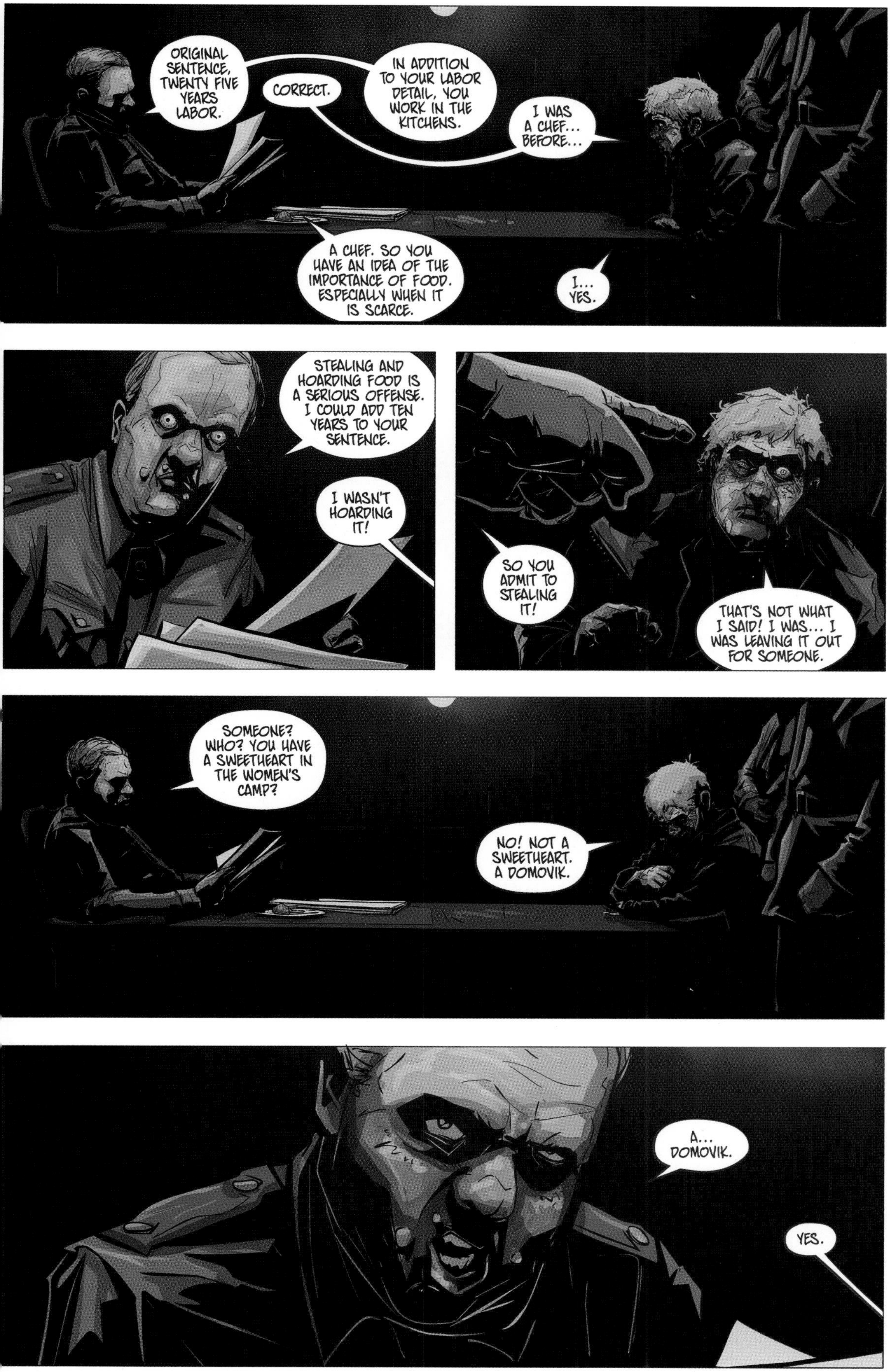
ORIGINAL SENTENCE, TWENTY FIVE YEARS LABOR.
CORRECT.
IN ADDITION TO YOUR LABOR DETAIL, YOU WORK IN THE KITCHENS.
I WAS A CHEF... BEFORE...
A CHEF. SO YOU HAVE AN IDEA OF THE IMPORTANCE OF FOOD. ESPECIALLY WHEN IT IS SCARCE.
I... YES.
STEALING AND HOARDING FOOD IS A SERIOUS OFFENSE. I COULD ADD TEN YEARS TO YOUR SENTENCE.
I WASN'T HOARDING IT!
SO YOU ADMIT TO STEALING IT!
THAT'S NOT WHAT I SAID! I WAS... I WAS LEAVING IT OUT FOR SOMEONE.
SOMEONE? WHO? YOU HAVE A SWEETHEART IN THE WOMEN'S CAMP?
NO! NOT A SWEETHEART. A DOMOVIK.
A... DOMOVIK.
YES.

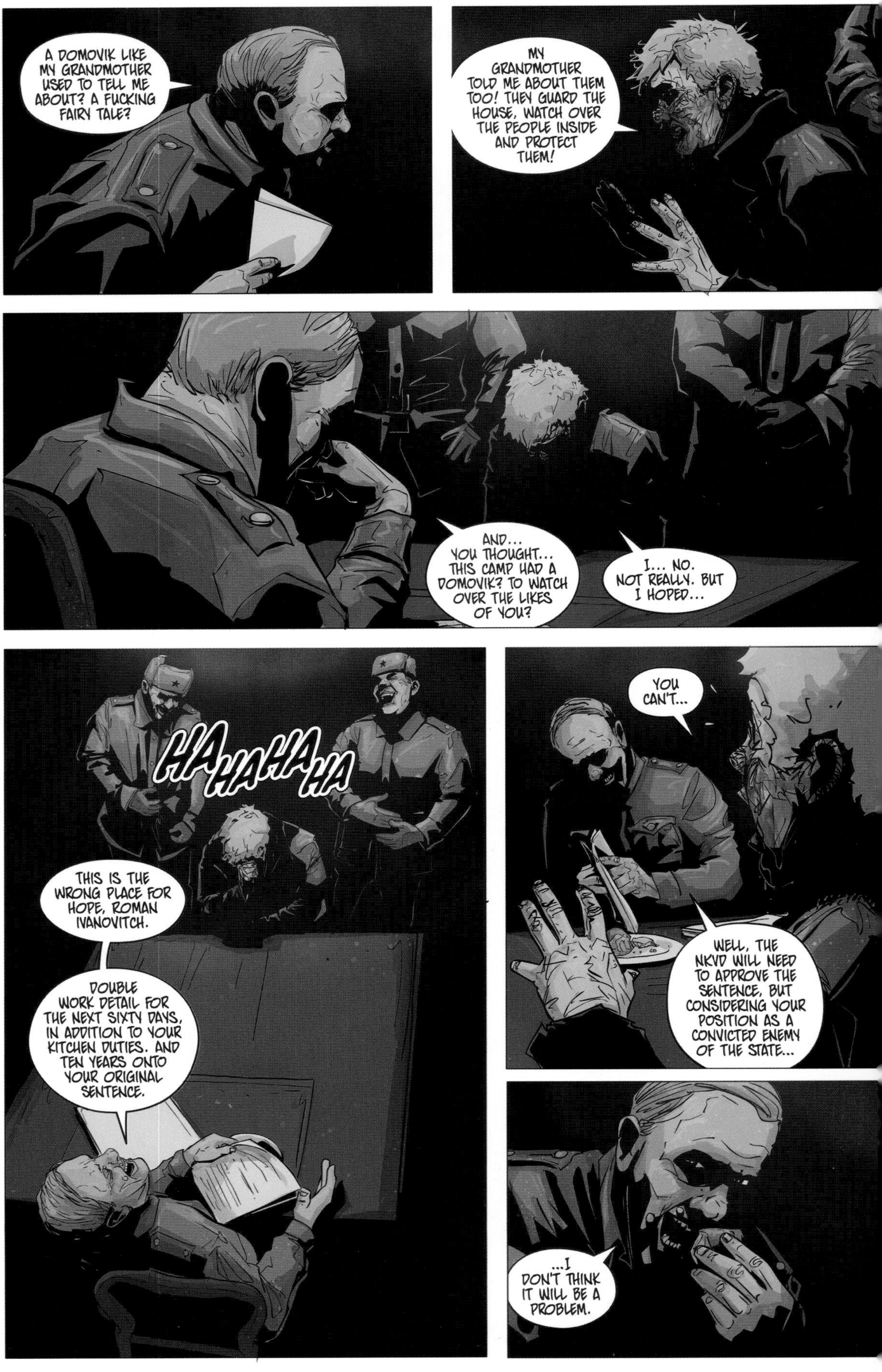
A DOMOVIK LIKE MY GRANDMOTHER USED TO TELL ME ABOUT? A FUCKING FAIRY TALE?
MY GRANDMOTHER TOLD ME ABOUT THEM TOO! THEY GUARD THE HOUSE, WATCH OVER THE PEOPLE INSIDE AND PROTECT THEM!
AND... YOU THOUGHT... THIS CAMP HAD A DOMOVIK? TO WATCH OVER THE LIKES OF YOU?
I... NO. NOT REALLY. BUT I HOPED...
HAHAHAHAHA
THIS IS THE WRONG PLACE FOR HOPE, ROMAN IVANOVITCH.
DOUBLE WORK DETAIL FOR THE NEXT SIXTY DAYS, IN ADDITION TO YOUR KITCHEN DUTIES. AND TEN YEARS ONTO YOUR ORIGINAL SENTENCE.
YOU CAN'T...
WELL, THE NKVD WILL NEED TO APPROVE THE SENTENCE, BUT CONSIDERING YOUR POSITION AS A CONVICTED ENEMY OF THE STATE...
...I DON'T THINK IT WILL BE A PROBLEM.

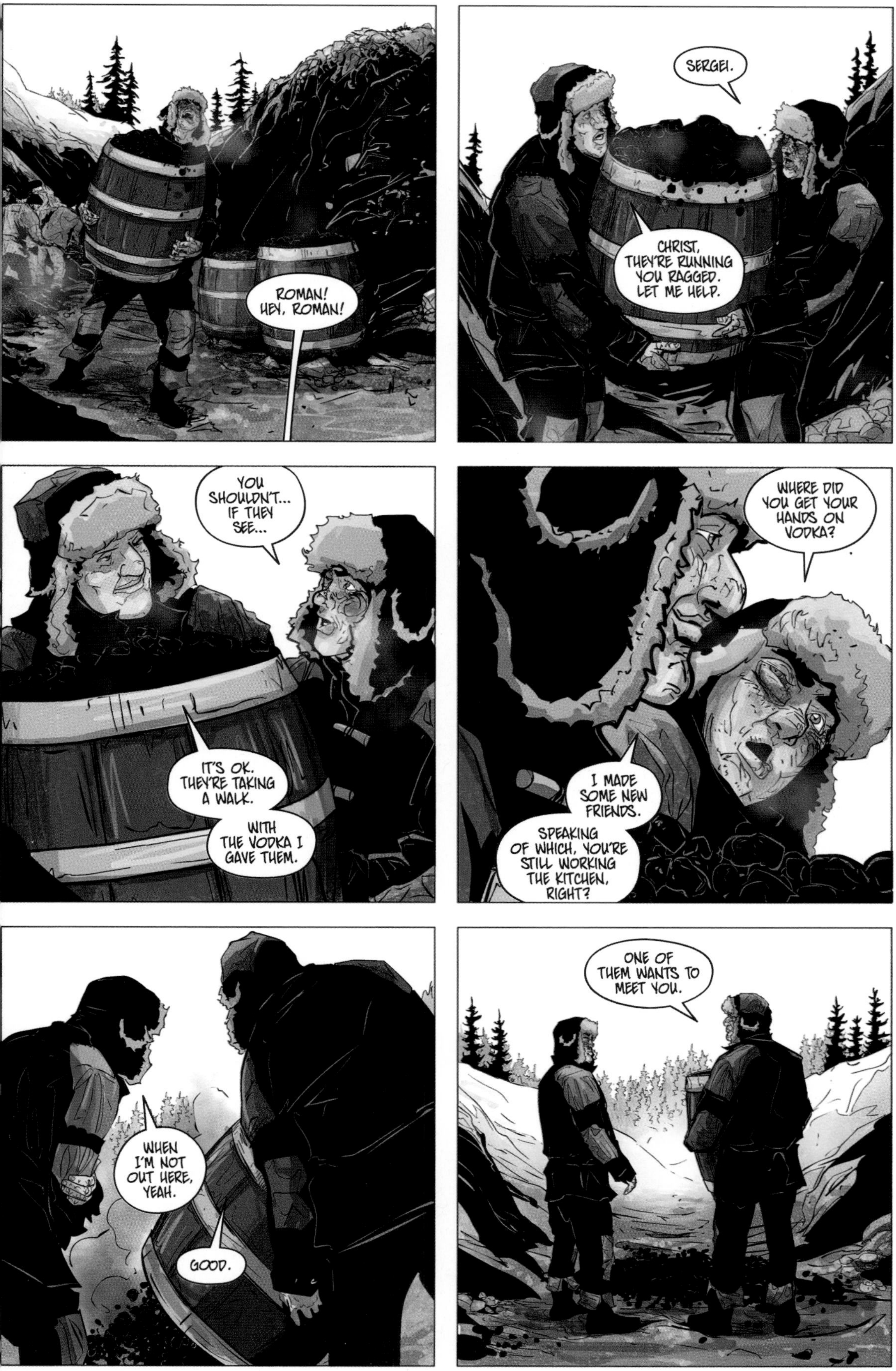
ROMAN! HEY, ROMAN!
SERGEI.
CHRIST, THEY'RE RUNNING YOU RAGGED. LET ME HELP.
YOU SHOULDN'T... IF THEY SEE...
IT'S OK. THEY'RE TAKING A WALK.
WITH THE VODKA I GAVE THEM.
WHERE DID YOU GET YOUR HANDS ON VODKA?
I MADE SOME NEW FRIENDS.
SPEAKING OF WHICH, YOU'RE STILL WORKING THE KITCHEN, RIGHT?
WHEN I'M NOT OUT HERE, YEAH.
GOOD.
ONE OF THEM WANTS TO MEET YOU.

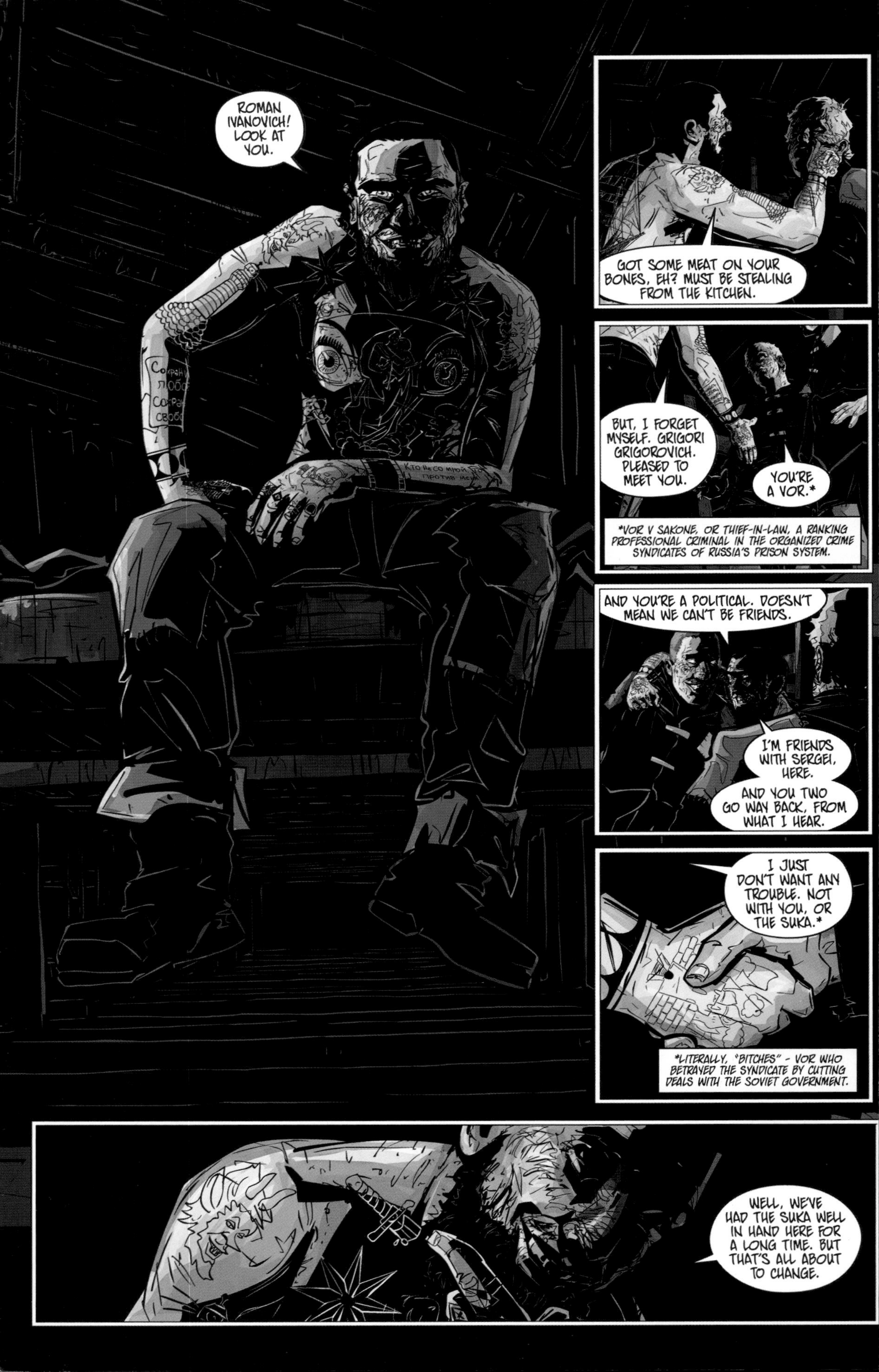
ROMAN IVANOVICH! LOOK AT YOU.
GOT SOME MEAT ON YOUR BONES, EH? MUST BE STEALING FROM THE KITCHEN.
BUT, I FORGET MYSELF. GRIGORI GRIGOROVICH. PLEASED TO MEET YOU.
YOU'RE A VOR.*
*VOR V SAKONE, OR THIEF-IN-LAW, A RANKING PROFESSIONAL CRIMINAL IN THE ORGANIZED CRIME SYNDICATES OF RUSSIA'S PRISON SYSTEM.
AND YOU'RE A POLITICAL. DOESN'T MEAN WE CAN'T BE FRIENDS.
I'M FRIENDS WITH SERGEI, HERE.
AND YOU TWO GO WAY BACK, FROM WHAT I HEAR.
I JUST DON'T WANT ANY TROUBLE. NOT WITH YOU, OR THE SUKA.*
*LITERALLY, "BITCHES" - VOR WHO BETRAYED THE SYNDICATE BY CUTTING DEALS WITH THE SOVIET GOVERNMENT.
WELL, WE'VE HAD THE SUKA WELL IN HAND HERE FOR A LONG TIME. BUT THAT'S ALL ABOUT TO CHANGE.

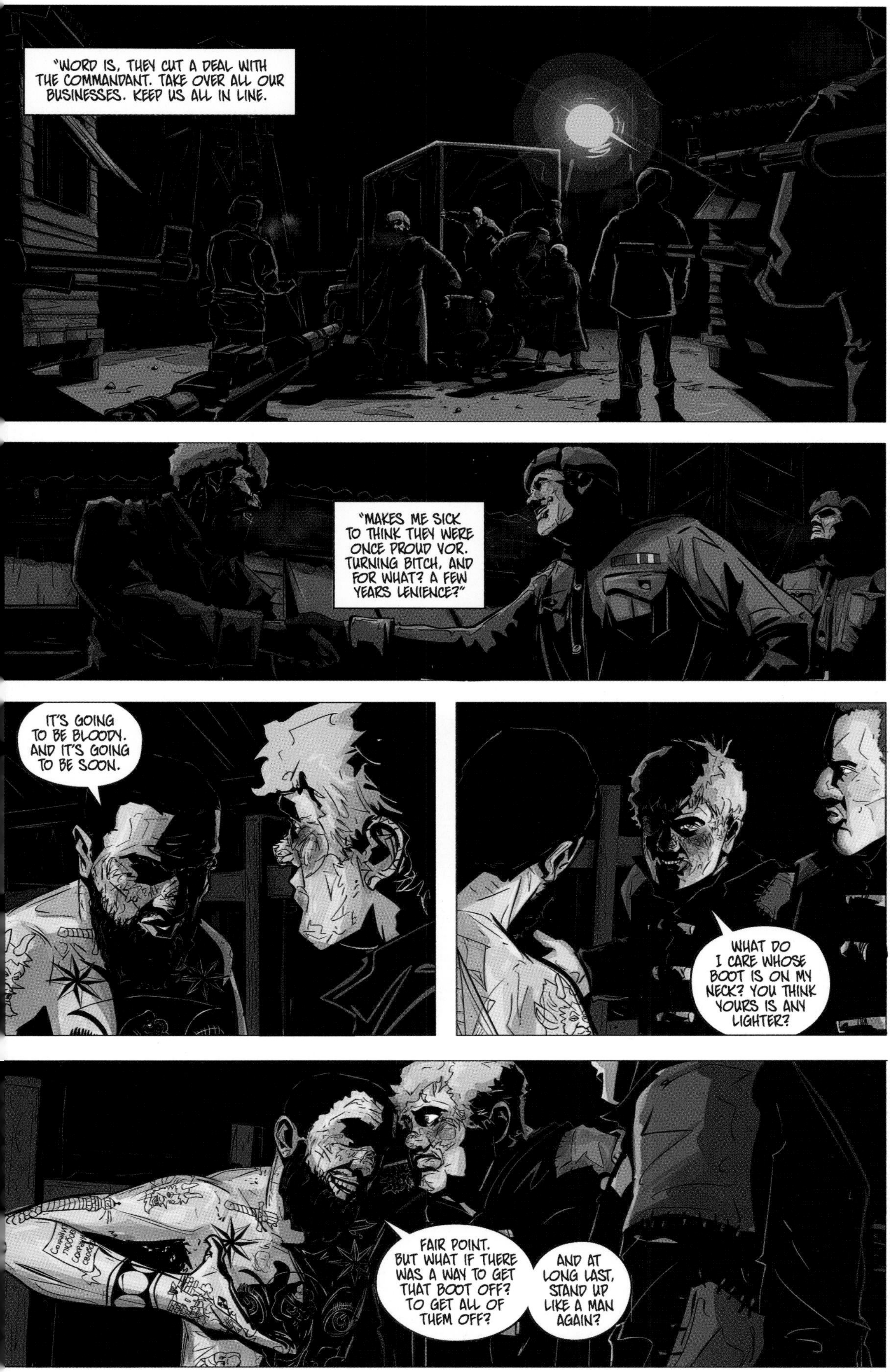
"WORD IS, THEY CUT A DEAL WITH THE COMMANDANT. TAKE OVER ALL OUR BUSINESSES. KEEP US ALL IN LINE.
"MAKES ME SICK TO THINK THEY WERE ONCE PROUD VOR. TURNING BITCH, AND FOR WHAT? A FEW YEARS LENIENCE?"
IT'S GOING TO BE BLOODY. AND IT'S GOING TO BE SOON.
WHAT DO I CARE WHOSE BOOT IS ON MY NECK? YOU THINK YOURS IS ANY LIGHTER?
FAIR POINT. BUT WHAT IF THERE WAS A WAY TO GET THAT BOOT OFF? TO GET ALL OF THEM OFF?
AND AT LONG LAST, STAND UP LIKE A MAN AGAIN?

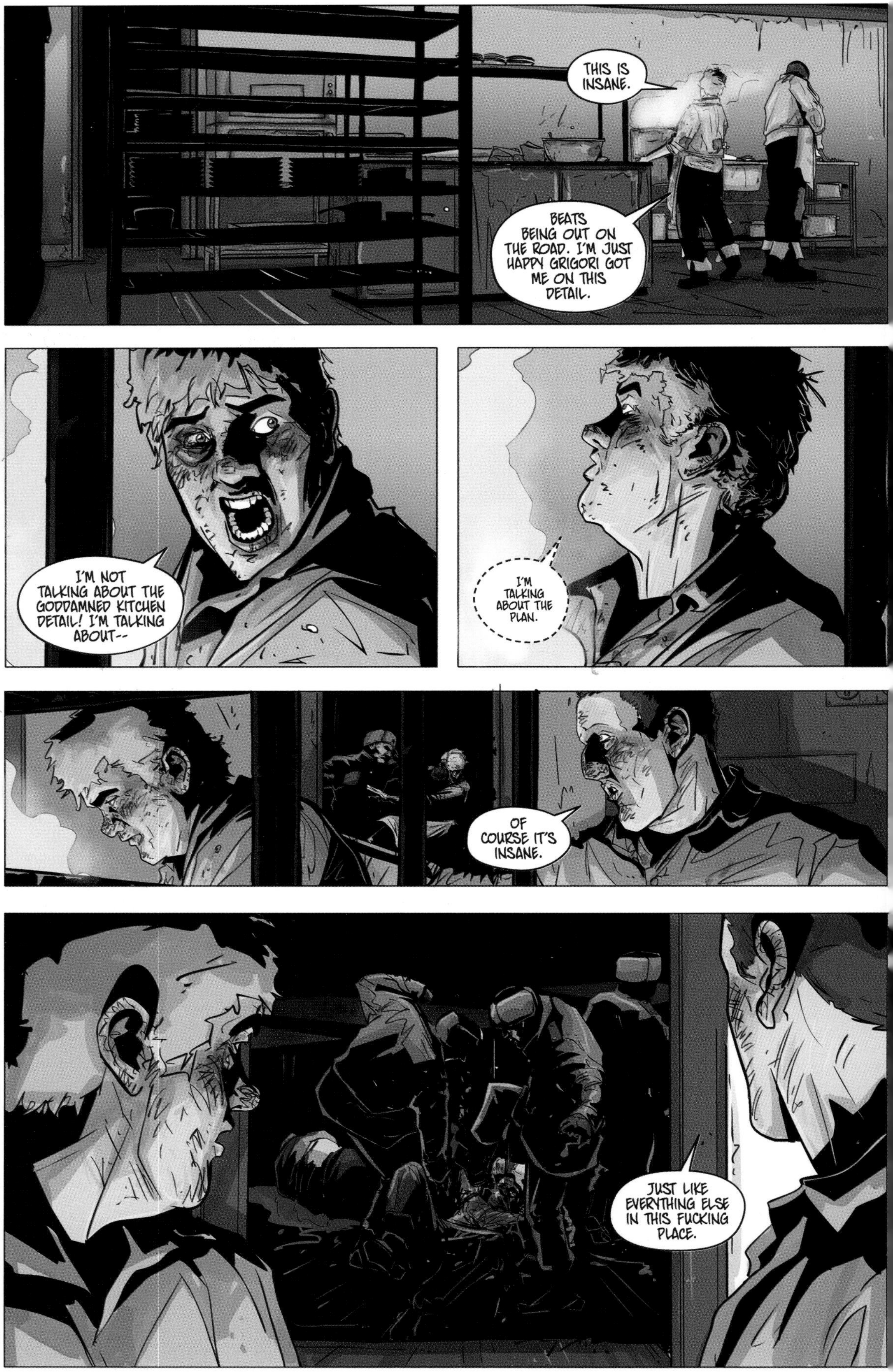
THIS IS INSANE.
BEATS BEING OUT ON THE ROAD. I'M JUST HAPPY GRIGORI GOT ME ON THIS DETAIL.
I'M NOT TALKING ABOUT THE GODDAMNED KITCHEN DETAIL! I'M TALKING ABOUT--
I'M TALKING ABOUT THE PLAN.
OF COURSE IT'S INSANE.
JUST LIKE EVERYTHING ELSE IN THIS FUCKING PLACE.

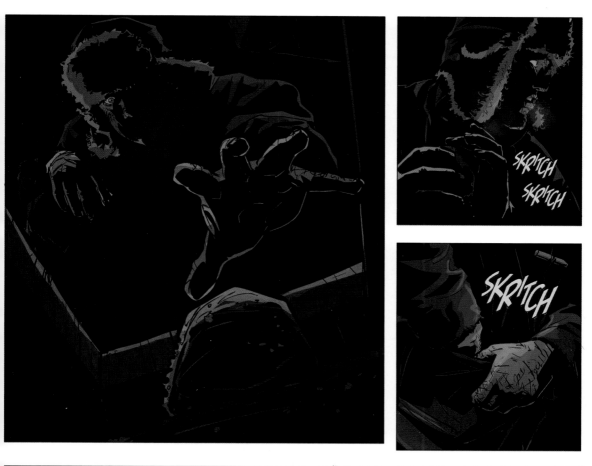

SKRITCH
SKRITCH

SKRITCH

SKRI

SKIMMING OFF THE TOP, I SEE.

AND YOU SAID YOU WEREN'T A CRIMINAL.

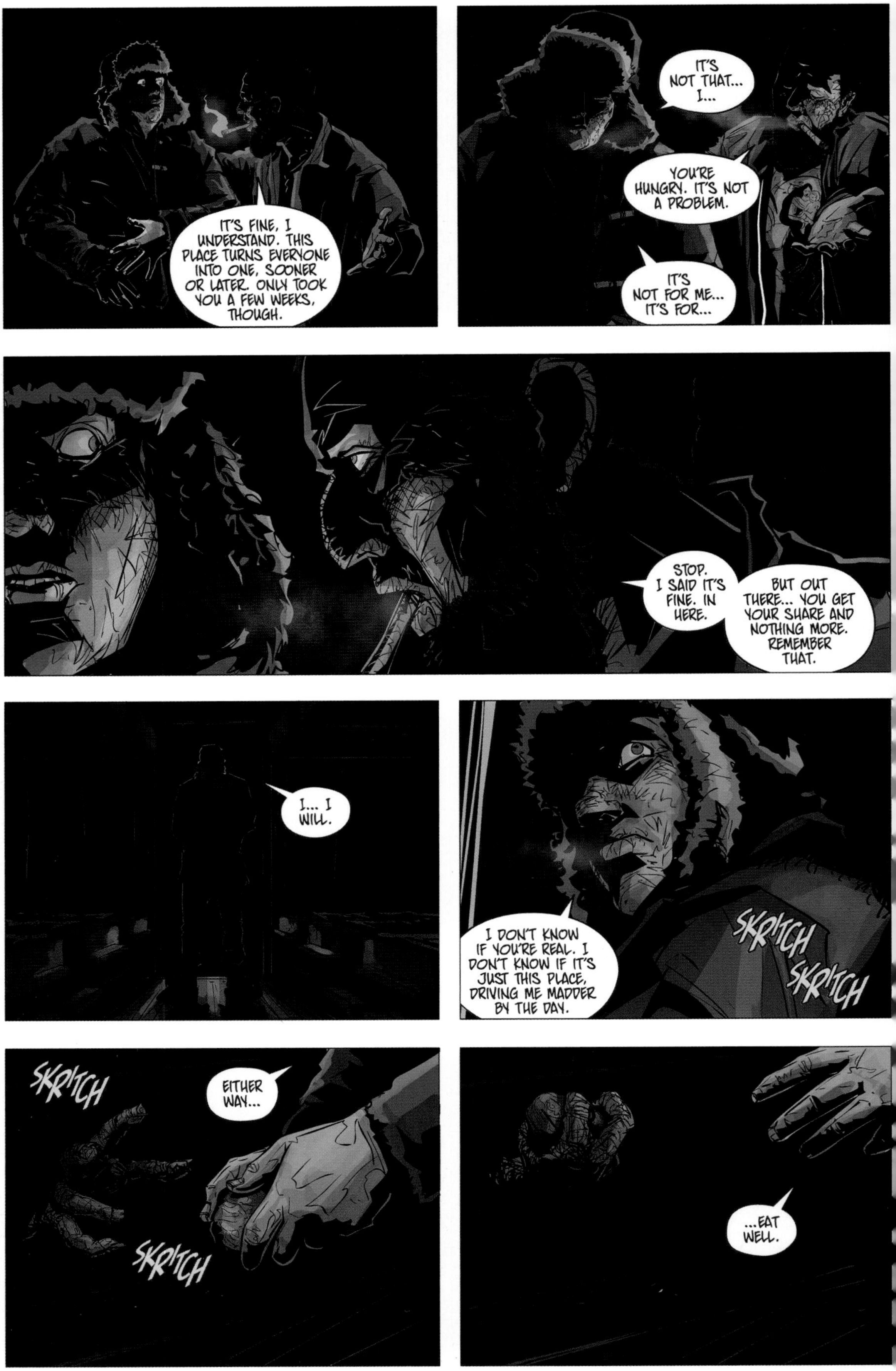
IT'S FINE, I UNDERSTAND. THIS PLACE TURNS EVERYONE INTO ONE, SOONER OR LATER. ONLY TOOK YOU A FEW WEEKS, THOUGH.
IT'S NOT THAT... I...
YOU'RE HUNGRY. IT'S NOT A PROBLEM.
IT'S NOT FOR ME... IT'S FOR...
STOP. I SAID IT'S FINE. IN HERE.
BUT OUT THERE... YOU GET YOUR SHARE AND NOTHING MORE. REMEMBER THAT.
I... I WILL.
I DON'T KNOW IF YOU'RE REAL. I DON'T KNOW IF IT'S JUST THIS PLACE, DRIVING ME MADDER BY THE DAY.
SKRITCH
SKRITCH
SKRITCH
EITHER WAY...
SKRITCH
...EAT WELL.

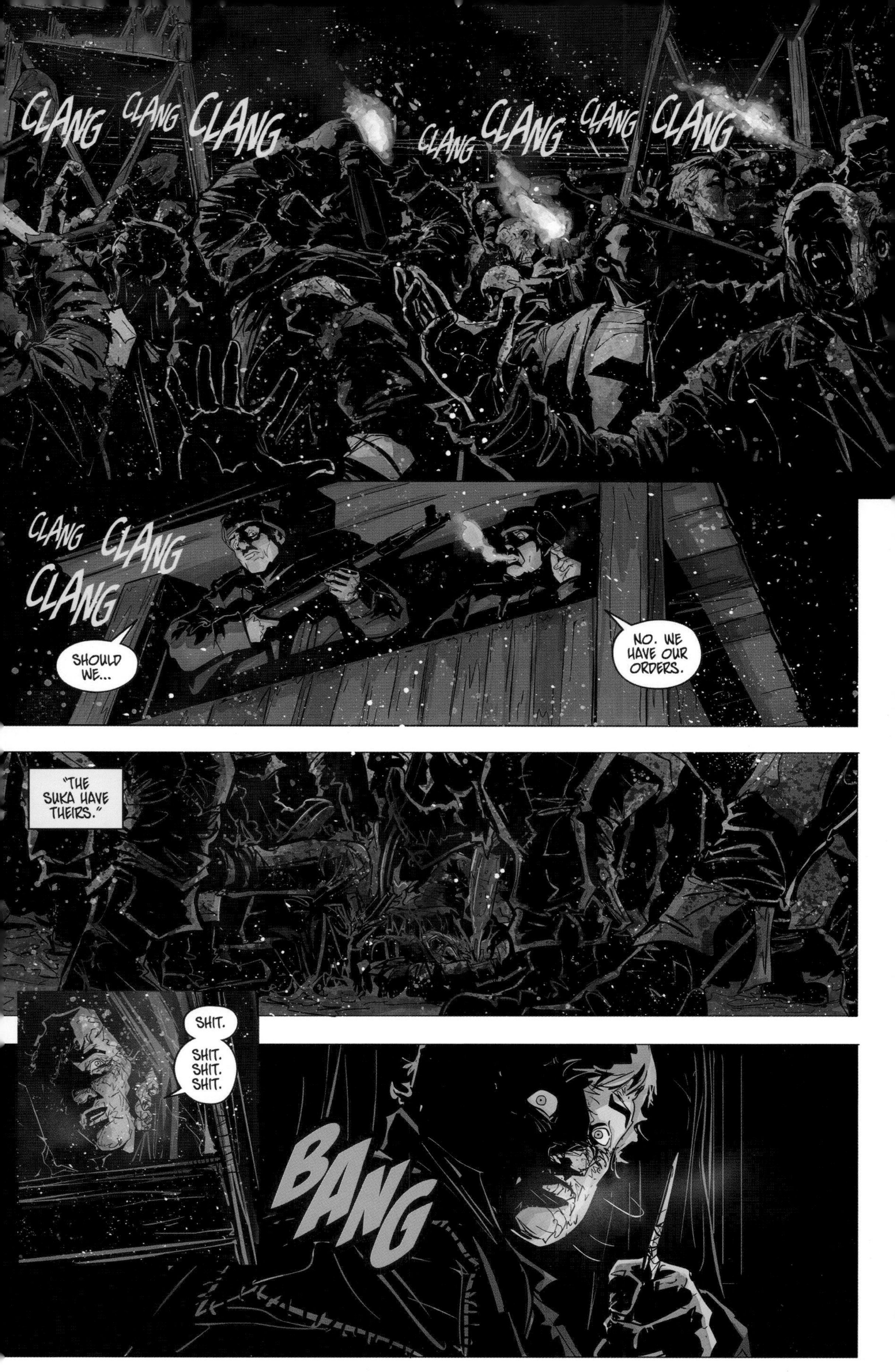
CLANG CLANG CLANG
CLANG CLANG CLANG CLANG
CLANG CLANG
CLANG
SHOULD WE...
NO. WE HAVE OUR ORDERS.
"THE SUKA HAVE THEIRS."
SHIT.
SHIT. SHIT. SHIT.
BANG

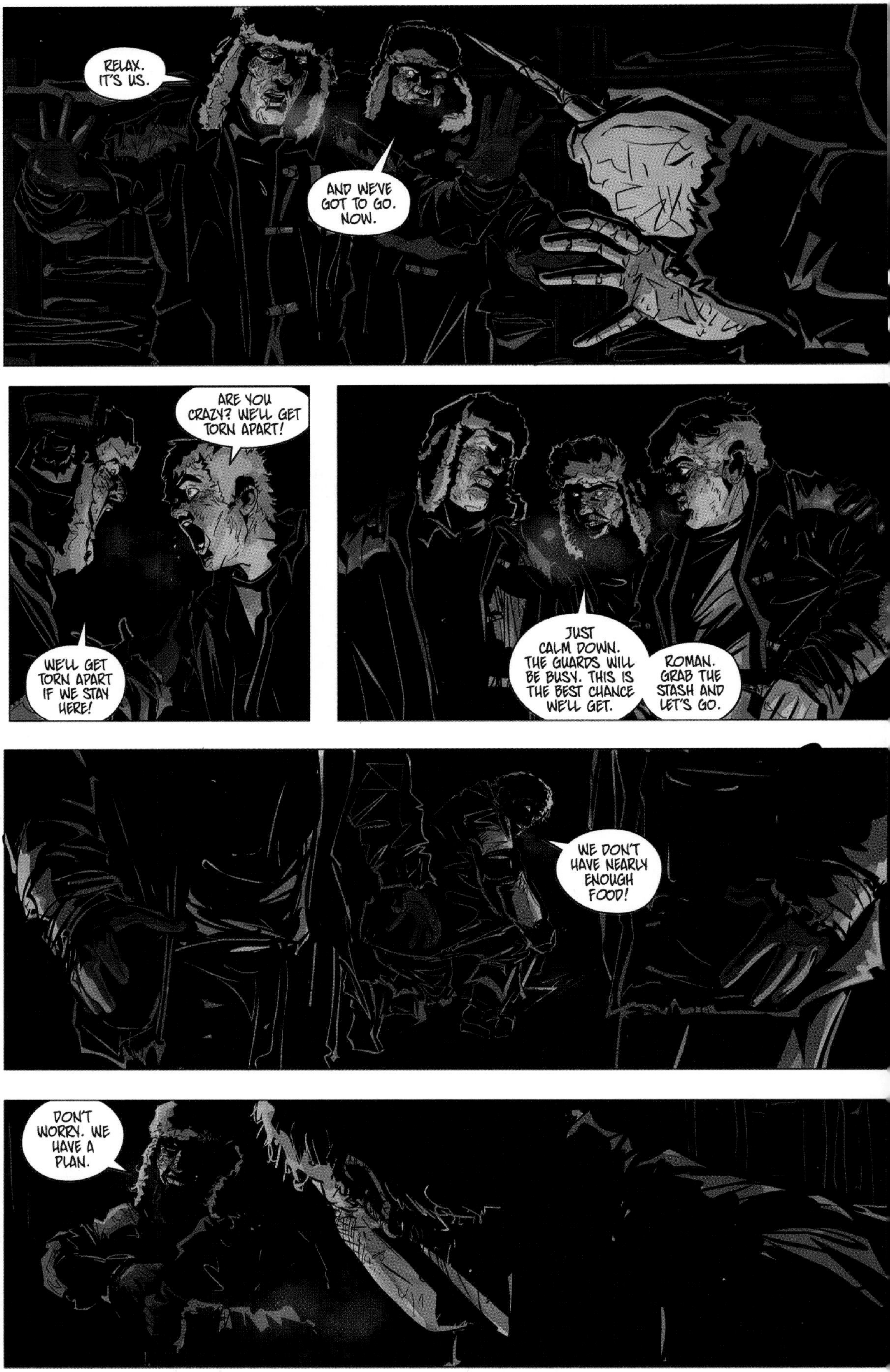
RELAX. IT'S US.
AND WE'VE GOT TO GO. NOW.
ARE YOU CRAZY? WE'LL GET TORN APART!
WE'LL GET TORN APART IF WE STAY HERE!
JUST CALM DOWN. THE GUARDS WILL BE BUSY. THIS IS THE BEST CHANCE WE'LL GET.
ROMAN. GRAB THE STASH AND LET'S GO.
WE DON'T HAVE NEARLY ENOUGH FOOD!
DON'T WORRY. WE HAVE A PLAN.

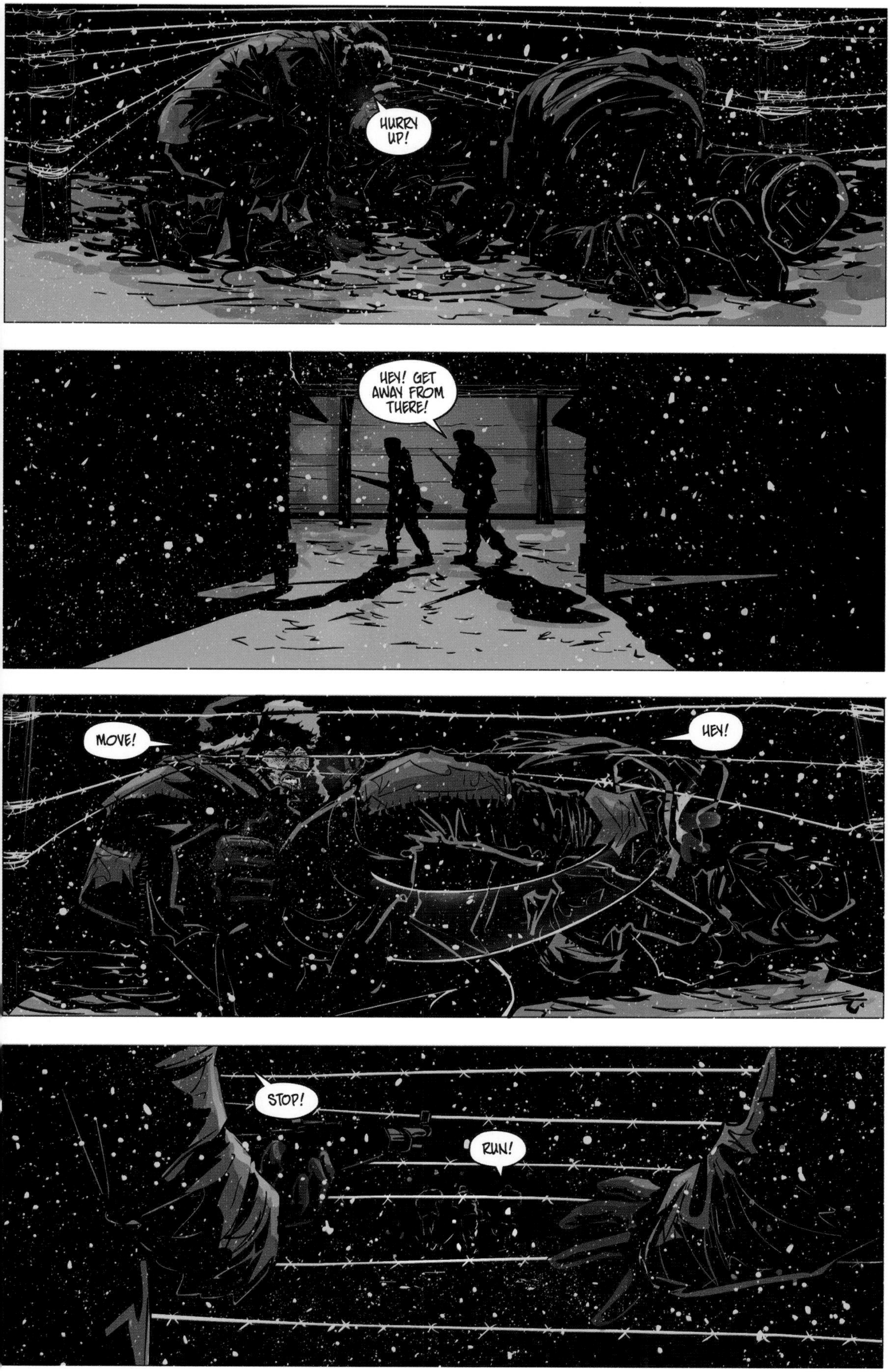
HURRY UP!
HEY! GET AWAY FROM THERE!
MOVE!
HEY!
STOP!
RUN!

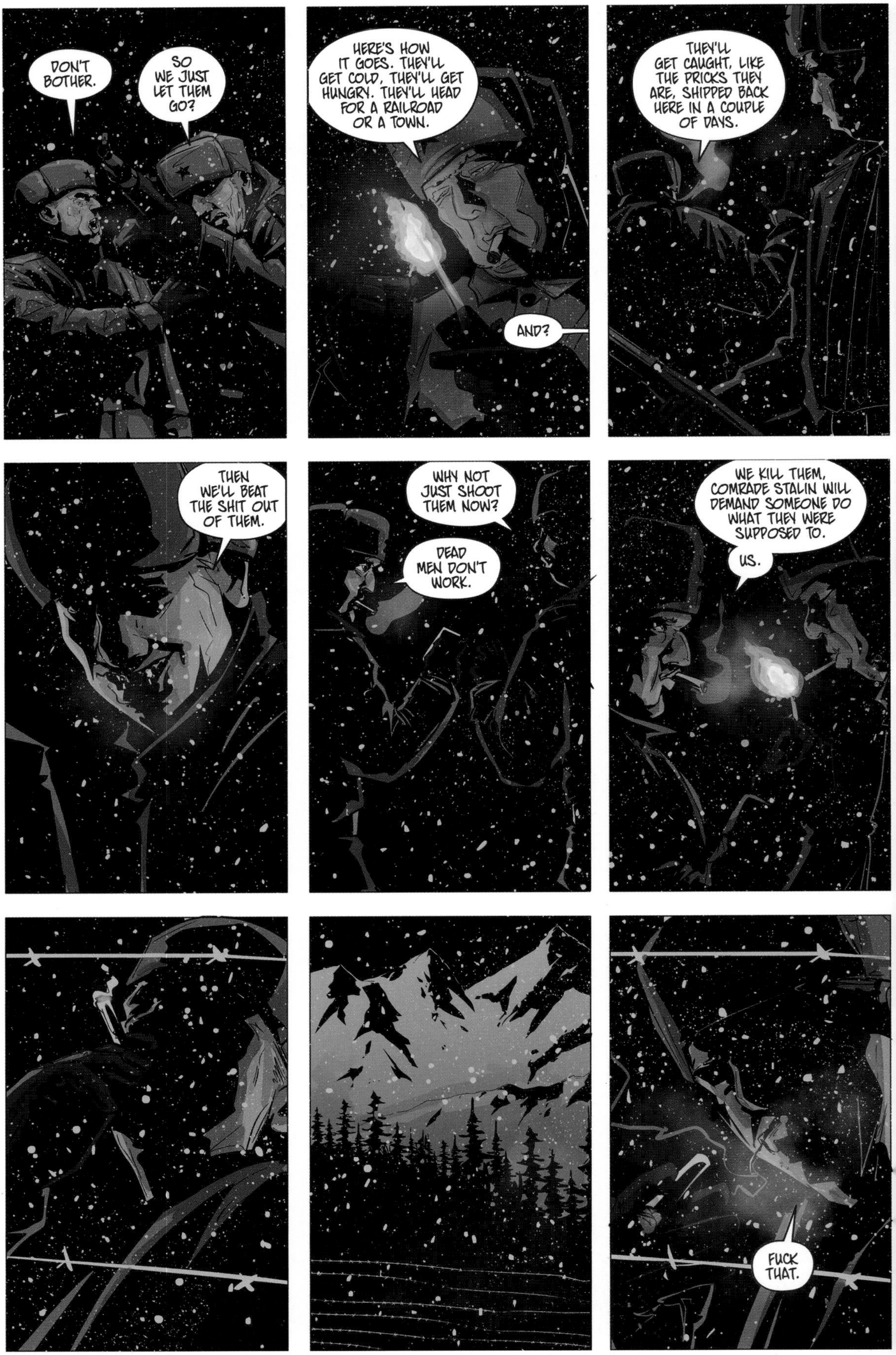
DON'T BOTHER.
SO WE JUST LET THEM GO?
HERE'S HOW IT GOES. THEY'LL GET COLD, THEY'LL GET HUNGRY. THEY'LL HEAD FOR A RAILROAD OR A TOWN.
AND?
THEY'LL GET CAUGHT, LIKE THE PRICKS THEY ARE, SHIPPED BACK HERE IN A COUPLE OF DAYS.
THEN WE'LL BEAT THE SHIT OUT OF THEM.
WHY NOT JUST SHOOT THEM NOW?
DEAD MEN DON'T WORK.
WE KILL THEM, COMRADE STALIN WILL DEMAND SOMEONE DO WHAT THEY WERE SUPPOSED TO.
US.
FUCK THAT.

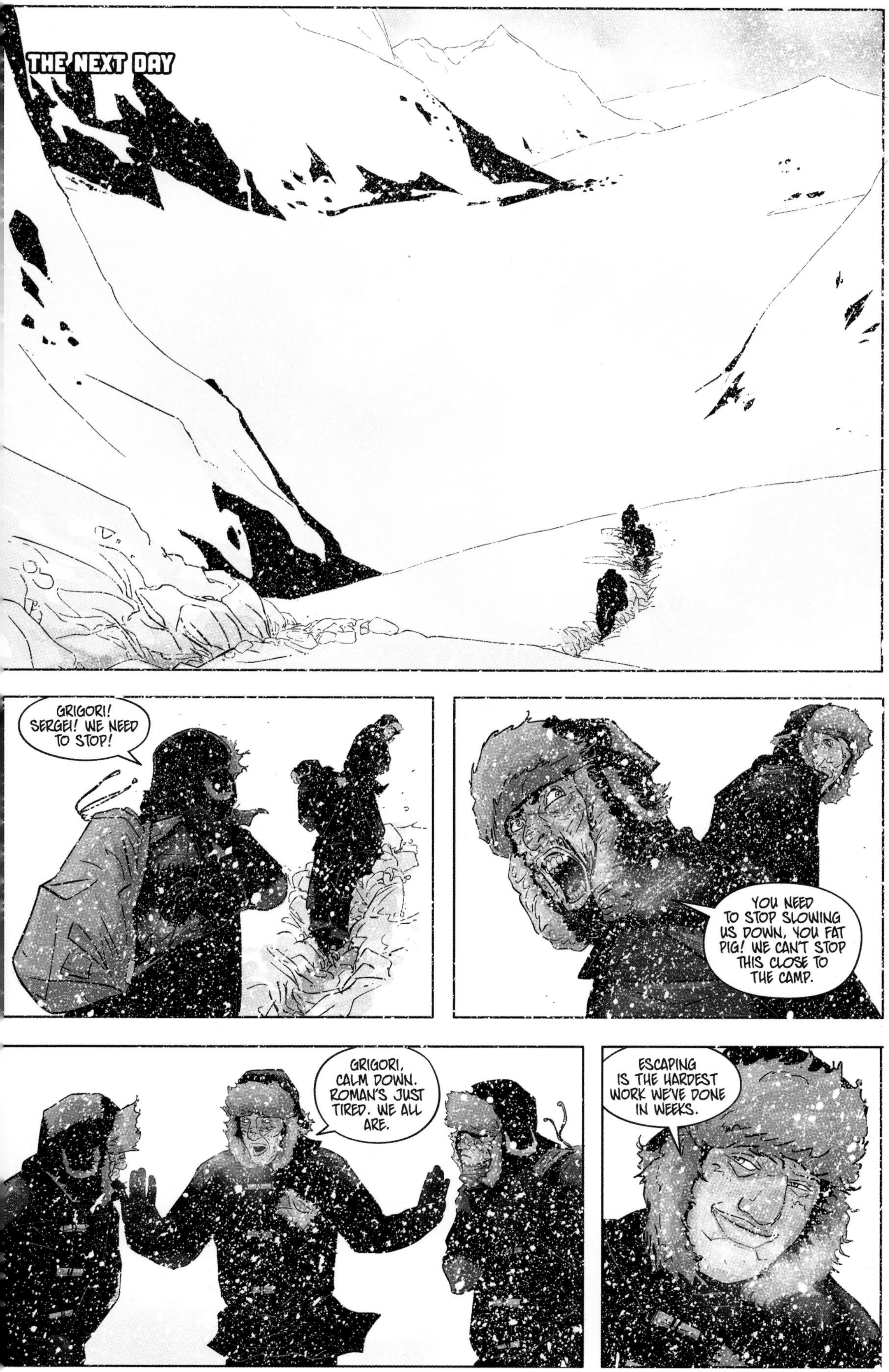
THE NEXT DAY
GRIGORI! SERGEI! WE NEED TO STOP!
YOU NEED TO STOP SLOWING US DOWN, YOU FAT PIG! WE CAN'T STOP THIS CLOSE TO THE CAMP.
GRIGORI, CALM DOWN. ROMAN'S JUST TIRED. WE ALL ARE.
ESCAPING IS THE HARDEST WORK WE'VE DONE IN WEEKS.

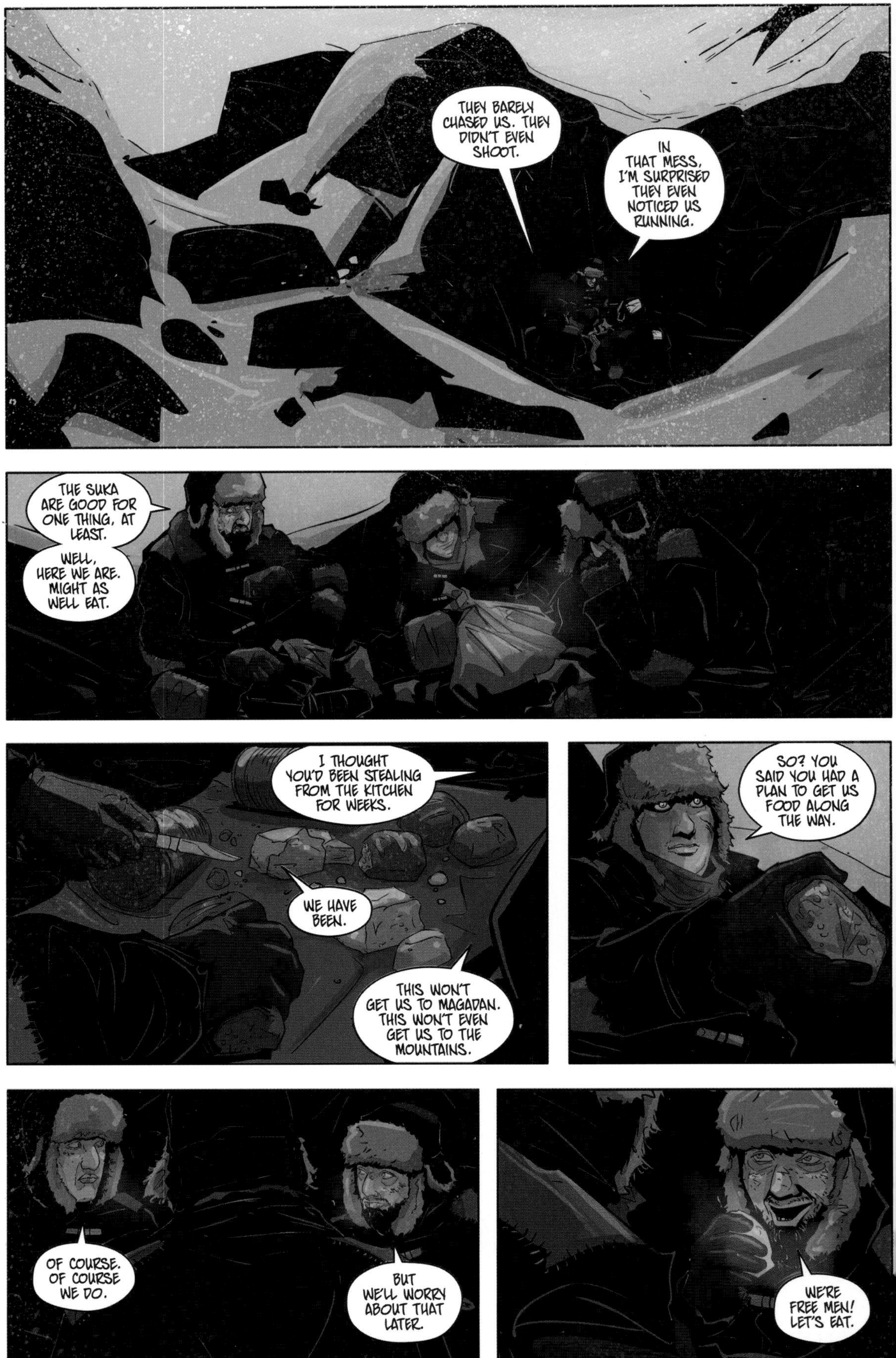
THEY BARELY CHASED US. THEY DIDN'T EVEN SHOOT.
IN THAT MESS, I'M SURPRISED THEY EVEN NOTICED US RUNNING.
THE SUKA ARE GOOD FOR ONE THING, AT LEAST.
WELL, HERE WE ARE. MIGHT AS WELL EAT.
I THOUGHT YOU'D BEEN STEALING FROM THE KITCHEN FOR WEEKS.
WE HAVE BEEN.
THIS WON'T GET US TO MAGADAN. THIS WON'T EVEN GET US TO THE MOUNTAINS.
SO? YOU SAID YOU HAD A PLAN TO GET US FOOD ALONG THE WAY.
OF COURSE. OF COURSE WE DO.
BUT WE'LL WORRY ABOUT THAT LATER.
WE'RE FREE MEN! LET'S EAT.

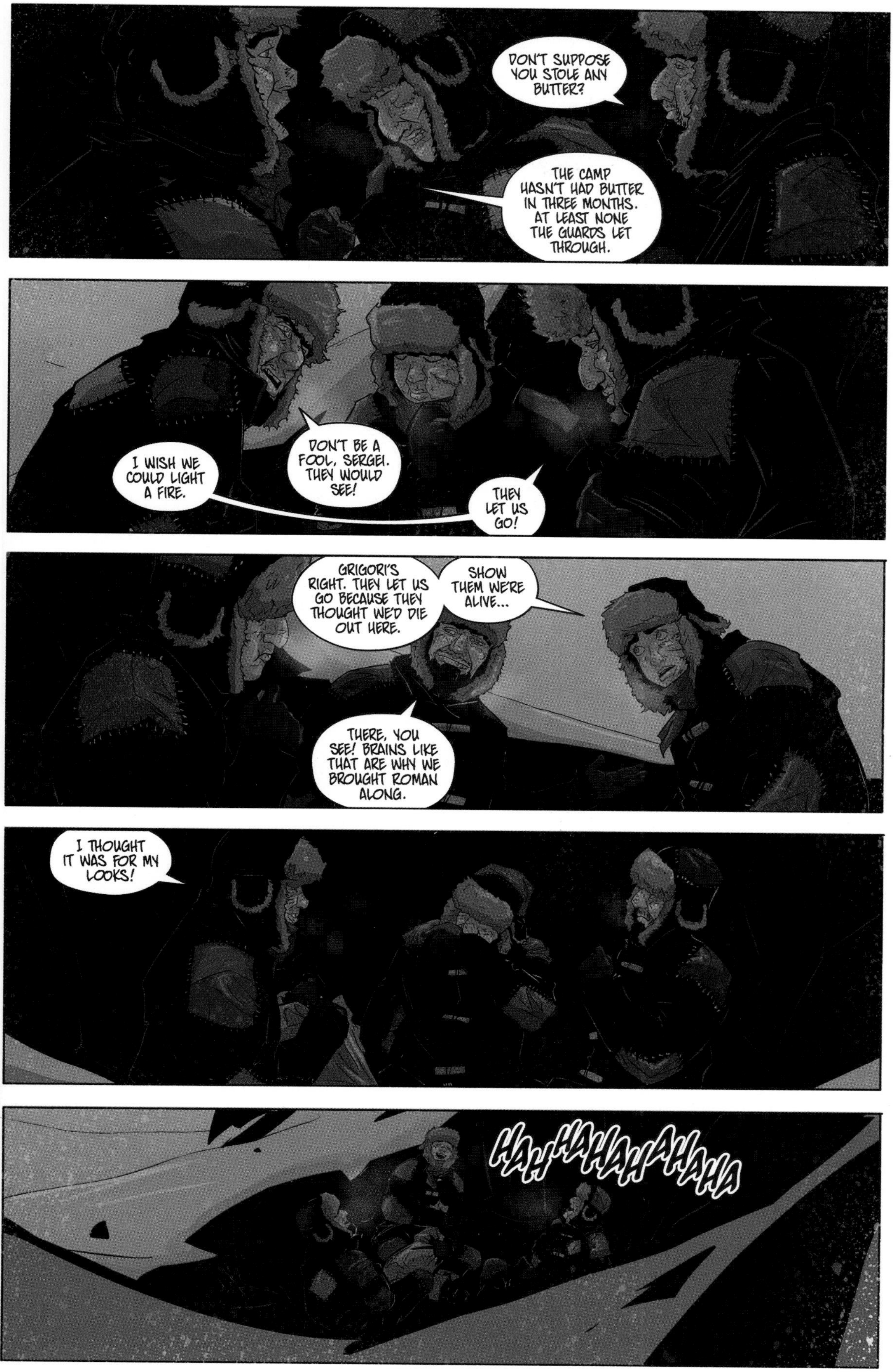
DON'T SUPPOSE YOU STOLE ANY BUTTER?
THE CAMP HASN'T HAD BUTTER IN THREE MONTHS. AT LEAST NONE THE GUARDS LET THROUGH.
I WISH WE COULD LIGHT A FIRE.
DON'T BE A FOOL, SERGEI. THEY WOULD SEE!
THEY LET US GO!
GRIGORI'S RIGHT. THEY LET US GO BECAUSE THEY THOUGHT WE'D DIE OUT HERE.
SHOW THEM WE'RE ALIVE...
THERE, YOU SEE! BRAINS LIKE THAT ARE WHY WE BROUGHT ROMAN ALONG.
I THOUGHT IT WAS FOR MY LOOKS!
HAH HAHAH AHAHA

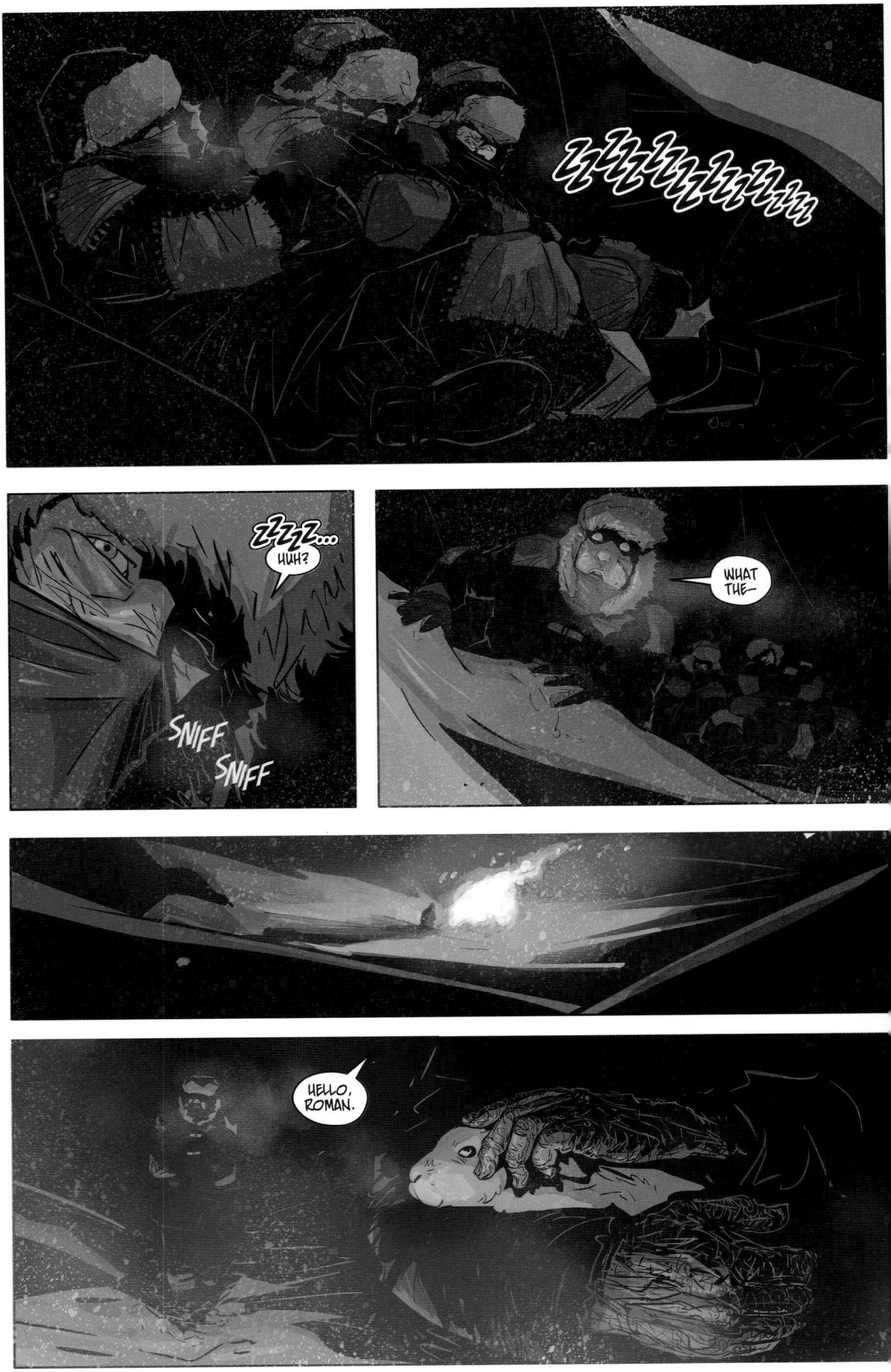
ZZZZZZZZZZZZzzz
ZZZZ...
HUH?
SNIFF
SNIFF
WHAT THE—
HELLO, ROMAN.

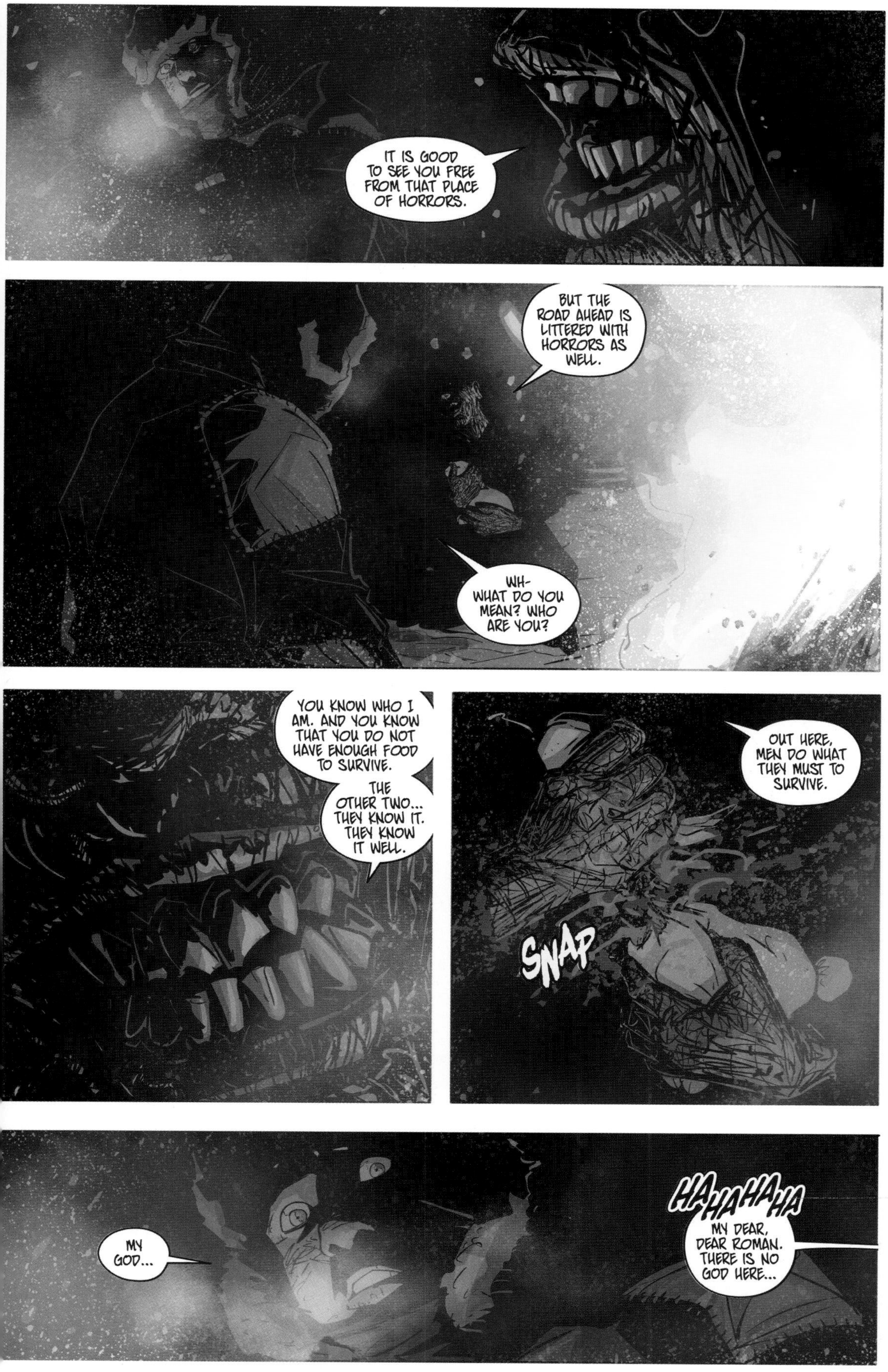
IT IS GOOD TO SEE YOU FREE FROM THAT PLACE OF HORRORS.
BUT THE ROAD AHEAD IS LITTERED WITH HORRORS AS WELL.
WH- WHAT DO YOU MEAN? WHO ARE YOU?
YOU KNOW WHO I AM. AND YOU KNOW THAT YOU DO NOT HAVE ENOUGH FOOD TO SURVIVE.
THE OTHER TWO... THEY KNOW IT. THEY KNOW IT WELL.
OUT HERE, MEN DO WHAT THEY MUST TO SURVIVE.
SNAP
MY GOD...
HAHAHAHAHA
MY DEAR, DEAR ROMAN. THERE IS NO GOD HERE...

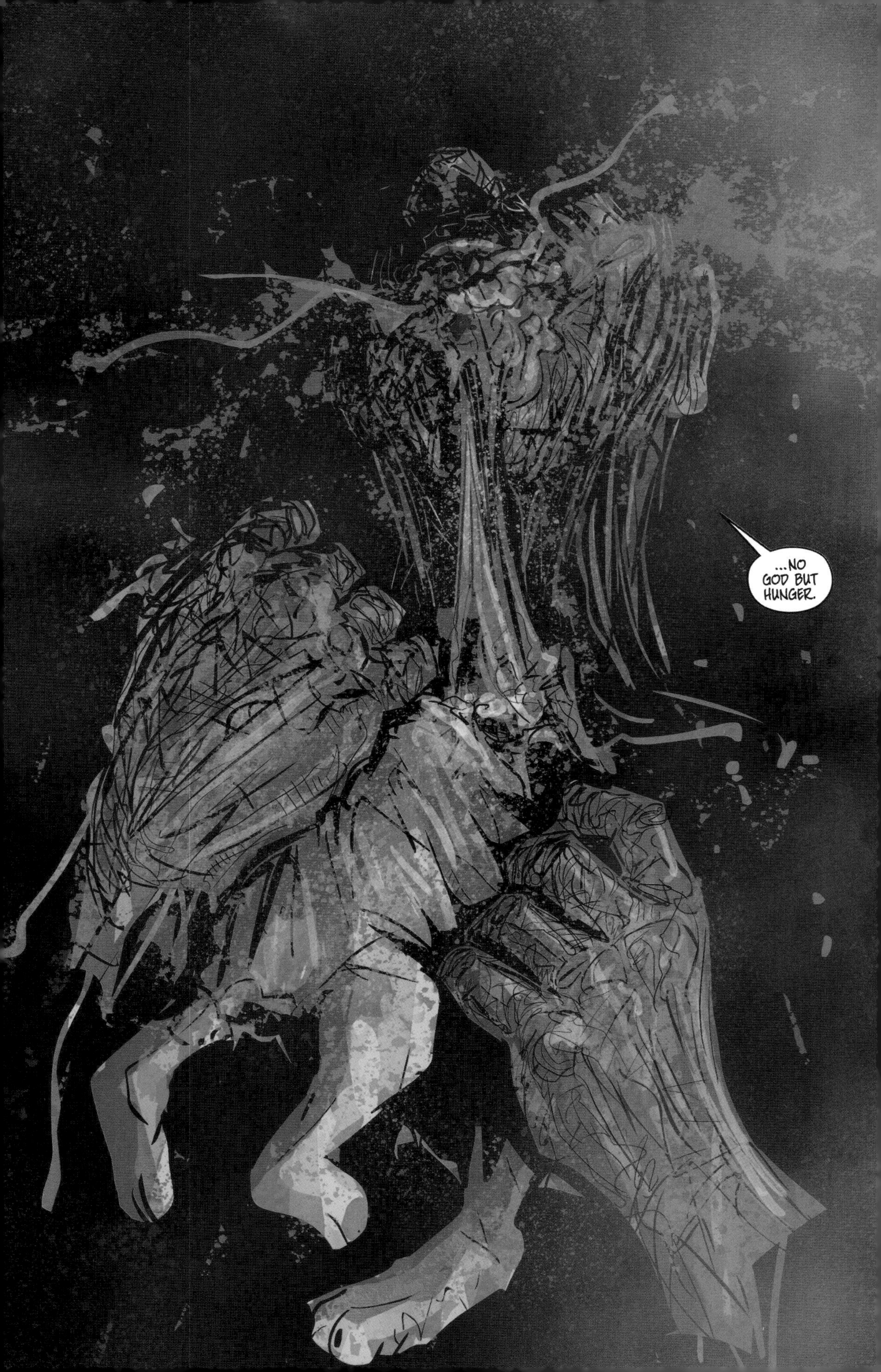
...NO GOD BUT HUNGER.

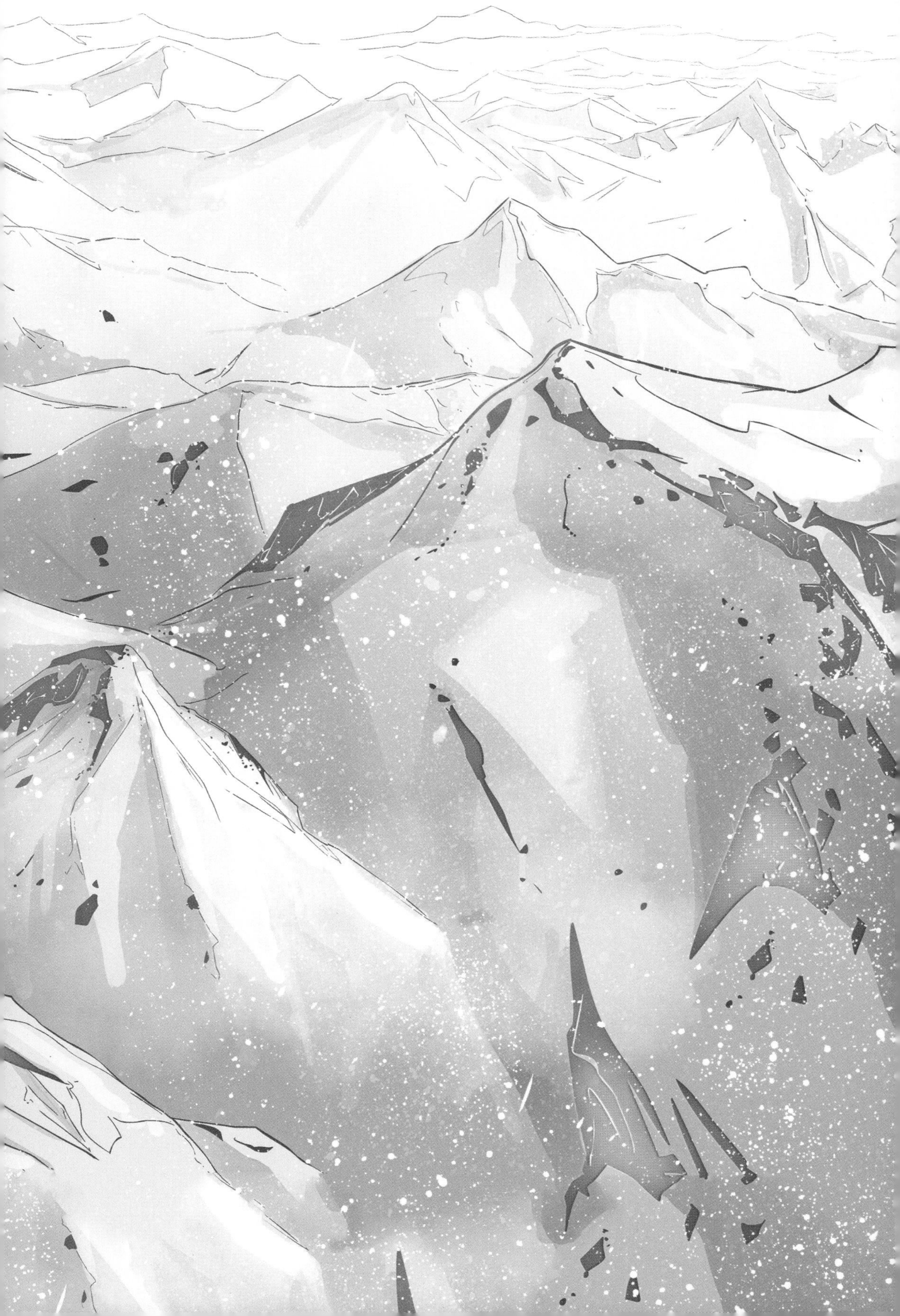

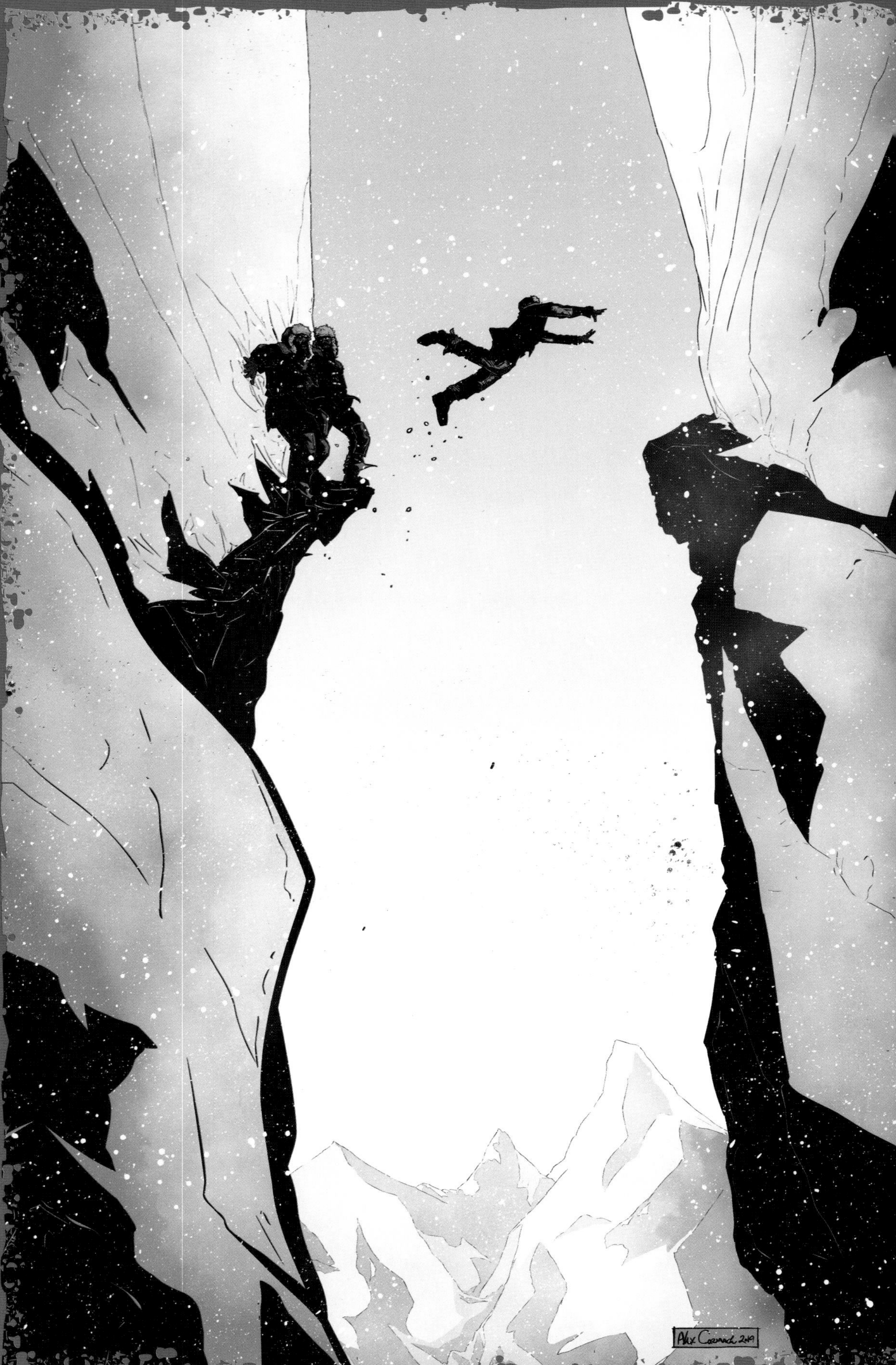
Alex Cormack 2019

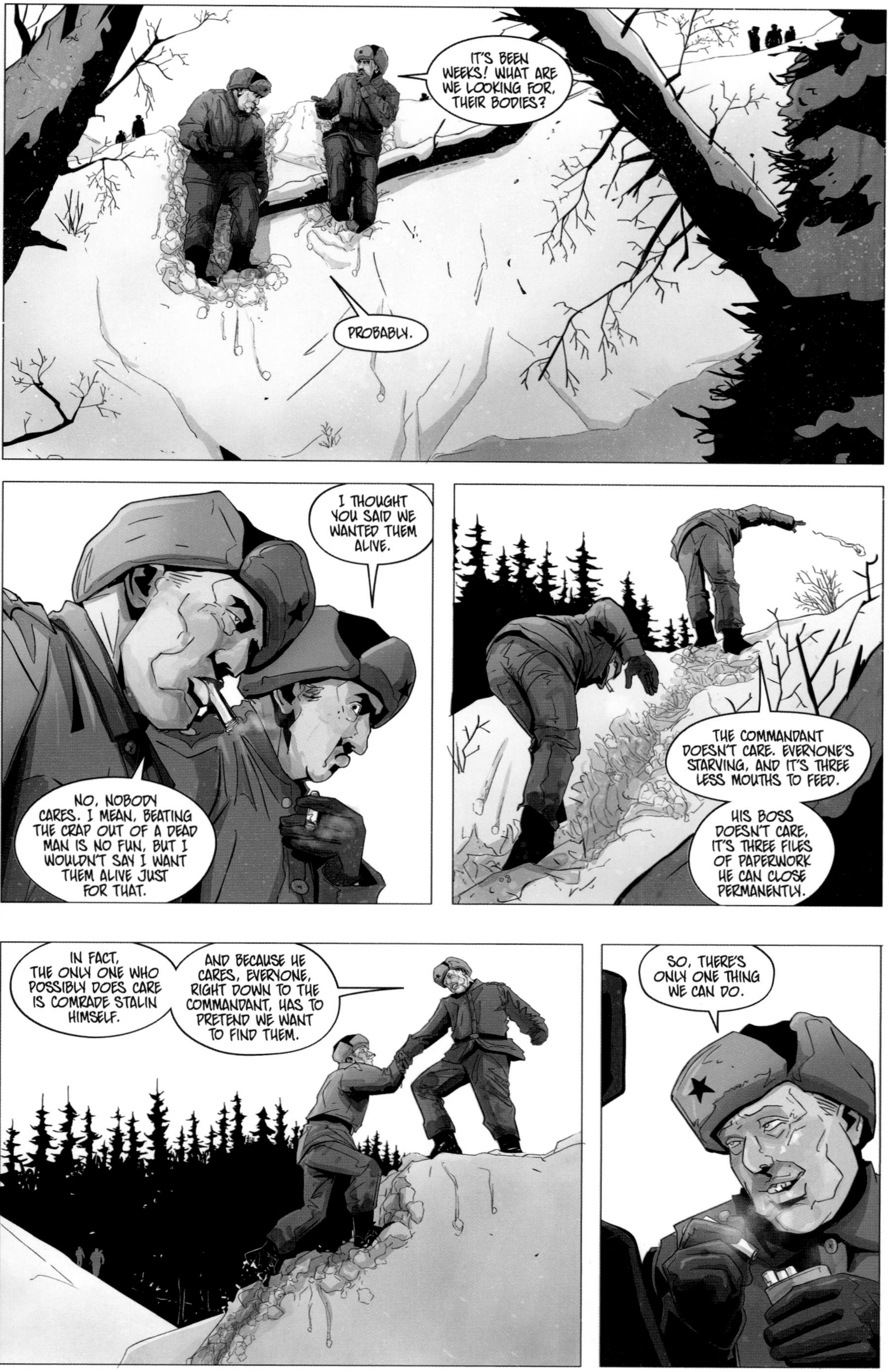
IT'S BEEN WEEKS! WHAT ARE WE LOOKING FOR, THEIR BODIES?
PROBABLY.
I THOUGHT YOU SAID WE WANTED THEM ALIVE.
NO, NOBODY CARES. I MEAN, BEATING THE CRAP OUT OF A DEAD MAN IS NO FUN, BUT I WOULDN'T SAY I WANT THEM ALIVE JUST FOR THAT.
THE COMMANDANT DOESN'T CARE. EVERYONE'S STARVING, AND IT'S THREE LESS MOUTHS TO FEED.
HIS BOSS DOESN'T CARE, IT'S THREE FILES OF PAPERWORK HE CAN CLOSE PERMANENTLY.
IN FACT, THE ONLY ONE WHO POSSIBLY DOES CARE IS COMRADE STALIN HIMSELF.
AND BECAUSE HE CARES, EVERYONE, RIGHT DOWN TO THE COMMANDANT, HAS TO PRETEND WE WANT TO FIND THEM.
SO, THERE'S ONLY ONE THING WE CAN DO.

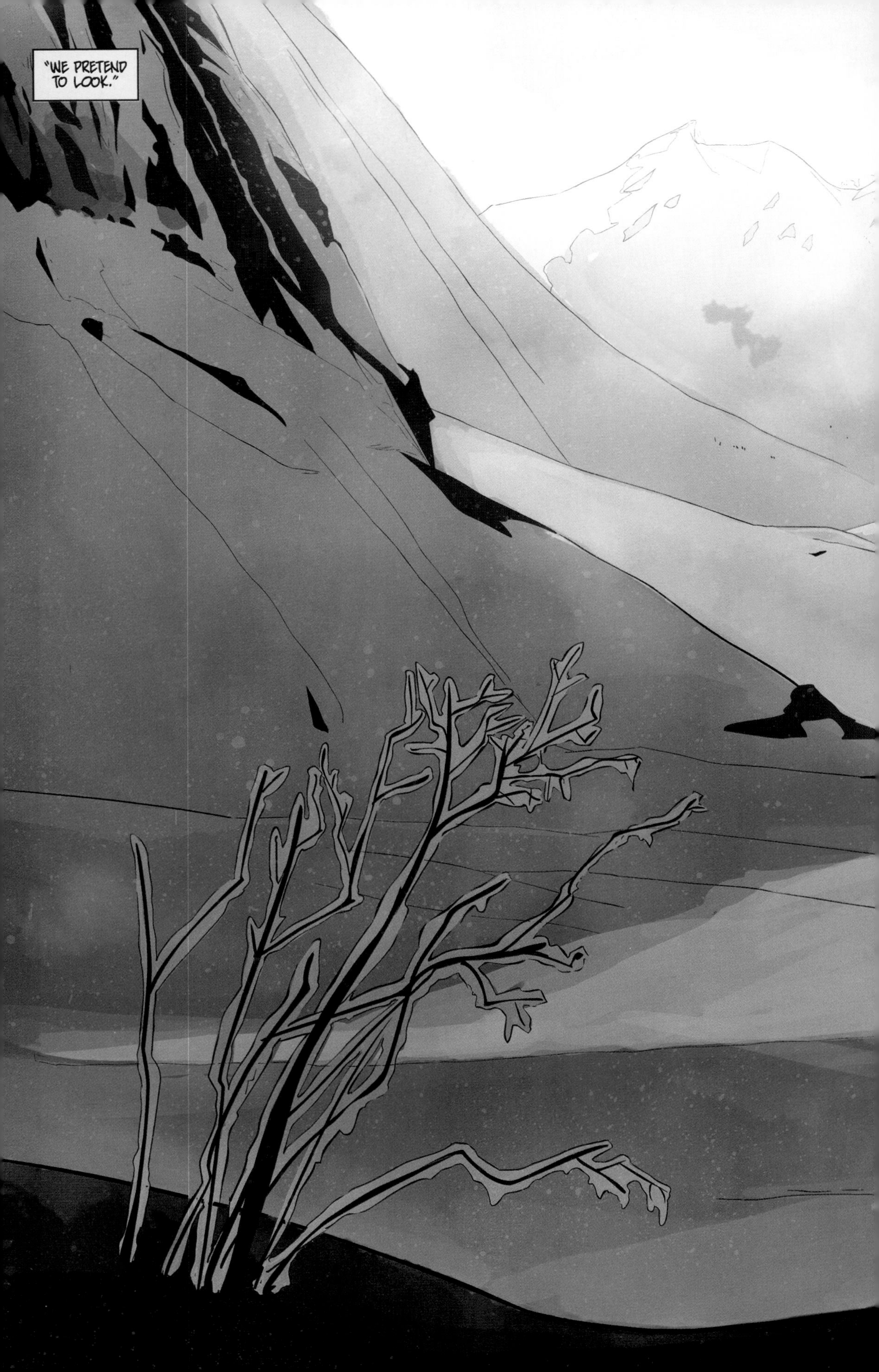
"WE PRETEND TO LOOK."

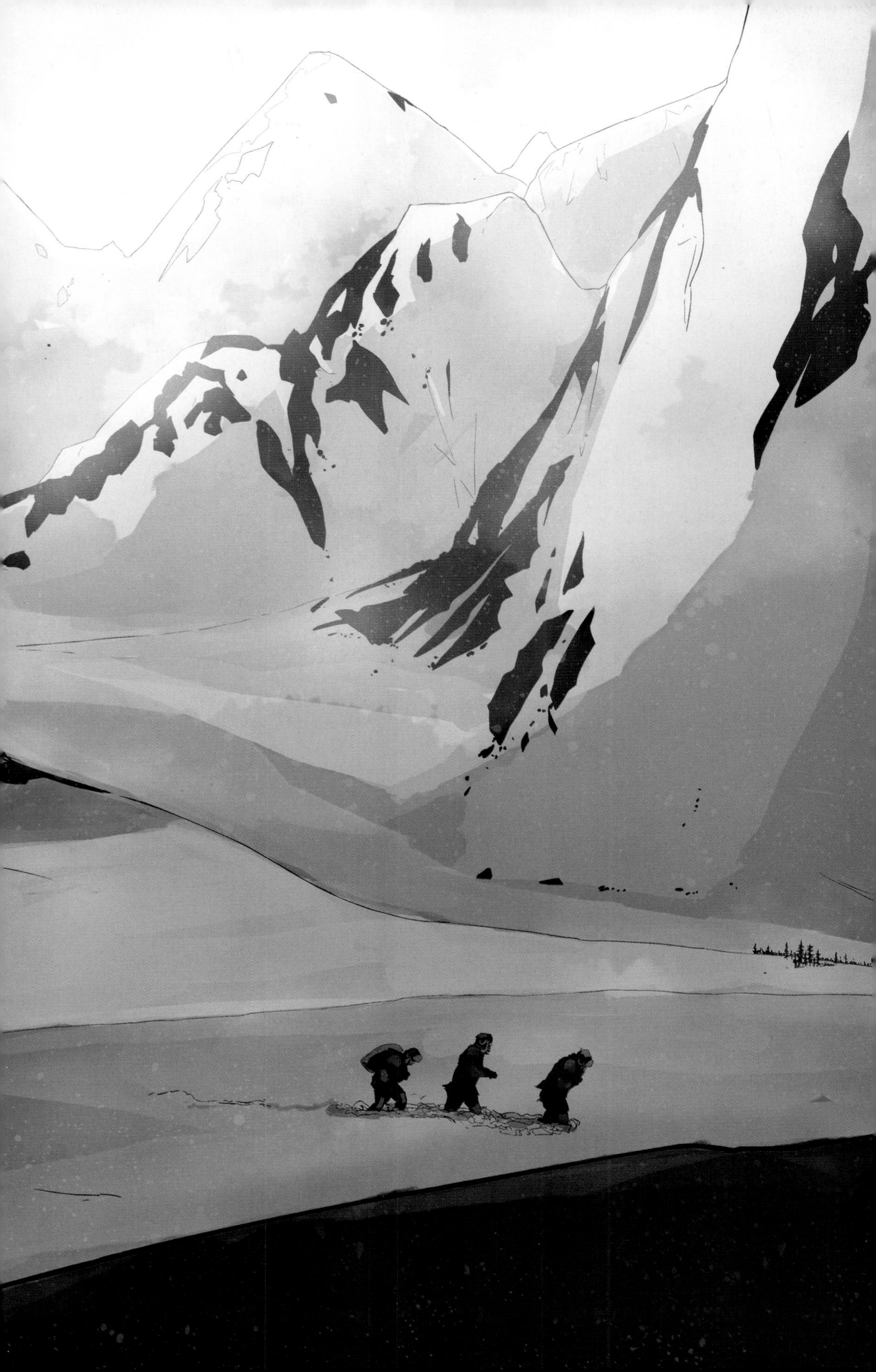

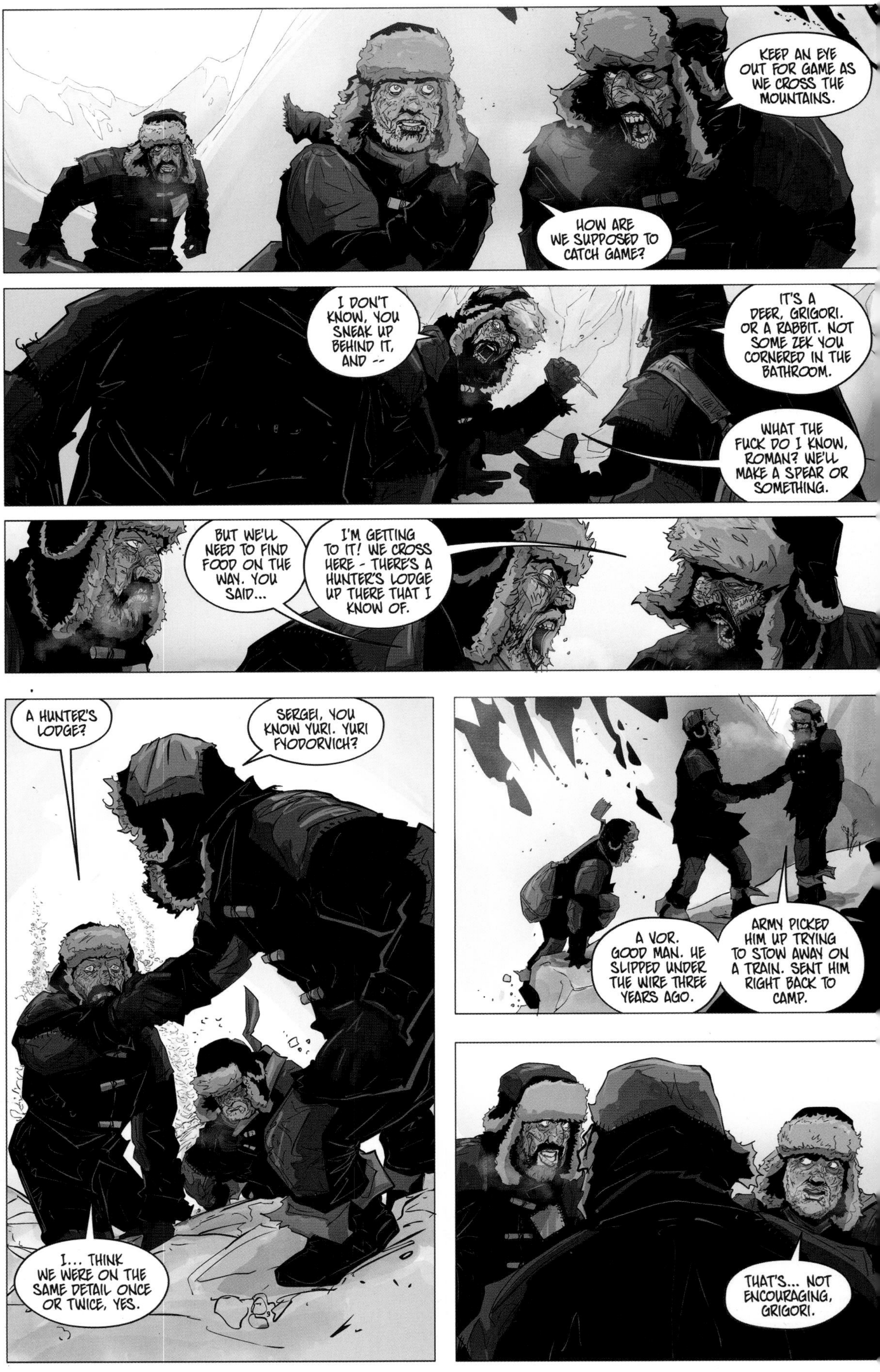
KEEP AN EYE OUT FOR GAME AS WE CROSS THE MOUNTAINS.
HOW ARE WE SUPPOSED TO CATCH GAME?
I DON'T KNOW, YOU SNEAK UP BEHIND IT, AND --
IT'S A DEER, GRIGORI. OR A RABBIT. NOT SOME ZEK YOU CORNERED IN THE BATHROOM.
WHAT THE FUCK DO I KNOW, ROMAN? WE'LL MAKE A SPEAR OR SOMETHING.
BUT WE'LL NEED TO FIND FOOD ON THE WAY. YOU SAID...
I'M GETTING TO IT! WE CROSS HERE - THERE'S A HUNTER'S LODGE UP THERE THAT I KNOW OF.
A HUNTER'S LODGE?
SERGEI, YOU KNOW YURI. YURI FYODORVICH?
I... THINK WE WERE ON THE SAME DETAIL ONCE OR TWICE, YES.
A VOR. GOOD MAN. HE SLIPPED UNDER THE WIRE THREE YEARS AGO.
ARMY PICKED HIM UP TRYING TO STOW AWAY ON A TRAIN. SENT HIM RIGHT BACK TO CAMP.
THAT'S... NOT ENCOURAGING, GRIGORI.

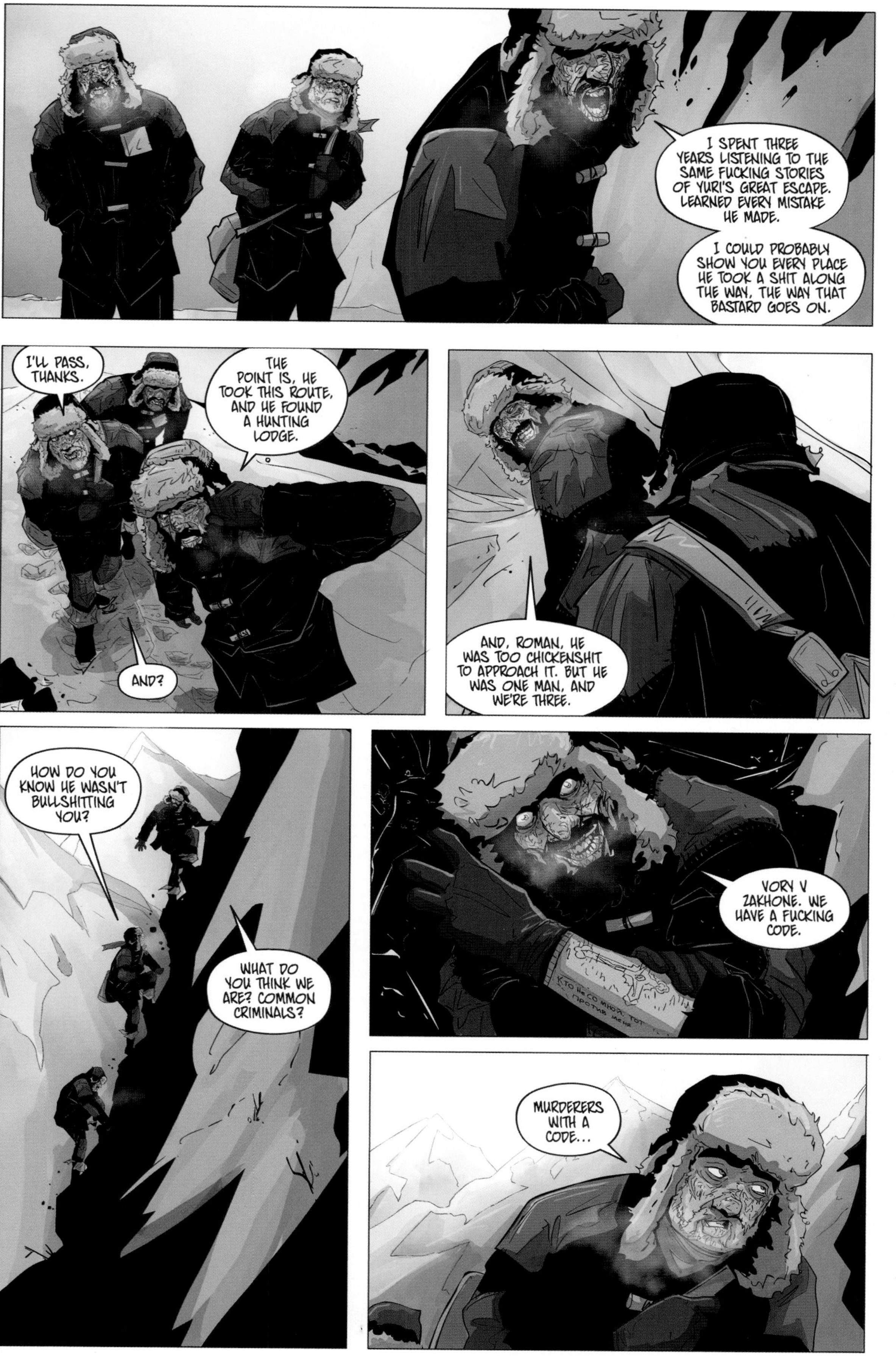
I SPENT THREE YEARS LISTENING TO THE SAME FUCKING STORIES OF YURI'S GREAT ESCAPE. LEARNED EVERY MISTAKE HE MADE.
I COULD PROBABLY SHOW YOU EVERY PLACE HE TOOK A SHIT ALONG THE WAY, THE WAY THAT BASTARD GOES ON.
I'LL PASS, THANKS.
THE POINT IS, HE TOOK THIS ROUTE, AND HE FOUND A HUNTING LODGE.
AND?
AND, ROMAN, HE WAS TOO CHICKENSHIT TO APPROACH IT. BUT HE WAS ONE MAN, AND WE'RE THREE.
HOW DO YOU KNOW HE WASN'T BULLSHITTING YOU?
WHAT DO YOU THINK WE ARE? COMMON CRIMINALS?
VORY V ZAKHONE. WE HAVE A FUCKING CODE.
MURDERERS WITH A CODE...

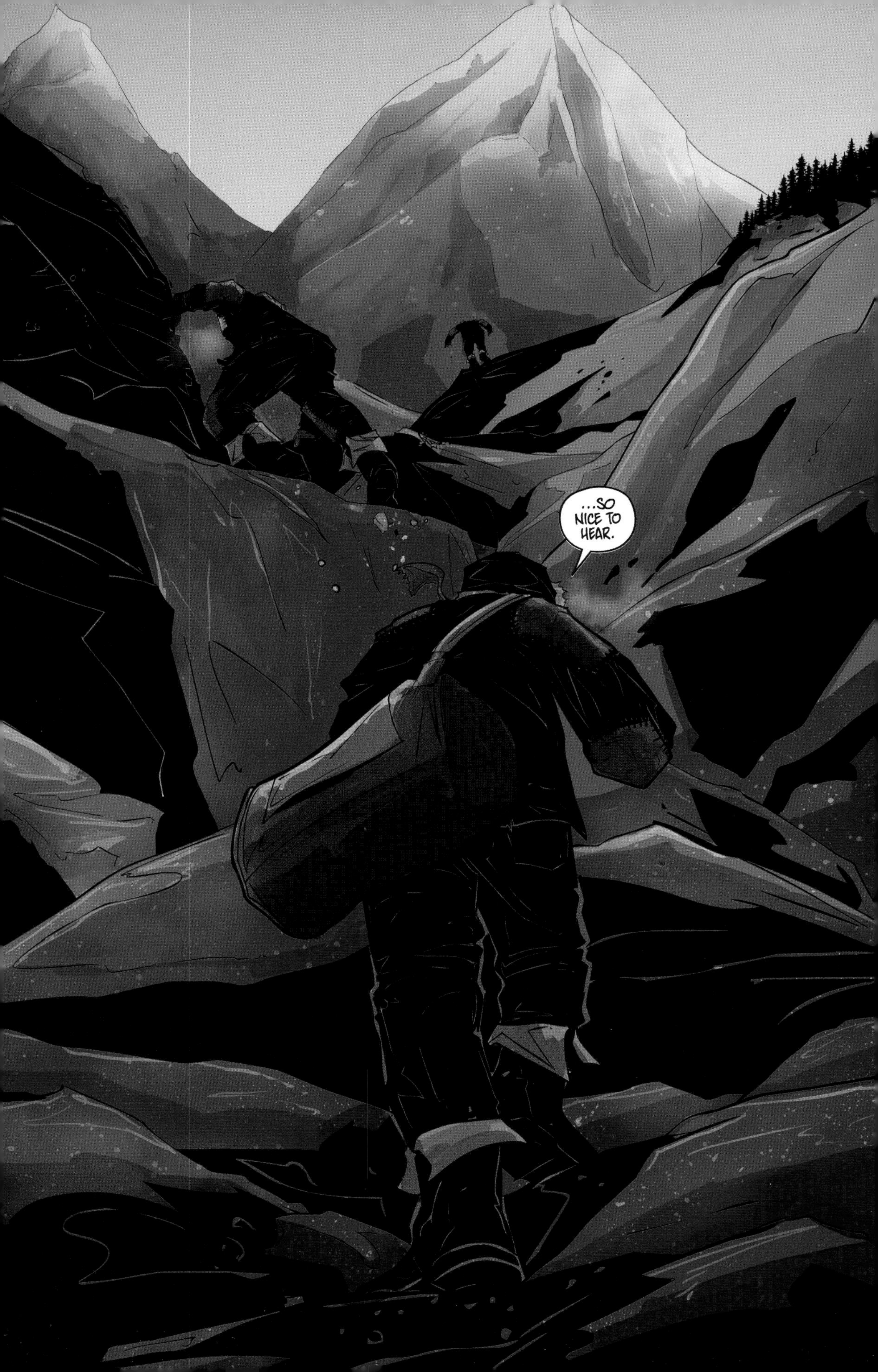
...SO NICE TO HEAR.

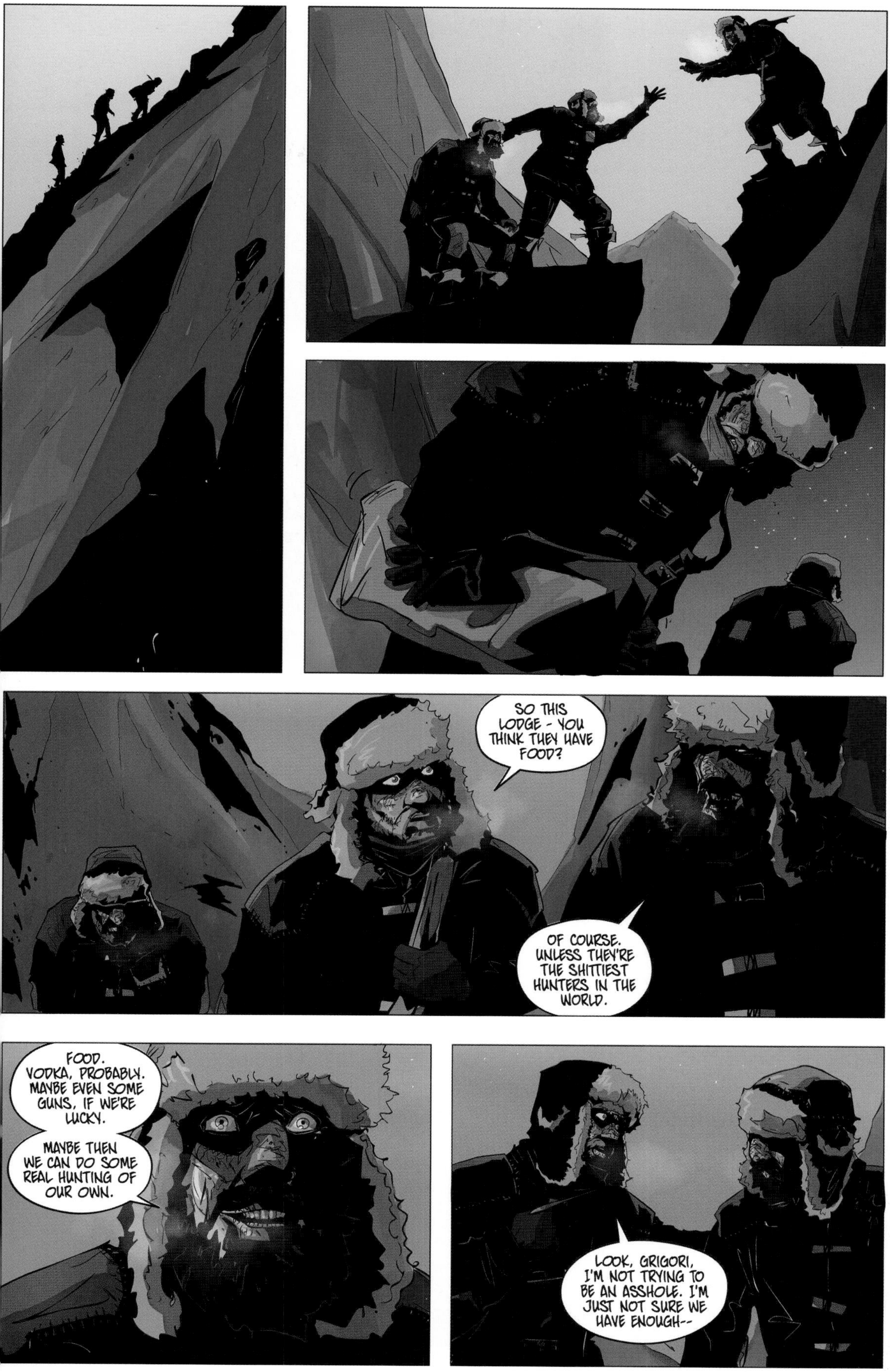
SO THIS LODGE - YOU THINK THEY HAVE FOOD?
OF COURSE. UNLESS THEY'RE THE SHITTIEST HUNTERS IN THE WORLD.
FOOD. VODKA, PROBABLY. MAYBE EVEN SOME GUNS, IF WE'RE LUCKY.
MAYBE THEN WE CAN DO SOME REAL HUNTING OF OUR OWN.
LOOK, GRIGORI, I'M NOT TRYING TO BE AN ASSHOLE. I'M JUST NOT SURE WE HAVE ENOUGH--

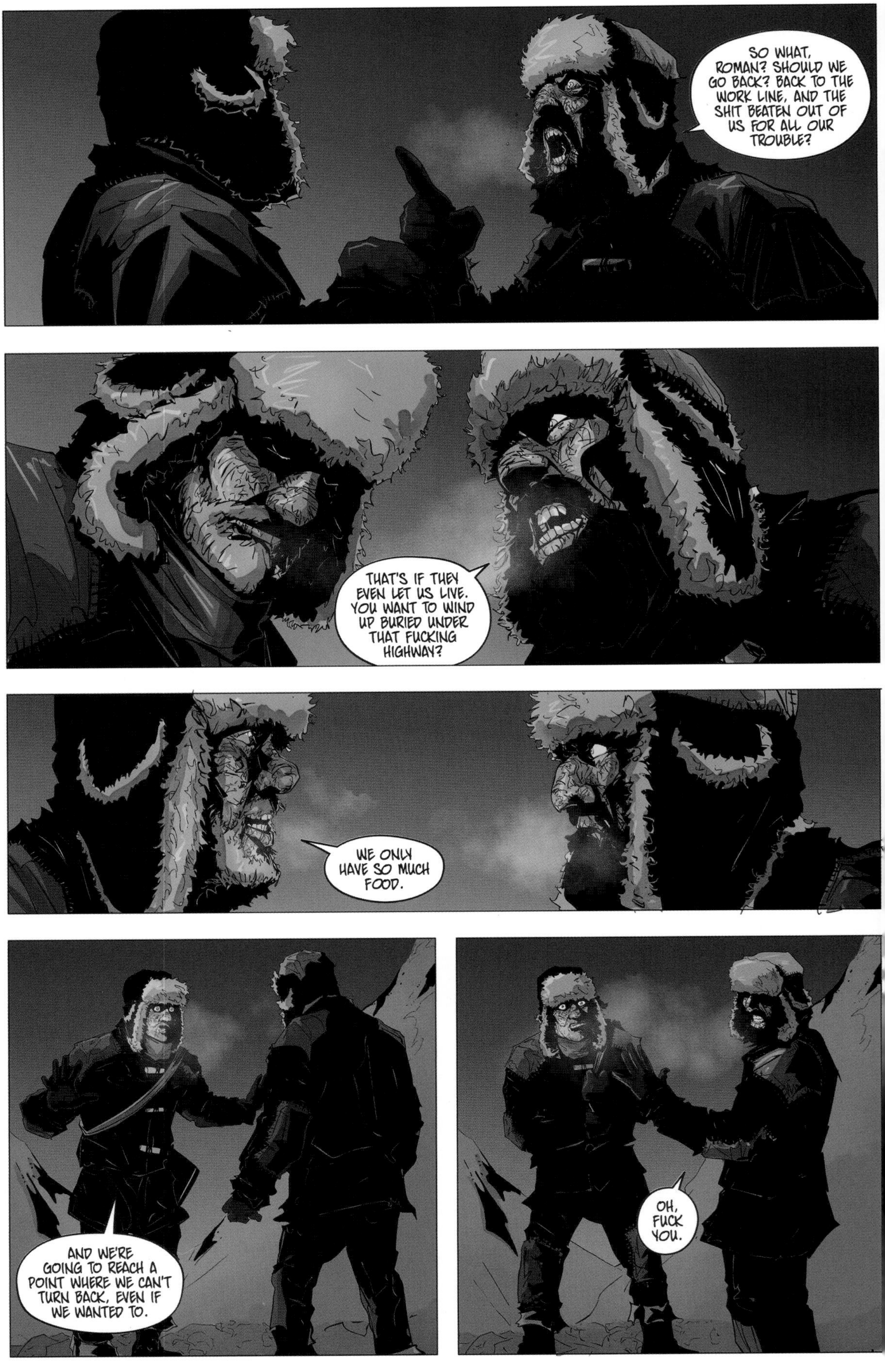
SO WHAT, ROMAN? SHOULD WE GO BACK? BACK TO THE WORK LINE, AND THE SHIT BEATEN OUT OF US FOR ALL OUR TROUBLE?
THAT'S IF THEY EVEN LET US LIVE. YOU WANT TO WIND UP BURIED UNDER THAT FUCKING HIGHWAY?
WE ONLY HAVE SO MUCH FOOD.
AND WE'RE GOING TO REACH A POINT WHERE WE CAN'T TURN BACK, EVEN IF WE WANTED TO.
OH, FUCK YOU.

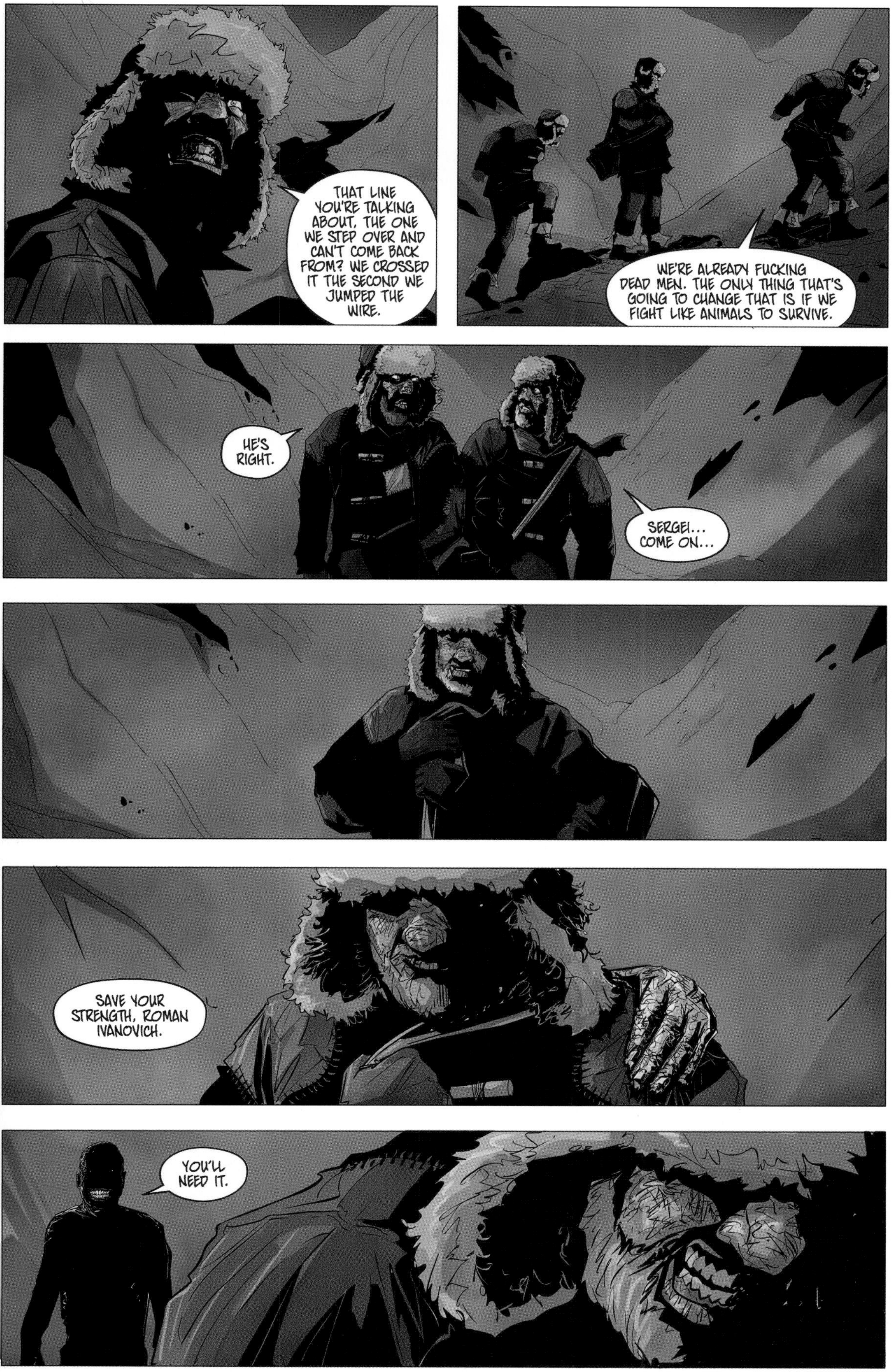
THAT LINE YOU'RE TALKING ABOUT, THE ONE WE STEP OVER AND CAN'T COME BACK FROM? WE CROSSED IT THE SECOND WE JUMPED THE WIRE.
WE'RE ALREADY FUCKING DEAD MEN. THE ONLY THING THAT'S GOING TO CHANGE THAT IS IF WE FIGHT LIKE ANIMALS TO SURVIVE.
HE'S RIGHT.
SERGEI... COME ON...
SAVE YOUR STRENGTH, ROMAN IVANOVICH.
YOU'LL NEED IT.

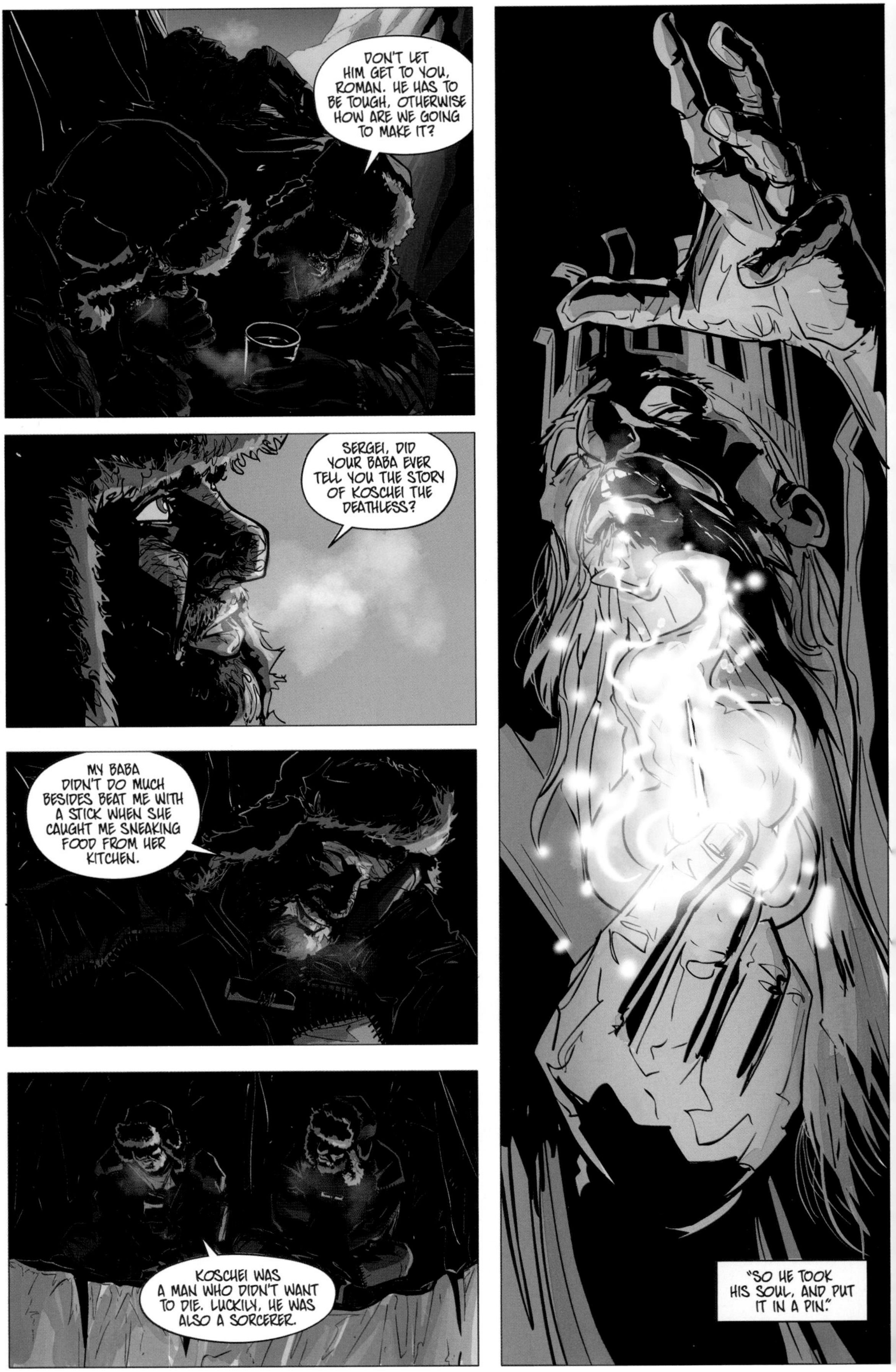
DON'T LET HIM GET TO YOU, ROMAN. HE HAS TO BE TOUGH, OTHERWISE HOW ARE WE GOING TO MAKE IT?
SERGEI, DID YOUR BABA EVER TELL YOU THE STORY OF KOSCHEI THE DEATHLESS?
MY BABA DIDN'T DO MUCH BESIDES BEAT ME WITH A STICK WHEN SHE CAUGHT ME SNEAKING FOOD FROM HER KITCHEN.
KOSCHEI WAS A MAN WHO DIDN'T WANT TO DIE. LUCKILY, HE WAS ALSO A SORCERER.
"SO HE TOOK HIS SOUL, AND PUT IT IN A PIN."

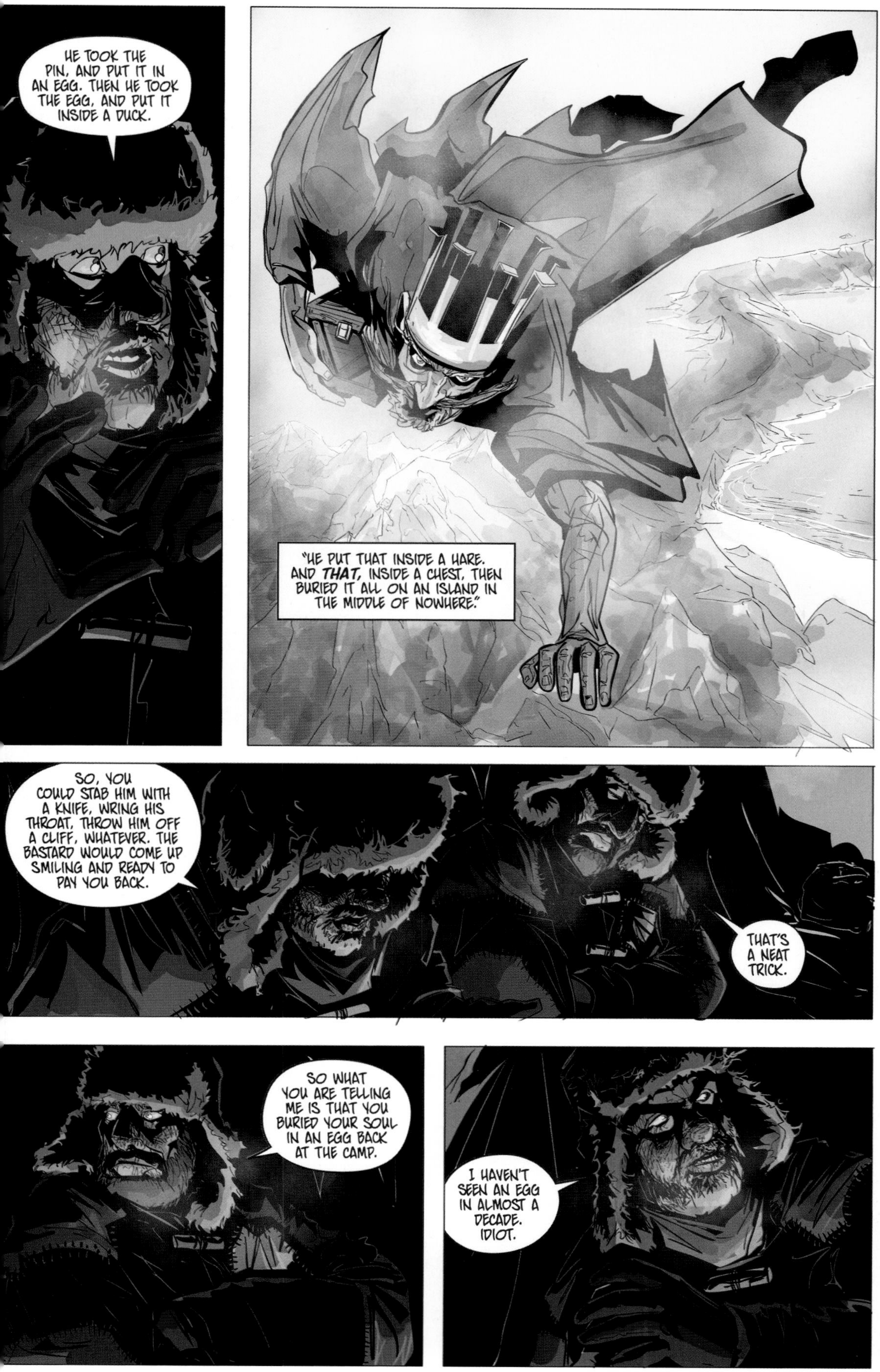
HE TOOK THE PIN, AND PUT IT IN AN EGG. THEN HE TOOK THE EGG, AND PUT IT INSIDE A DUCK.
"HE PUT THAT INSIDE A HARE. AND THAT, INSIDE A CHEST, THEN BURIED IT ALL ON AN ISLAND IN THE MIDDLE OF NOWHERE."
SO, YOU COULD STAB HIM WITH A KNIFE, WRING HIS THROAT, THROW HIM OFF A CLIFF, WHATEVER. THE BASTARD WOULD COME UP SMILING AND READY TO PAY YOU BACK.
THAT'S A NEAT TRICK.
SO WHAT YOU ARE TELLING ME IS THAT YOU BURIED YOUR SOUL IN AN EGG BACK AT THE CAMP.
I HAVEN'T SEEN AN EGG IN ALMOST A DECADE. IDIOT.

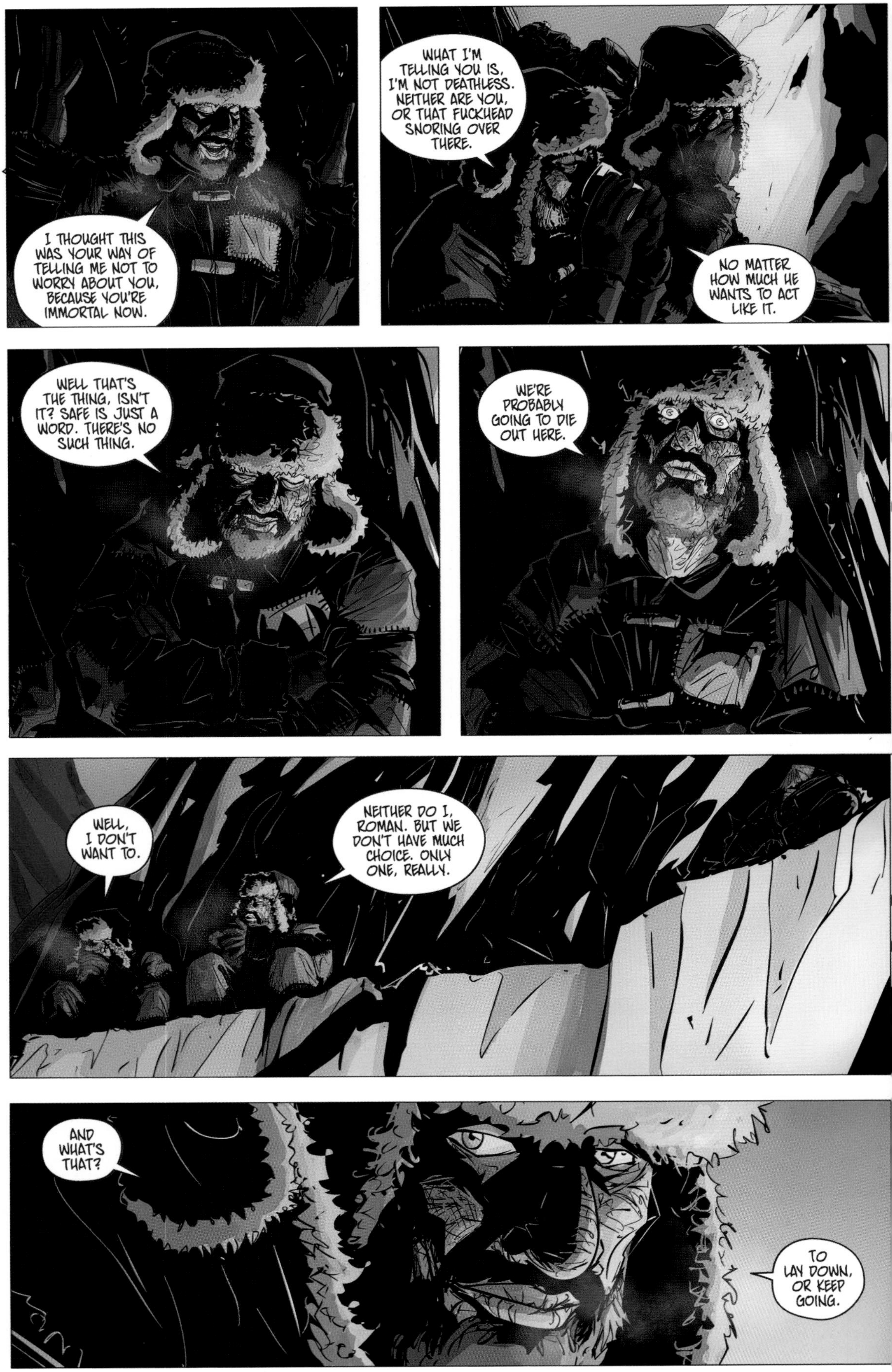
I THOUGHT THIS WAS YOUR WAY OF TELLING ME NOT TO WORRY ABOUT YOU, BECAUSE YOU'RE IMMORTAL NOW.
WHAT I'M TELLING YOU IS, I'M NOT DEATHLESS. NEITHER ARE YOU, OR THAT FUCKHEAD SNORING OVER THERE.
NO MATTER HOW MUCH HE WANTS TO ACT LIKE IT.
WELL THAT'S THE THING, ISN'T IT? SAFE IS JUST A WORD. THERE'S NO SUCH THING.
WE'RE PROBABLY GOING TO DIE OUT HERE.
WELL, I DON'T WANT TO.
NEITHER DO I, ROMAN. BUT WE DON'T HAVE MUCH CHOICE. ONLY ONE, REALLY.
AND WHAT'S THAT?
TO LAY DOWN, OR KEEP GOING.

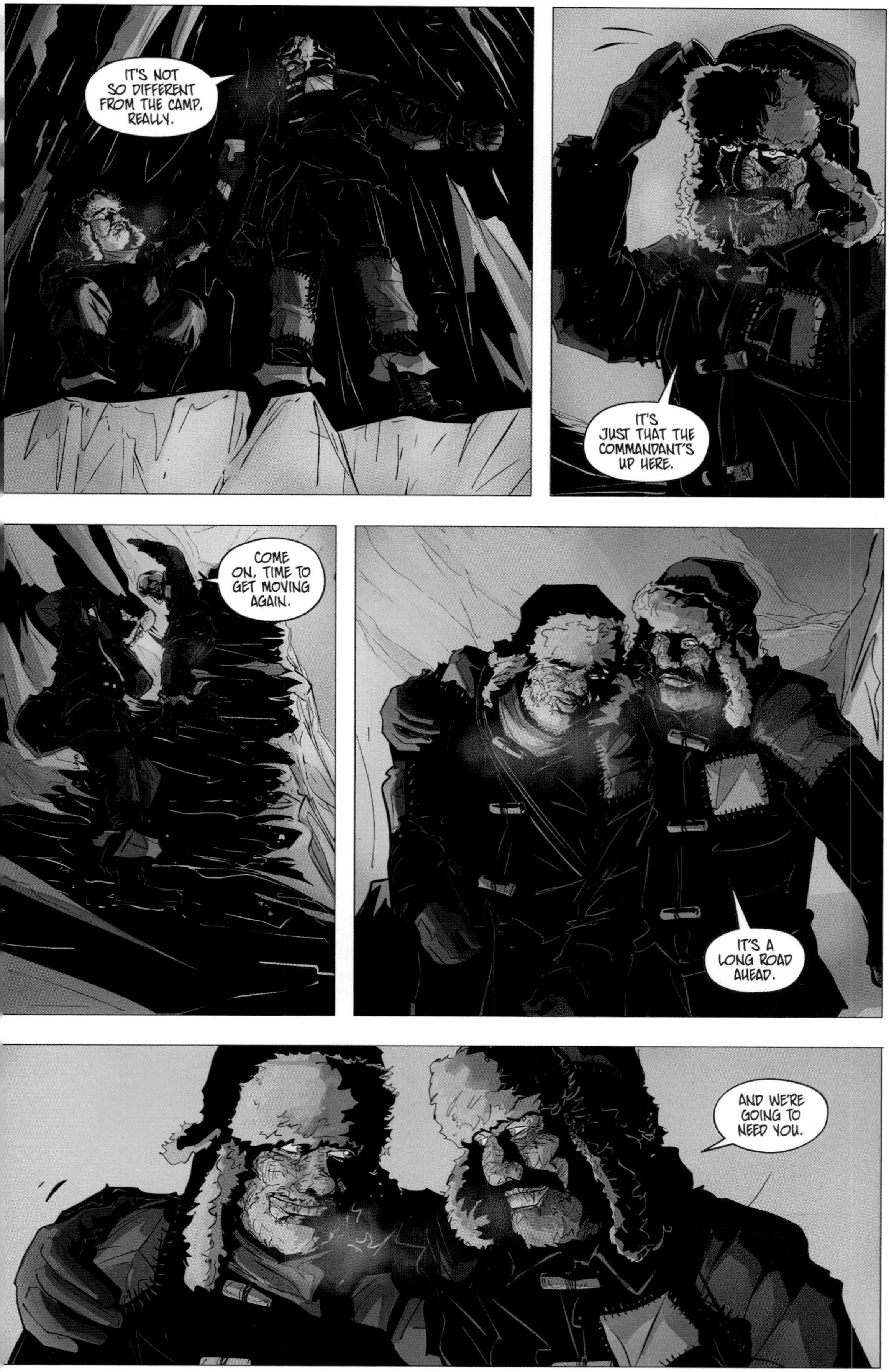
IT'S NOT SO DIFFERENT FROM THE CAMP, REALLY.
IT'S JUST THAT THE COMMANDANT'S UP HERE.
COME ON, TIME TO GET MOVING AGAIN.
IT'S A LONG ROAD AHEAD.
AND WE'RE GOING TO NEED YOU.

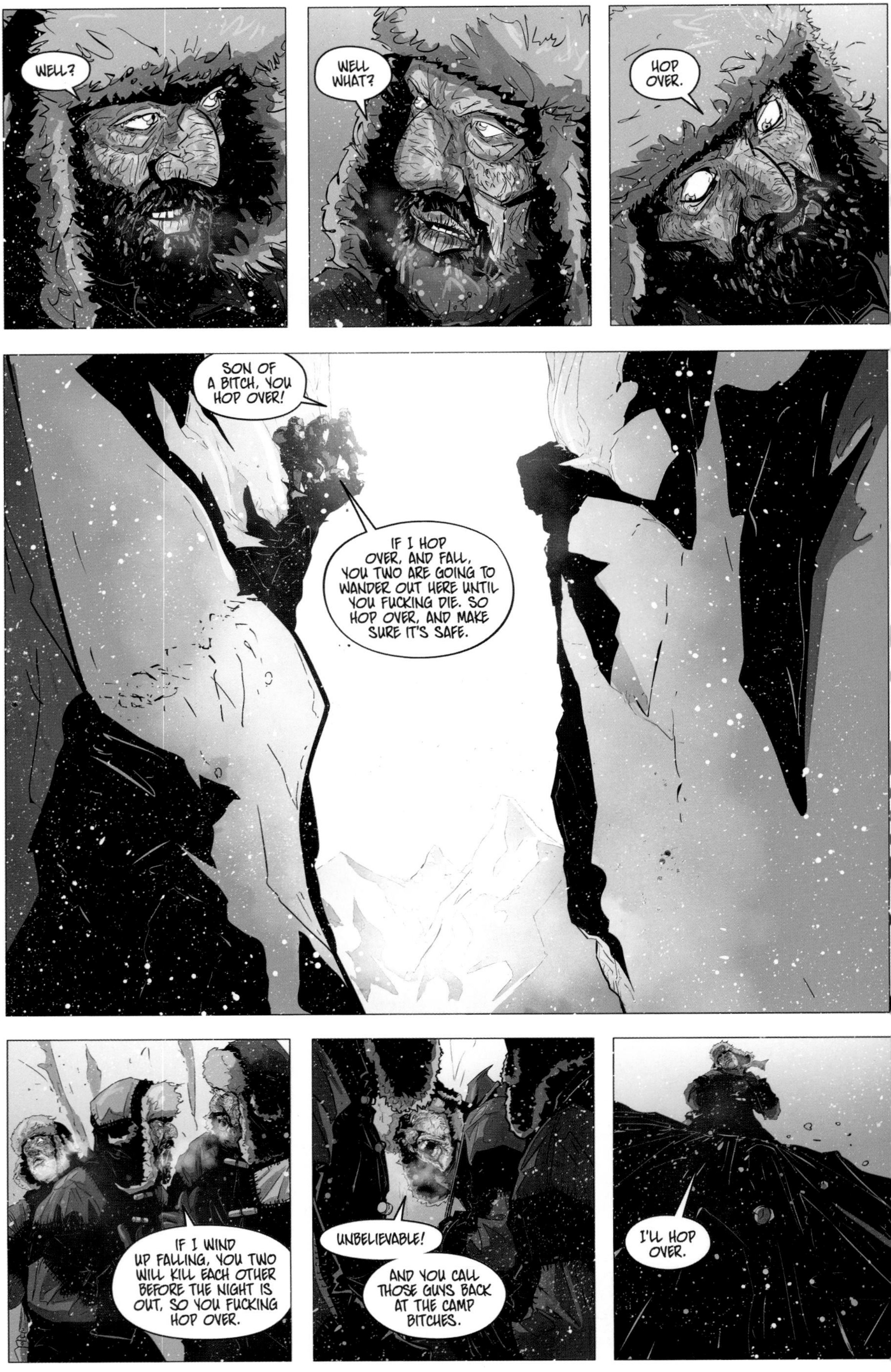
WELL?
WELL WHAT?
HOP OVER.
SON OF A BITCH, YOU HOP OVER!
IF I HOP OVER, AND FALL, YOU TWO ARE GOING TO WANDER OUT HERE UNTIL YOU FUCKING DIE. SO HOP OVER, AND MAKE SURE IT'S SAFE.
IF I WIND UP FALLING, YOU TWO WILL KILL EACH OTHER BEFORE THE NIGHT IS OUT, SO YOU FUCKING HOP OVER.
UNBELIEVABLE!
AND YOU CALL THOSE GUYS BACK AT THE CAMP BITCHES.
I'LL HOP OVER.

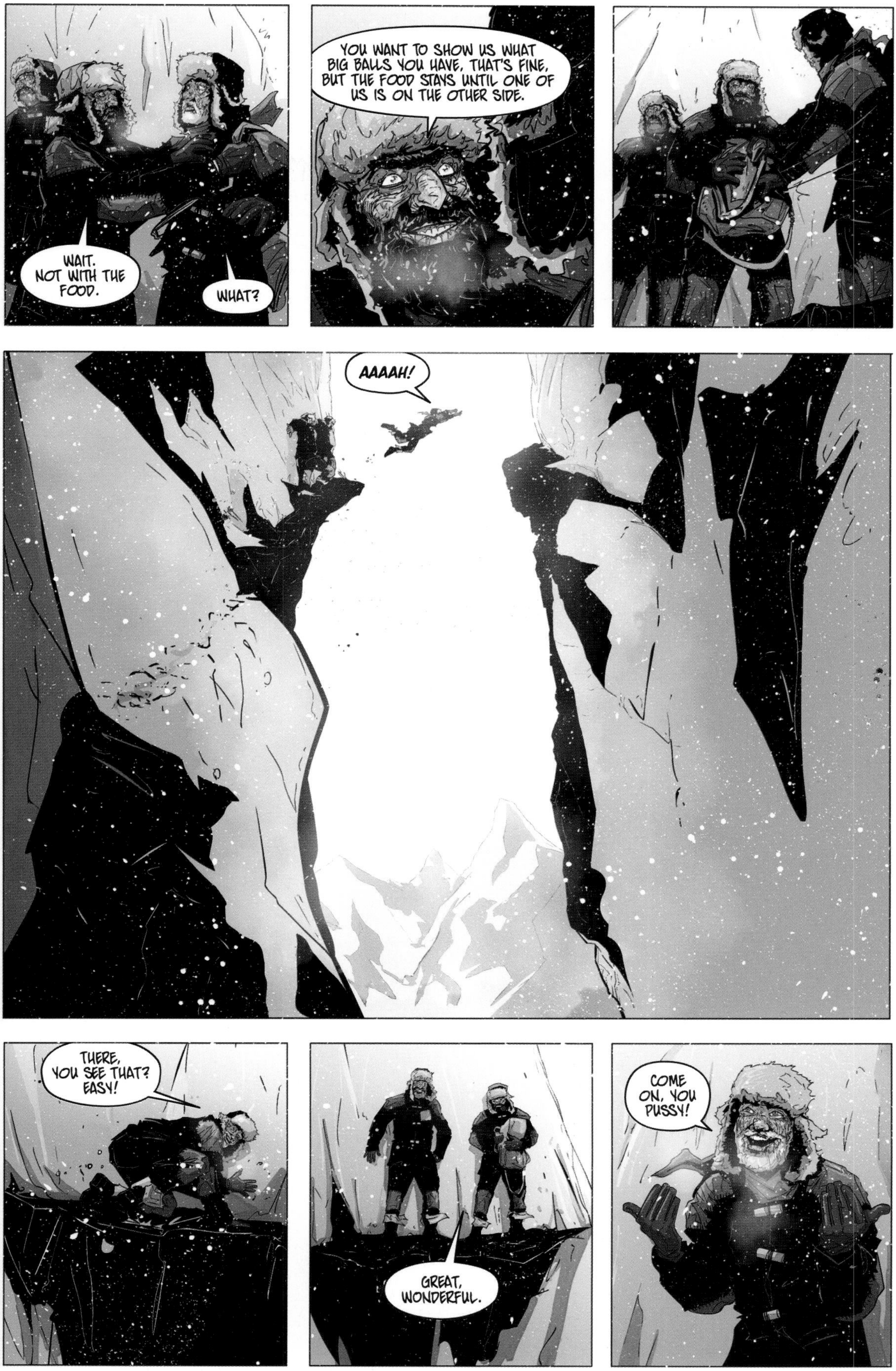
WAIT. NOT WITH THE FOOD.
WHAT?
YOU WANT TO SHOW US WHAT BIG BALLS YOU HAVE, THAT'S FINE, BUT THE FOOD STAYS UNTIL ONE OF US IS ON THE OTHER SIDE.
AAAAH!
THERE, YOU SEE THAT? EASY!
GREAT, WONDERFUL.
COME ON, YOU PUSSY!

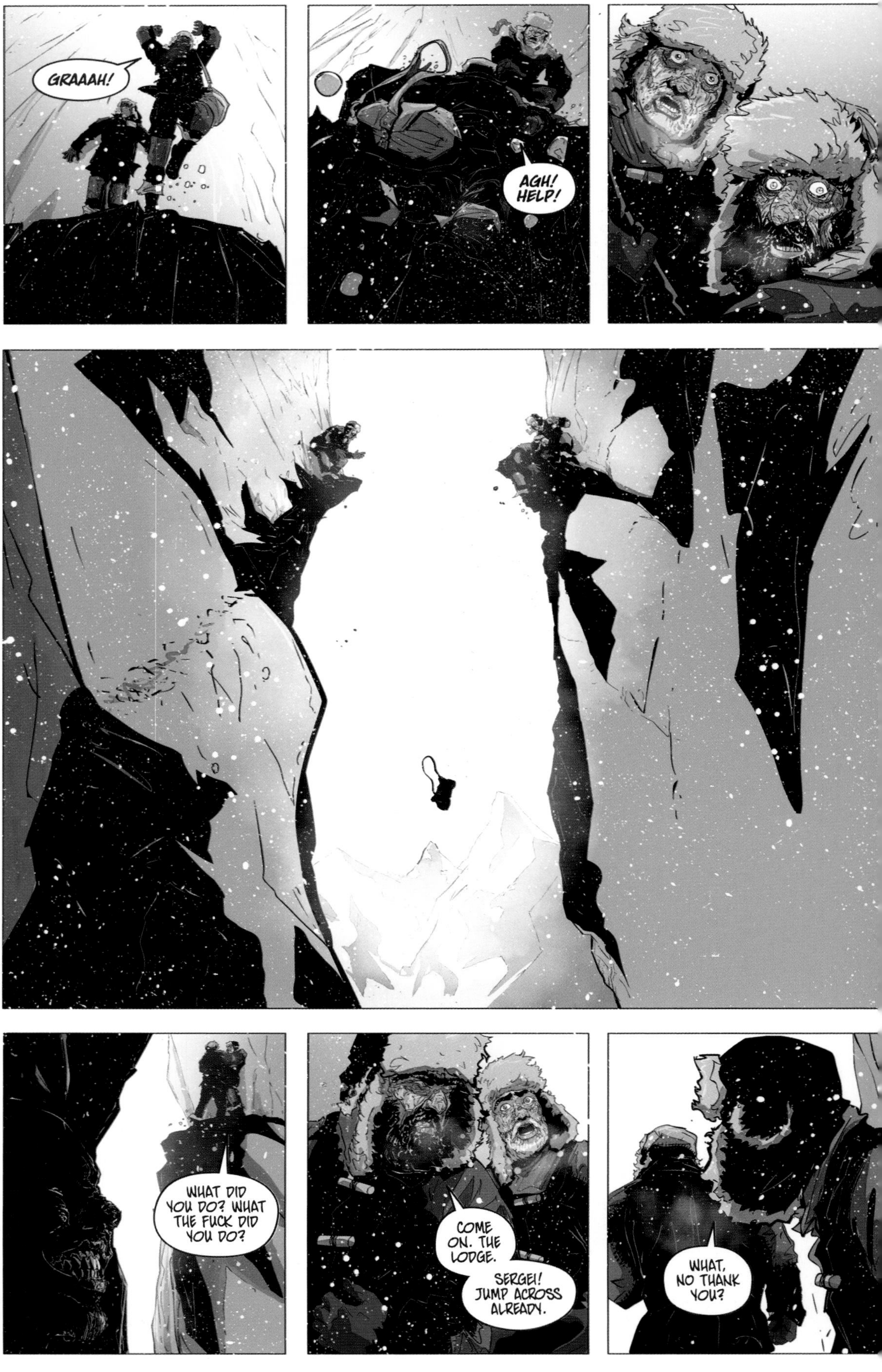
GRAAAH!
AGH! HELP!
WHAT DID YOU DO? WHAT THE FUCK DID YOU DO?
COME ON. THE LODGE.
SERGEI! JUMP ACROSS ALREADY.
WHAT, NO THANK YOU?

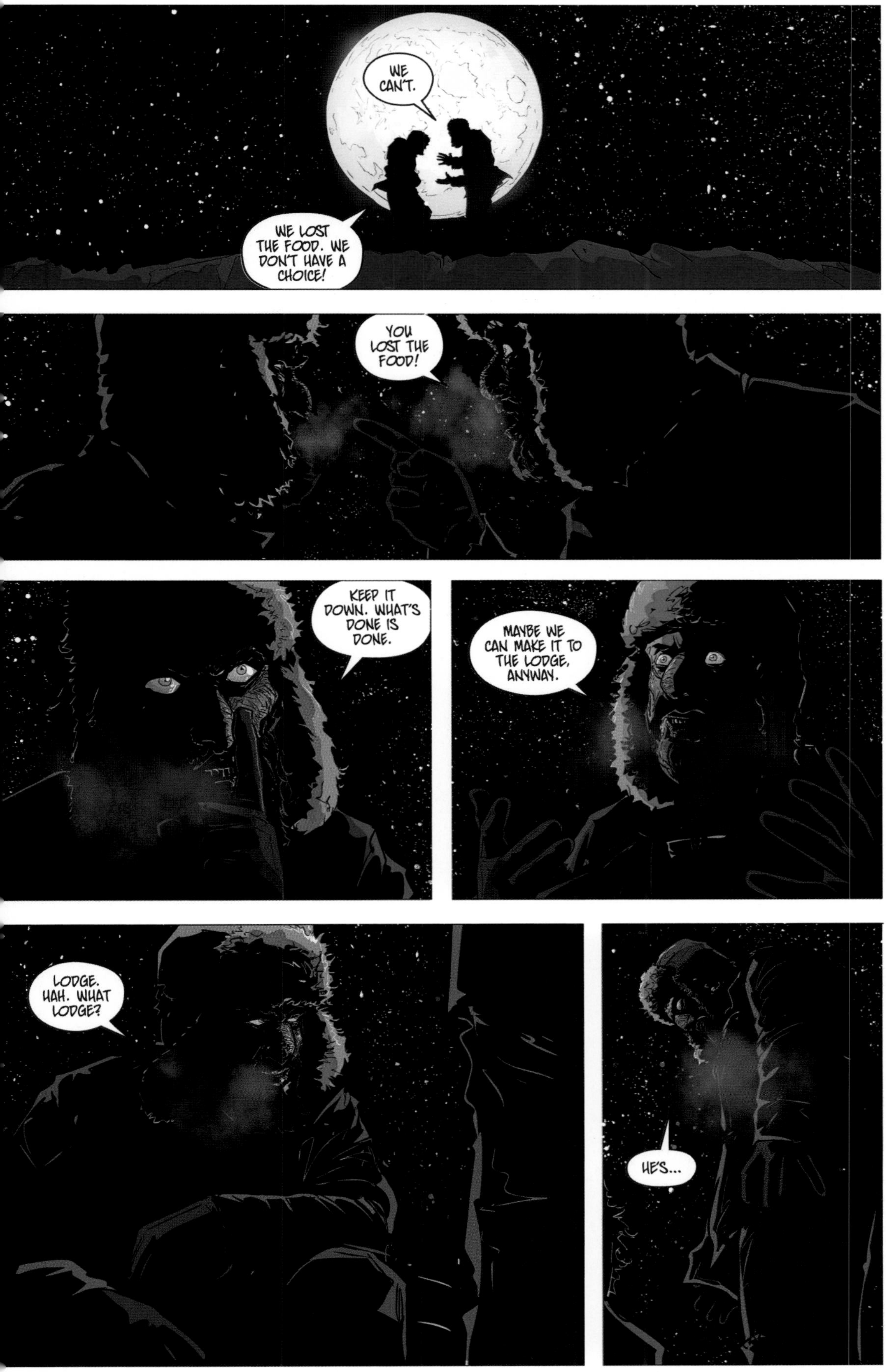
WE CAN'T.
WE LOST THE FOOD. WE DON'T HAVE A CHOICE!
YOU LOST THE FOOD!
KEEP IT DOWN. WHAT'S DONE IS DONE.
MAYBE WE CAN MAKE IT TO THE LODGE, ANYWAY.
LODGE. HAH. WHAT LODGE?
HE'S...

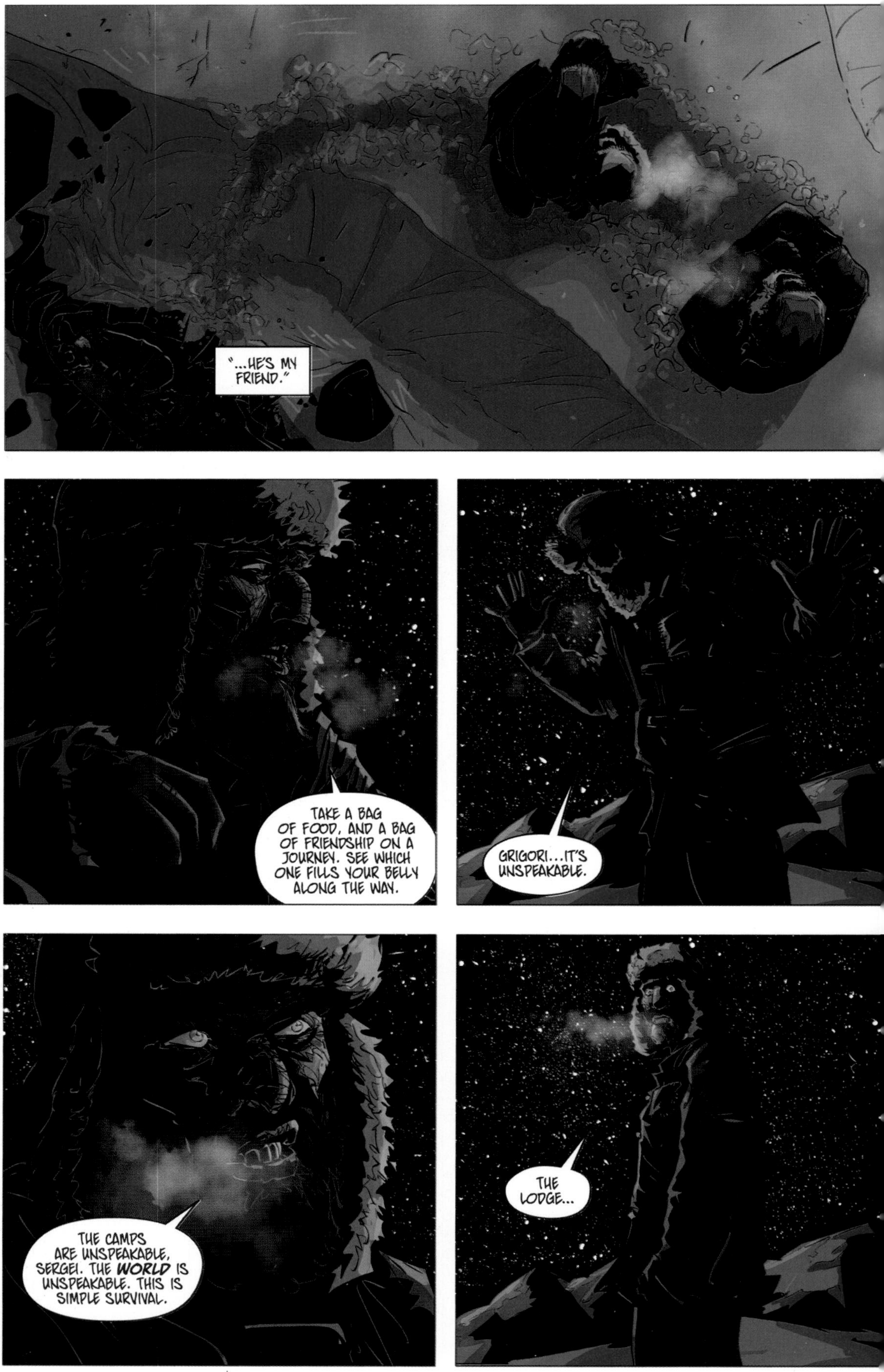
"...HE'S MY FRIEND."
TAKE A BAG OF FOOD, AND A BAG OF FRIENDSHIP ON A JOURNEY. SEE WHICH ONE FILLS YOUR BELLY ALONG THE WAY.
GRIGORI...IT'S UNSPEAKABLE.
THE CAMPS ARE UNSPEAKABLE, SERGEI. THE *WORLD* IS UNSPEAKABLE. THIS IS SIMPLE SURVIVAL.
THE LODGE...

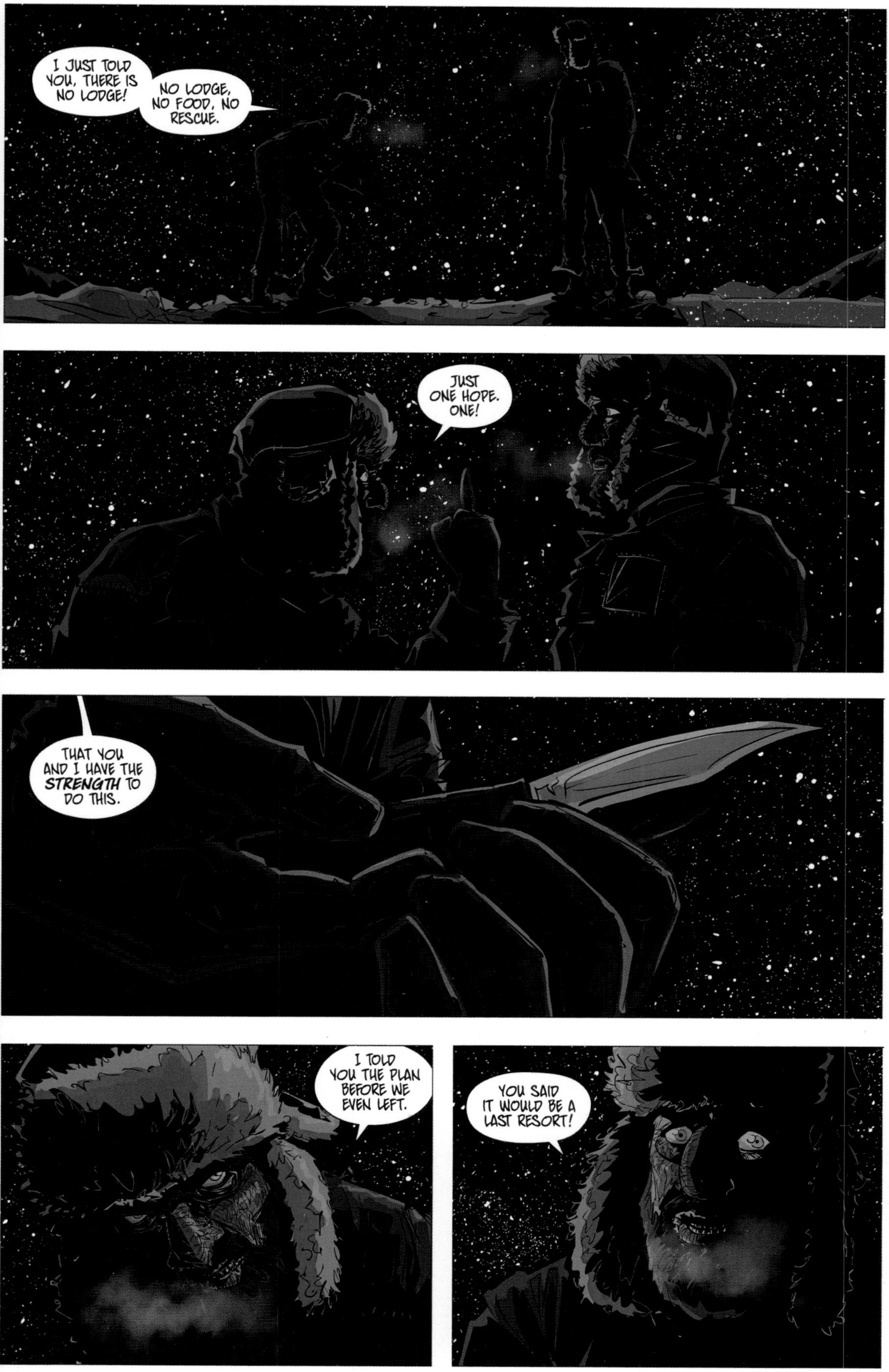
I JUST TOLD YOU, THERE IS NO LODGE!
NO LODGE, NO FOOD, NO RESCUE.
JUST ONE HOPE. ONE!
THAT YOU AND I HAVE THE *STRENGTH* TO DO THIS.
I TOLD YOU THE PLAN BEFORE WE EVEN LEFT.
YOU SAID IT WOULD BE A LAST RESORT!

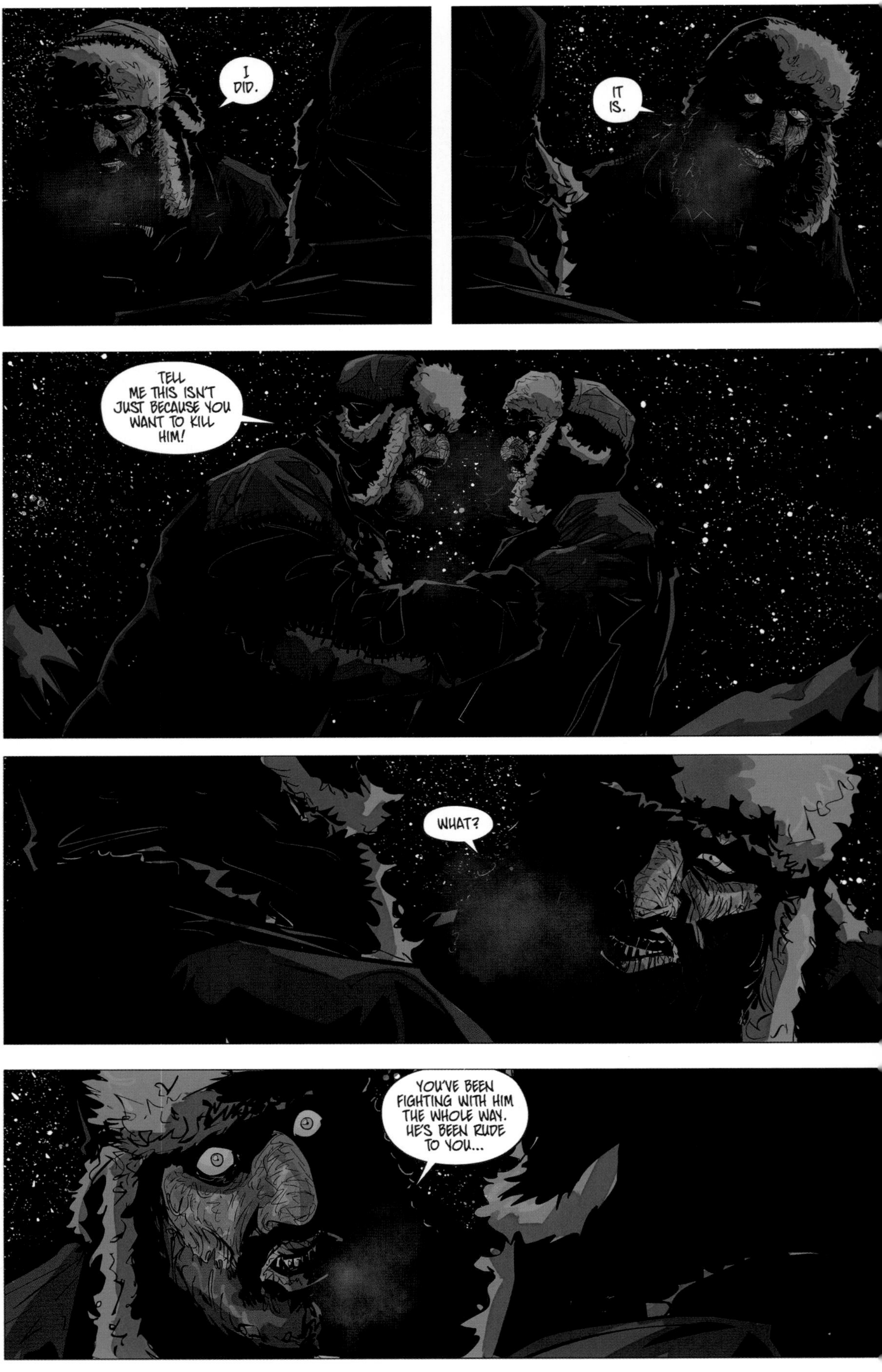
I DID.
IT IS.
TELL ME THIS ISN'T JUST BECAUSE YOU WANT TO KILL HIM!
WHAT?
YOU'VE BEEN FIGHTING WITH HIM THE WHOLE WAY. HE'S BEEN RUDE TO YOU...

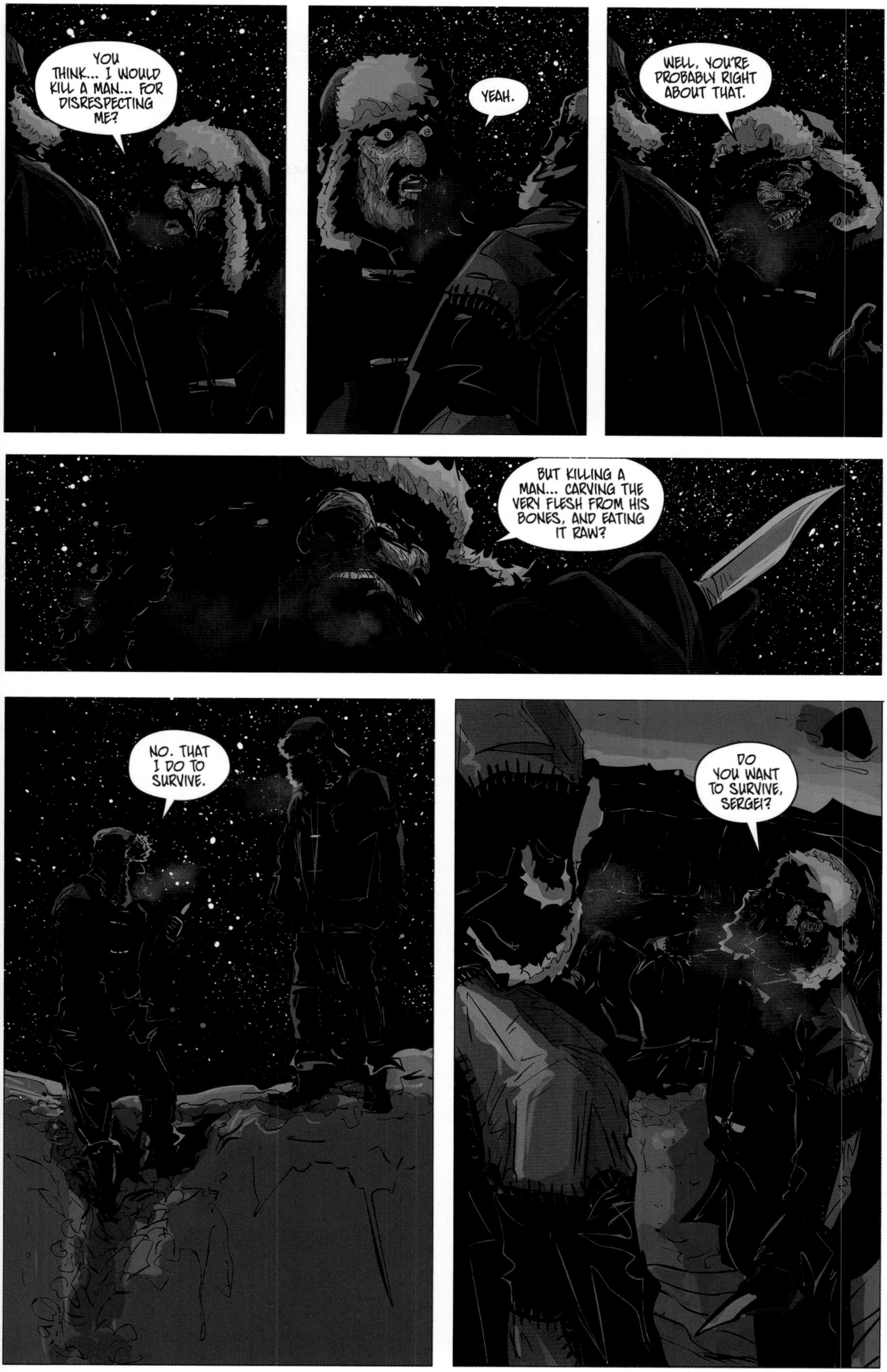
YOU THINK... I WOULD KILL A MAN... FOR DISRESPECTING ME?
YEAH.
WELL, YOU'RE PROBABLY RIGHT ABOUT THAT.
BUT KILLING A MAN... CARVING THE VERY FLESH FROM HIS BONES, AND EATING IT RAW?
NO. THAT I DO TO SURVIVE.
DO YOU WANT TO SURVIVE, SERGEI?

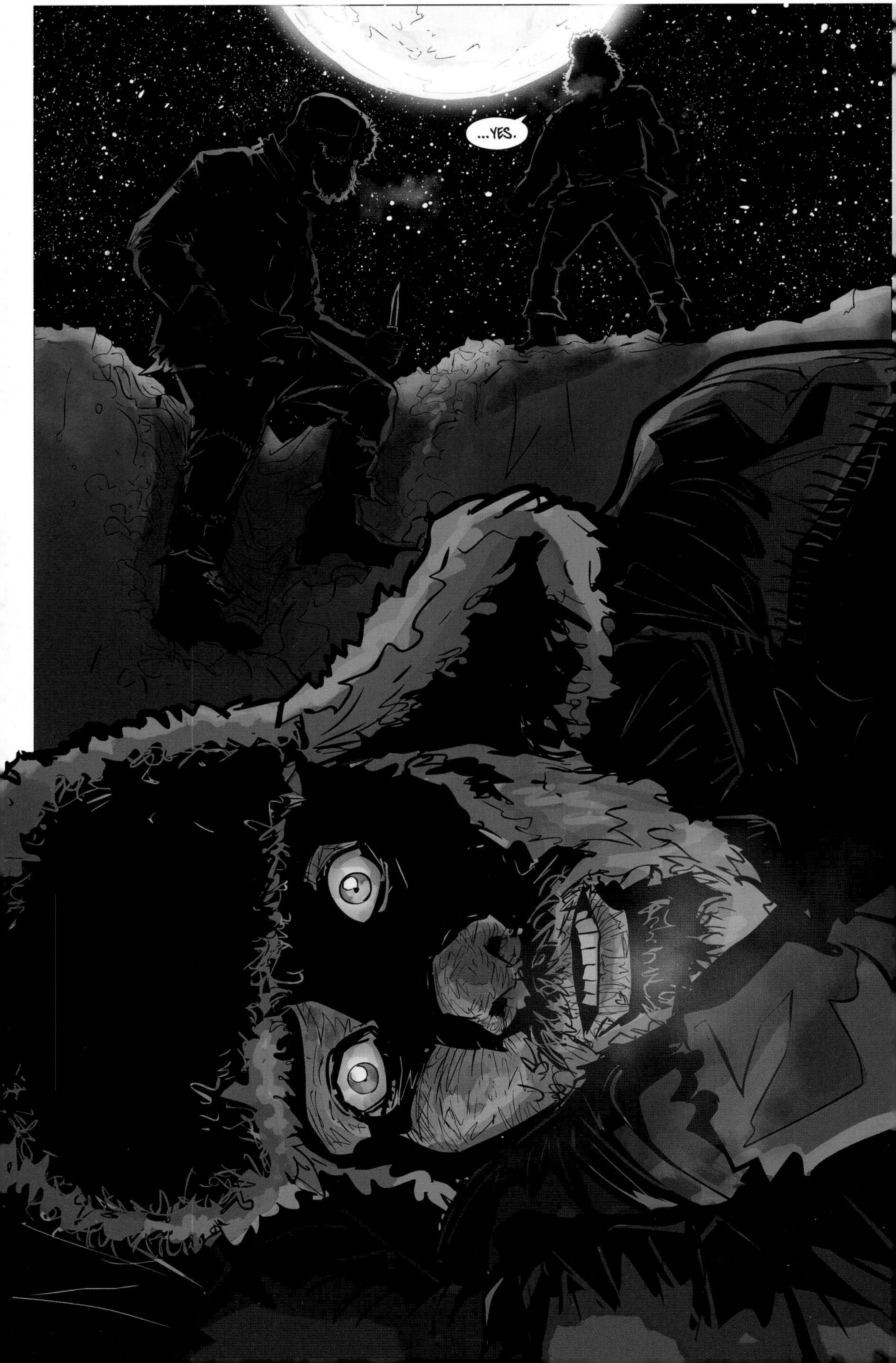
...YES.

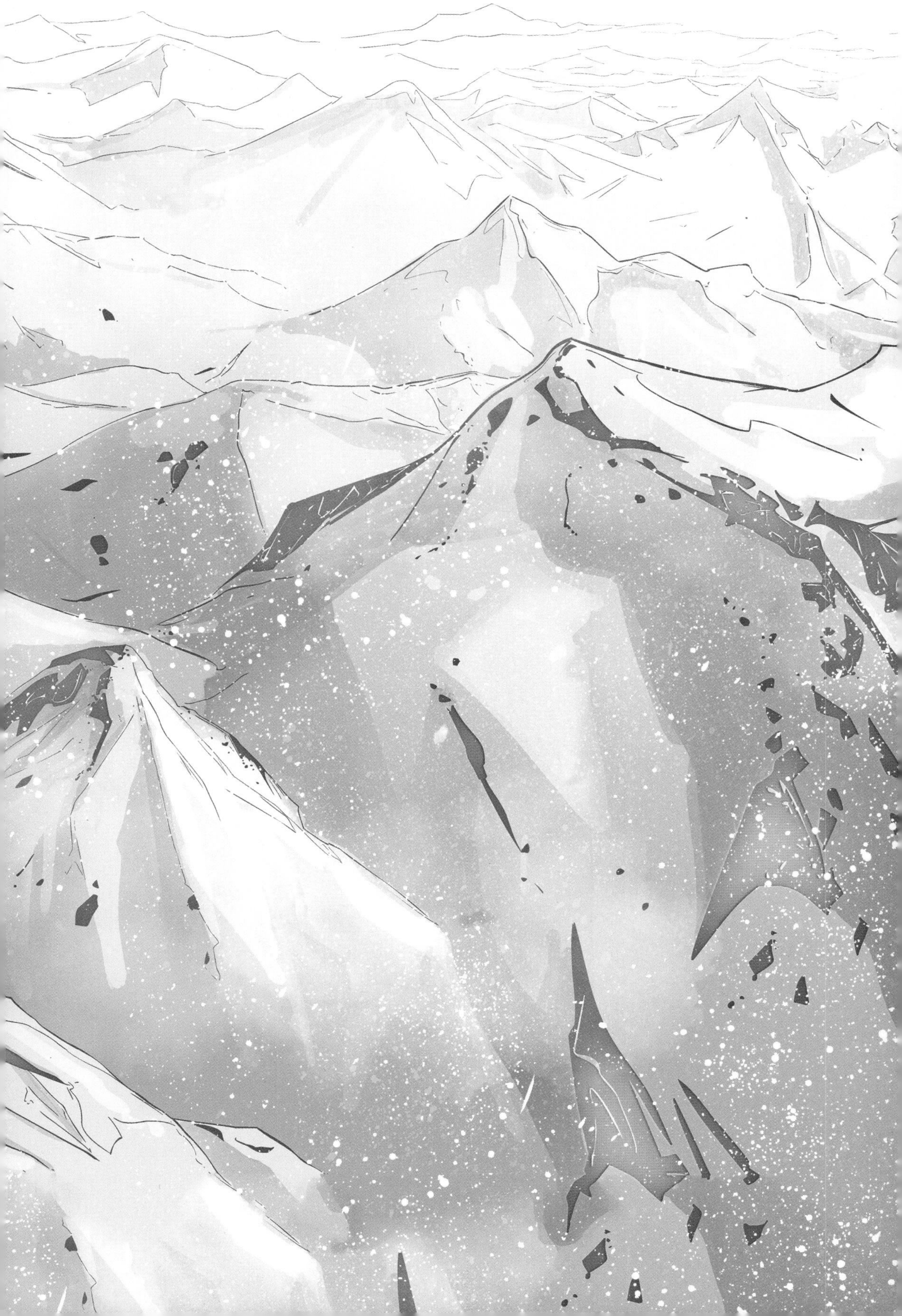

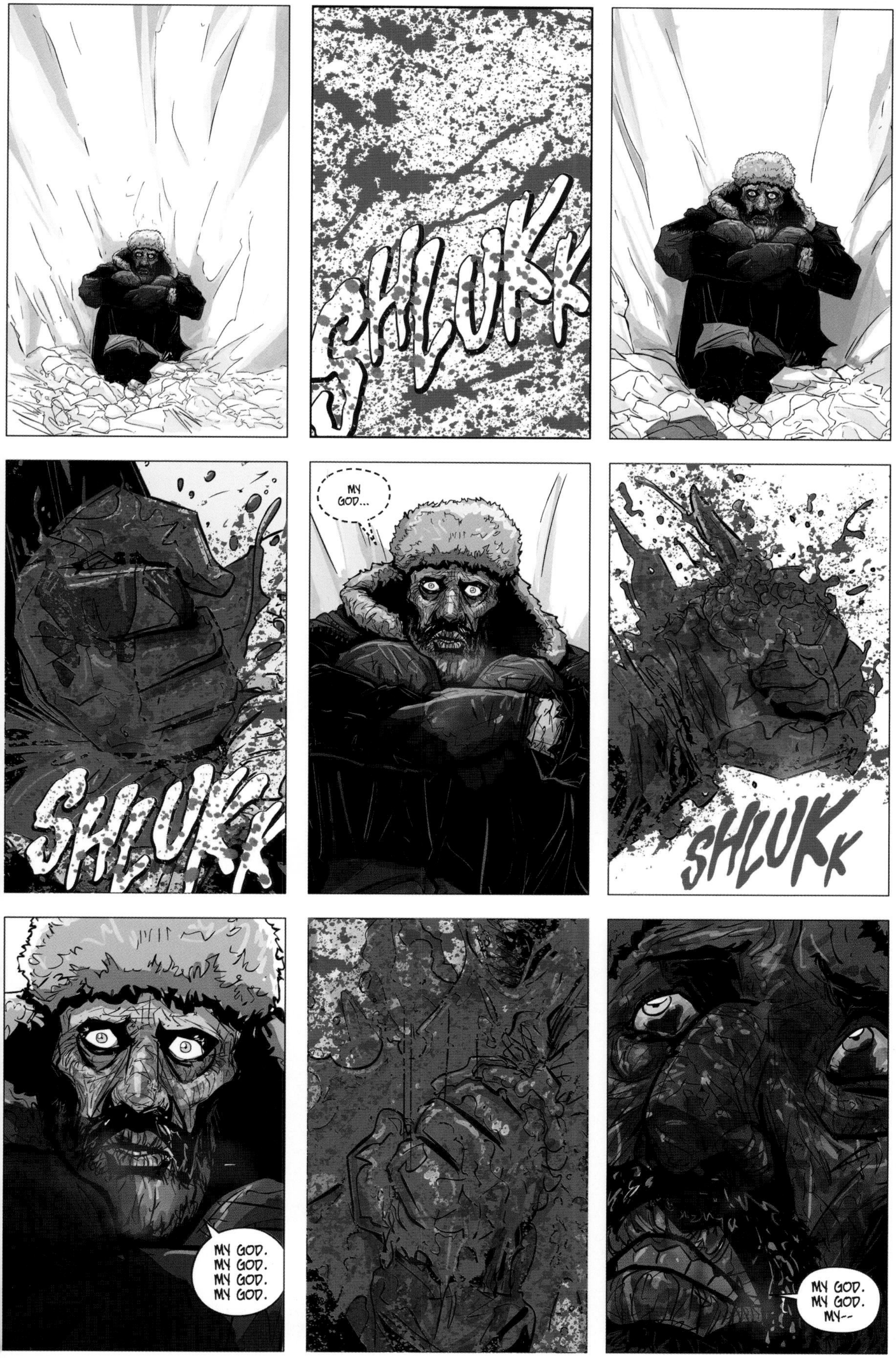
SHLOKK
MY GOD...
SHLUKK
SHLUKK
MY GOD. MY GOD. MY GOD. MY GOD.
MY GOD. MY GOD. MY--

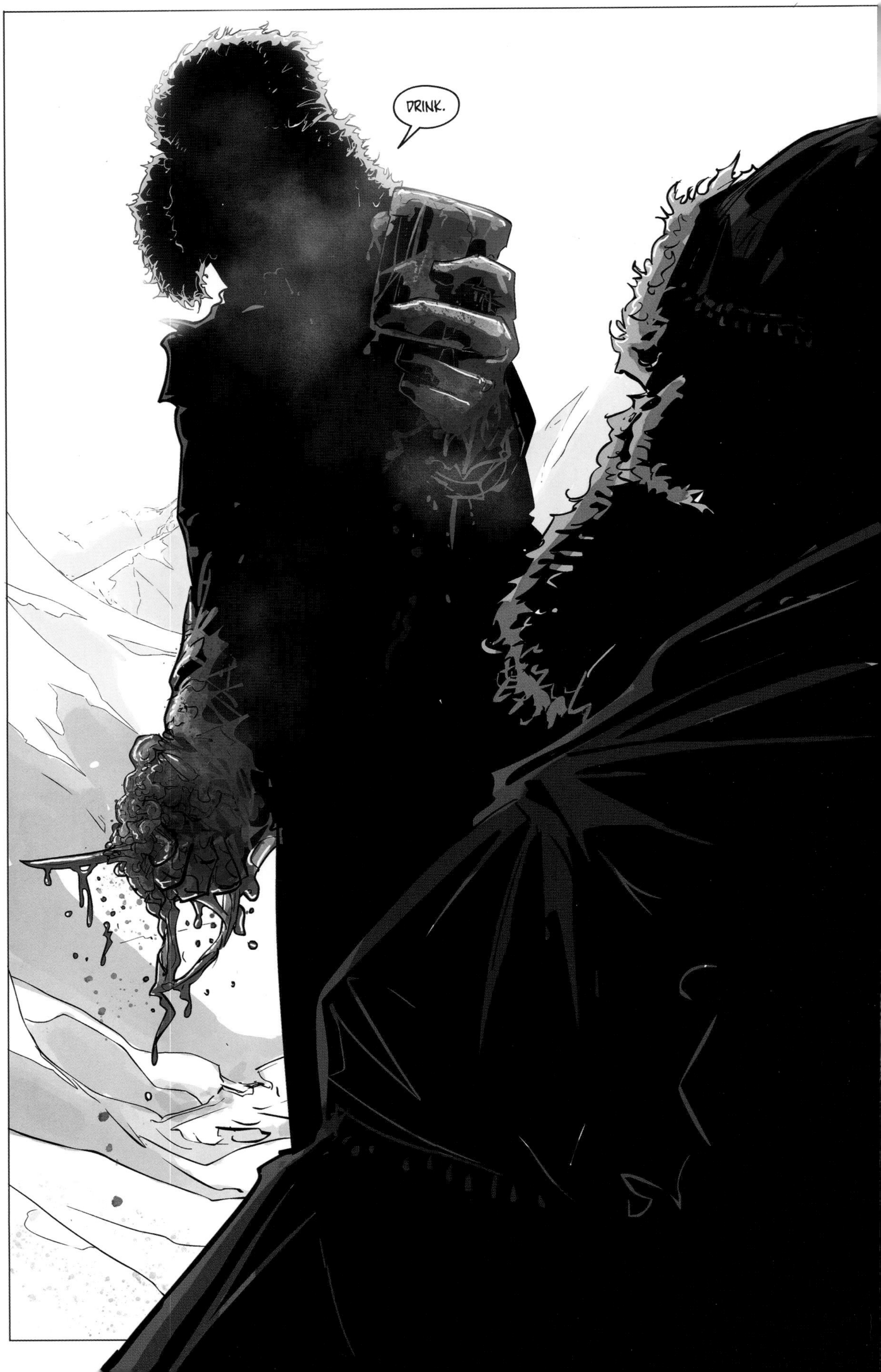
DRINK.

I DON'T WANT TO...

DRINK, SERGEI. A TOAST.

A TOAST?

A VOW.

WE WALK OUT OF THIS HELL TOGETHER.

TOGETHER.

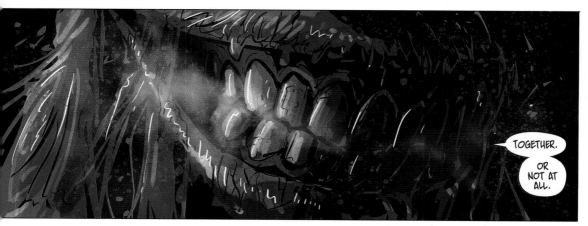

TOGETHER.

OR NOT AT ALL.

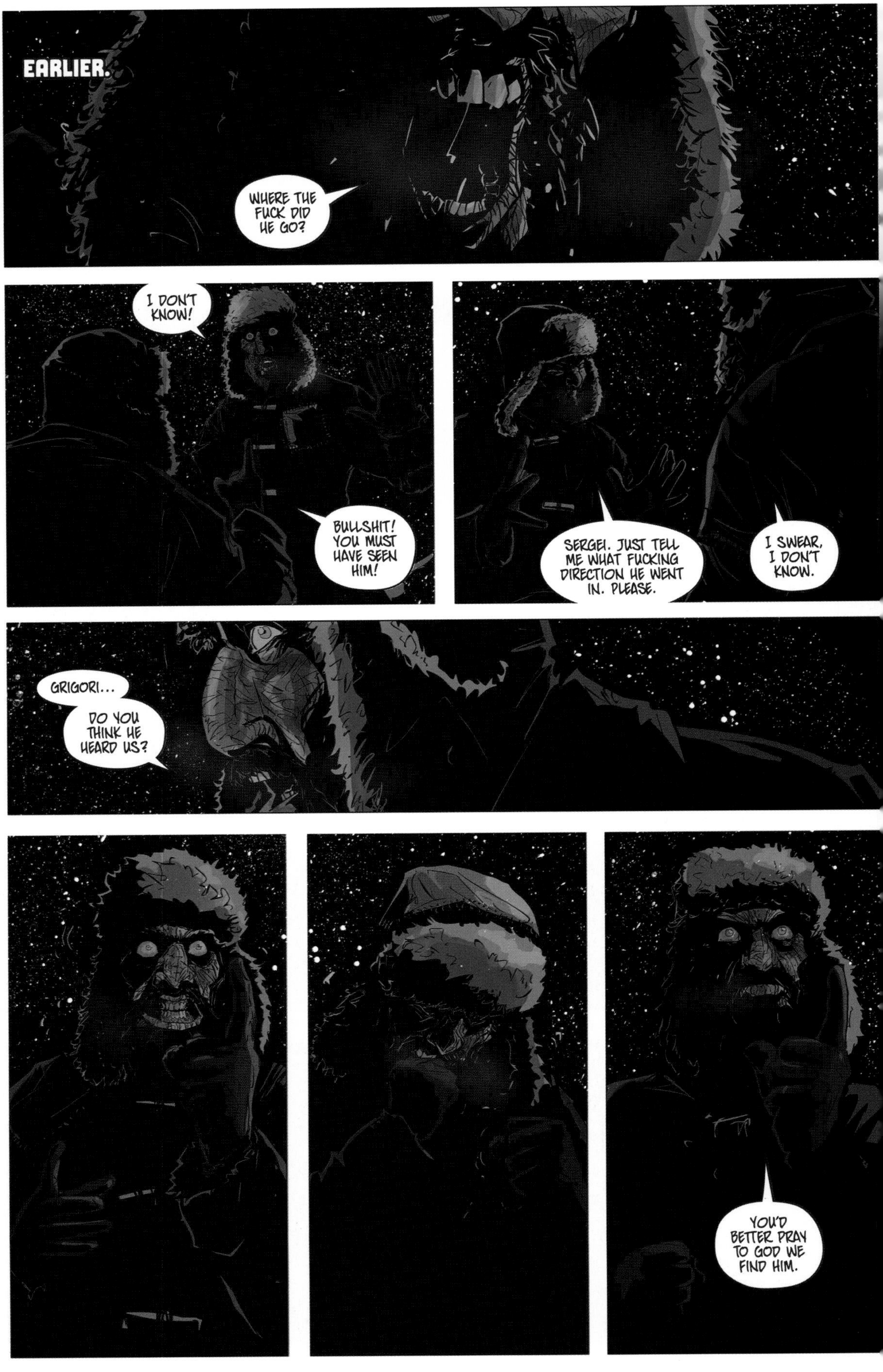
EARLIER.
WHERE THE FUCK DID HE GO?
I DON'T KNOW!
BULLSHIT! YOU MUST HAVE SEEN HIM!
SERGEI. JUST TELL ME WHAT FUCKING DIRECTION HE WENT IN. PLEASE.
I SWEAR, I DON'T KNOW.
GRIGORI...
DO YOU THINK HE HEARD US?
YOU'D BETTER PRAY TO GOD WE FIND HIM.

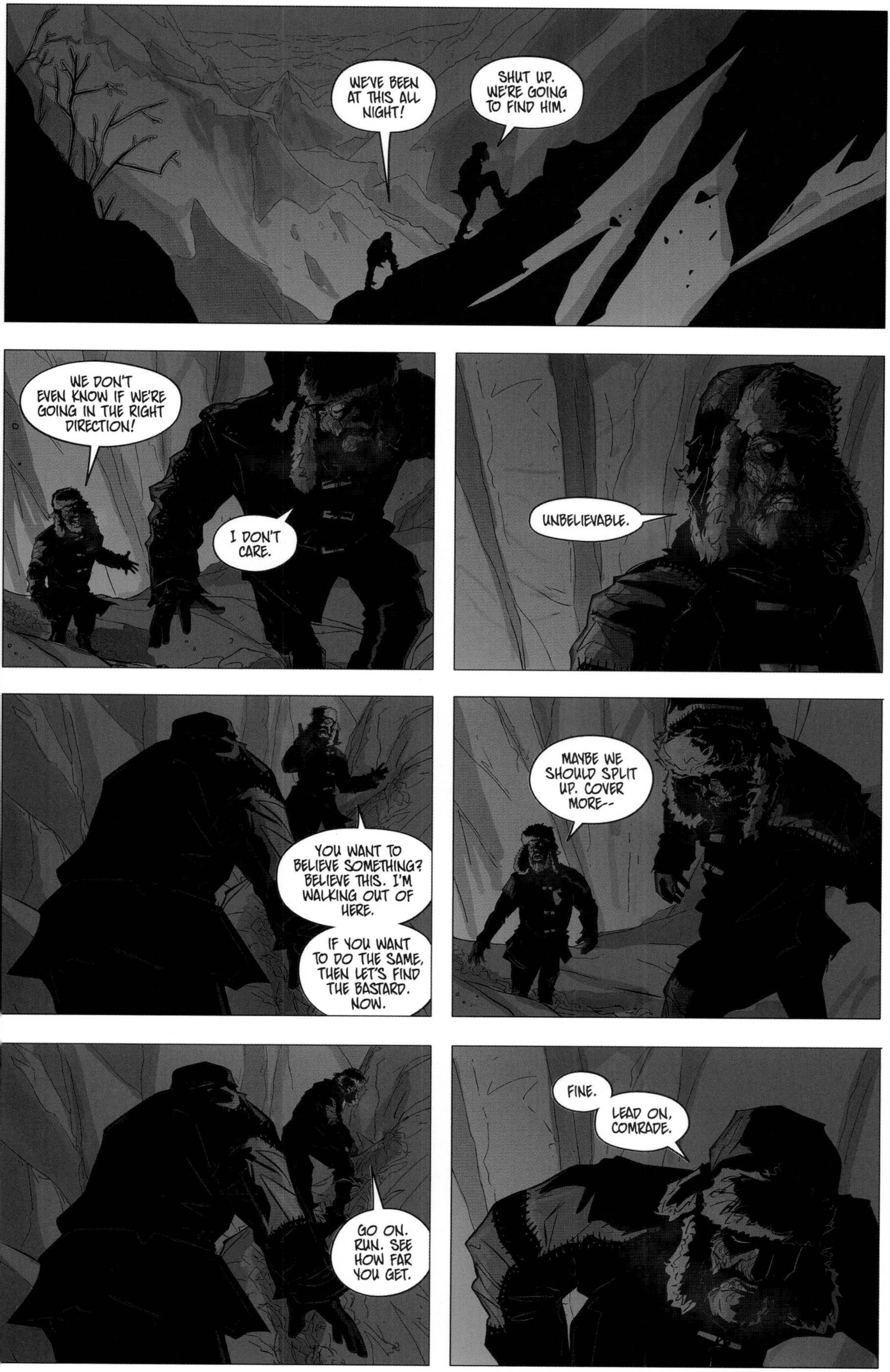
WE'VE BEEN AT THIS ALL NIGHT!
SHUT UP. WE'RE GOING TO FIND HIM.
WE DON'T EVEN KNOW IF WE'RE GOING IN THE RIGHT DIRECTION!
I DON'T CARE.
UNBELIEVABLE.
YOU WANT TO BELIEVE SOMETHING? BELIEVE THIS. I'M WALKING OUT OF HERE.
IF YOU WANT TO DO THE SAME, THEN LET'S FIND THE BASTARD. NOW.
MAYBE WE SHOULD SPLIT UP. COVER MORE--
GO ON. RUN. SEE HOW FAR YOU GET.
FINE.
LEAD ON, COMRADE.

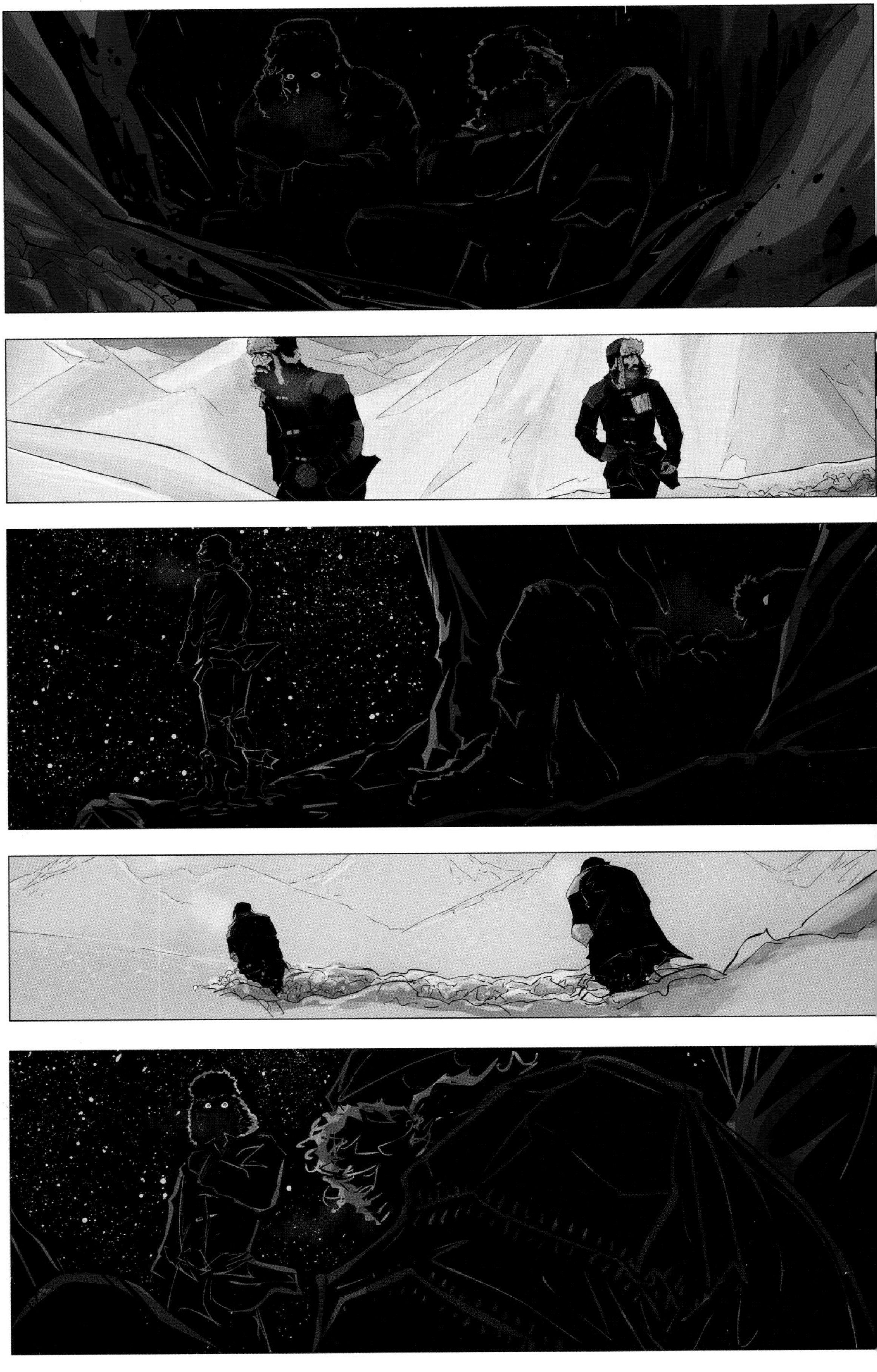

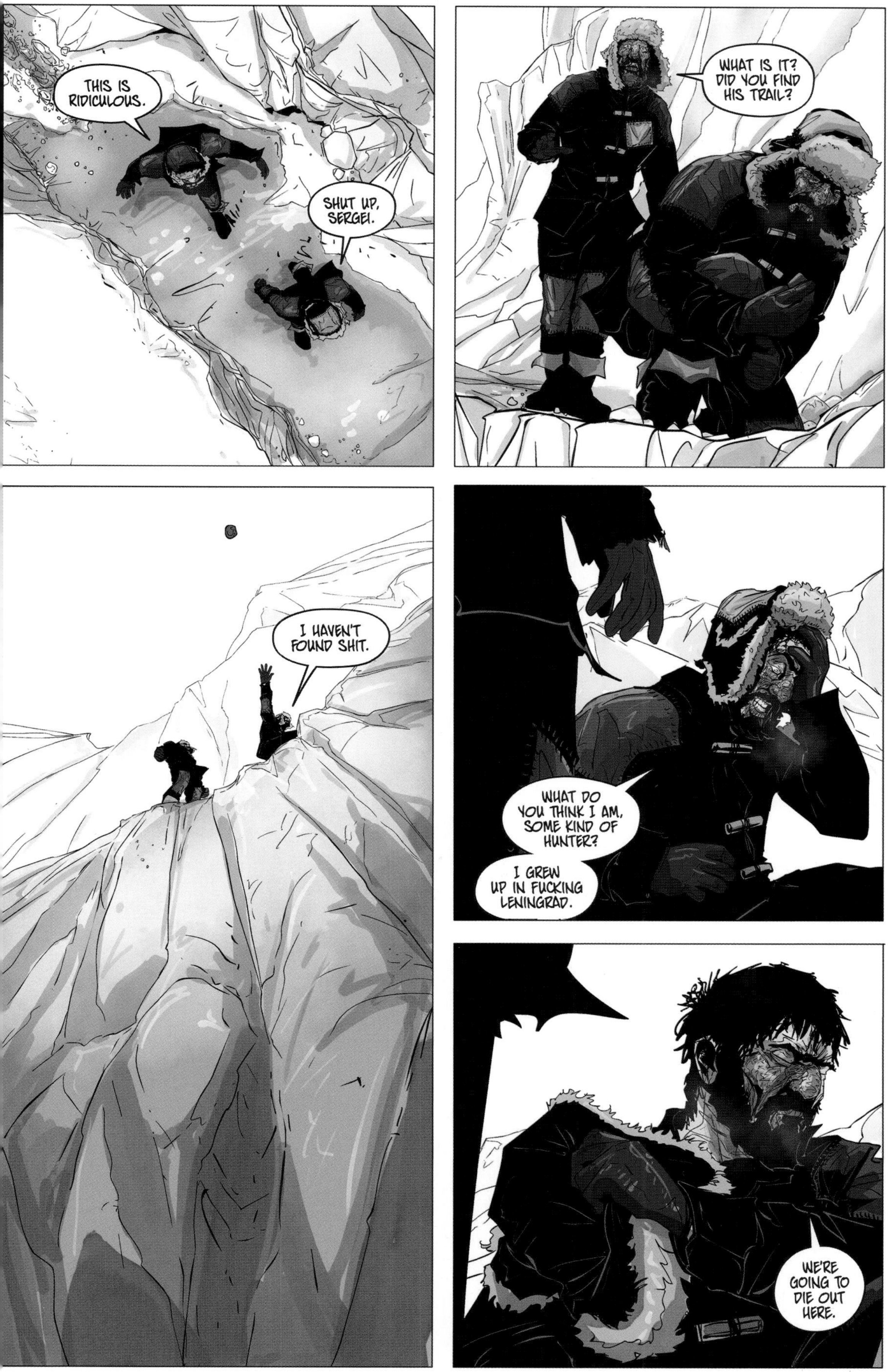
THIS IS RIDICULOUS.
SHUT UP, SERGEI.
WHAT IS IT? DID YOU FIND HIS TRAIL?
I HAVEN'T FOUND SHIT.
WHAT DO YOU THINK I AM, SOME KIND OF HUNTER?
I GREW UP IN FUCKING LENINGRAD.
WE'RE GOING TO DIE OUT HERE.

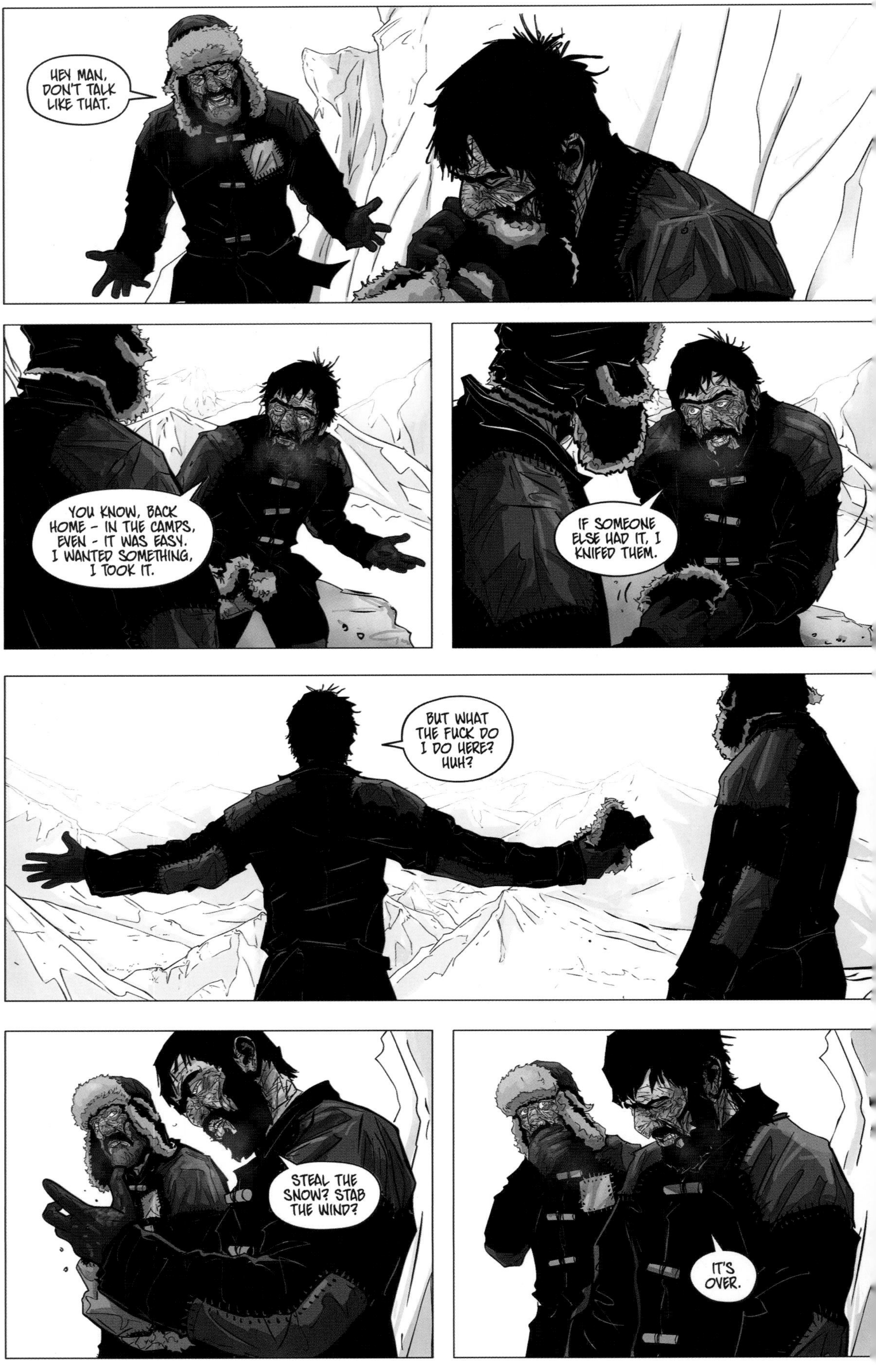
HEY MAN, DON'T TALK LIKE THAT.
YOU KNOW, BACK HOME - IN THE CAMPS, EVEN - IT WAS EASY. I WANTED SOMETHING, I TOOK IT.
IF SOMEONE ELSE HAD IT, I KNIFED THEM.
BUT WHAT THE FUCK DO I DO HERE? HUH?
STEAL THE SNOW? STAB THE WIND?
IT'S OVER.

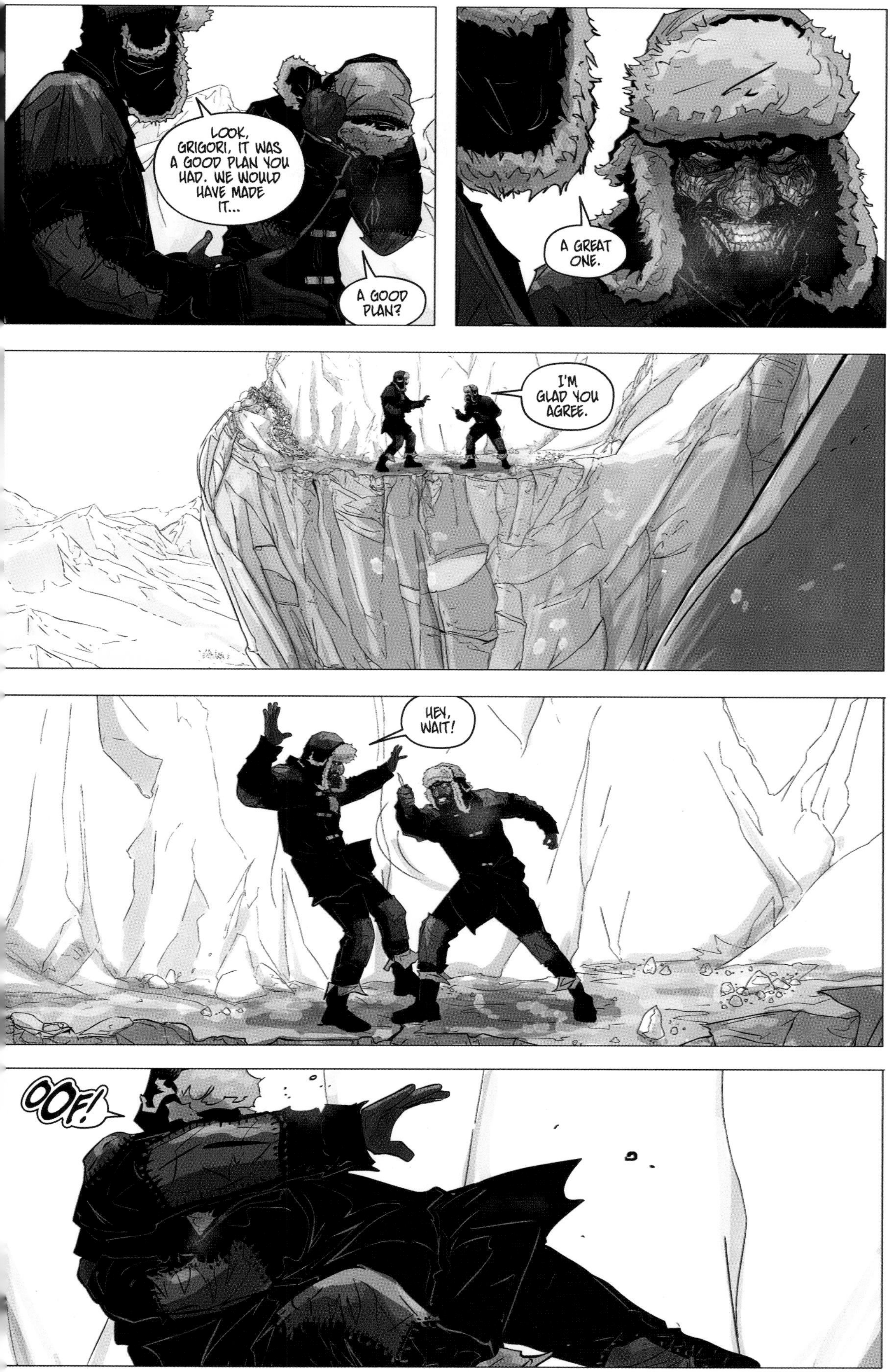
LOOK, GRIGORI, IT WAS A GOOD PLAN YOU HAD. WE WOULD HAVE MADE IT...
A GOOD PLAN?
A GREAT ONE.
I'M GLAD YOU AGREE.
HEY, WAIT!
OOF!

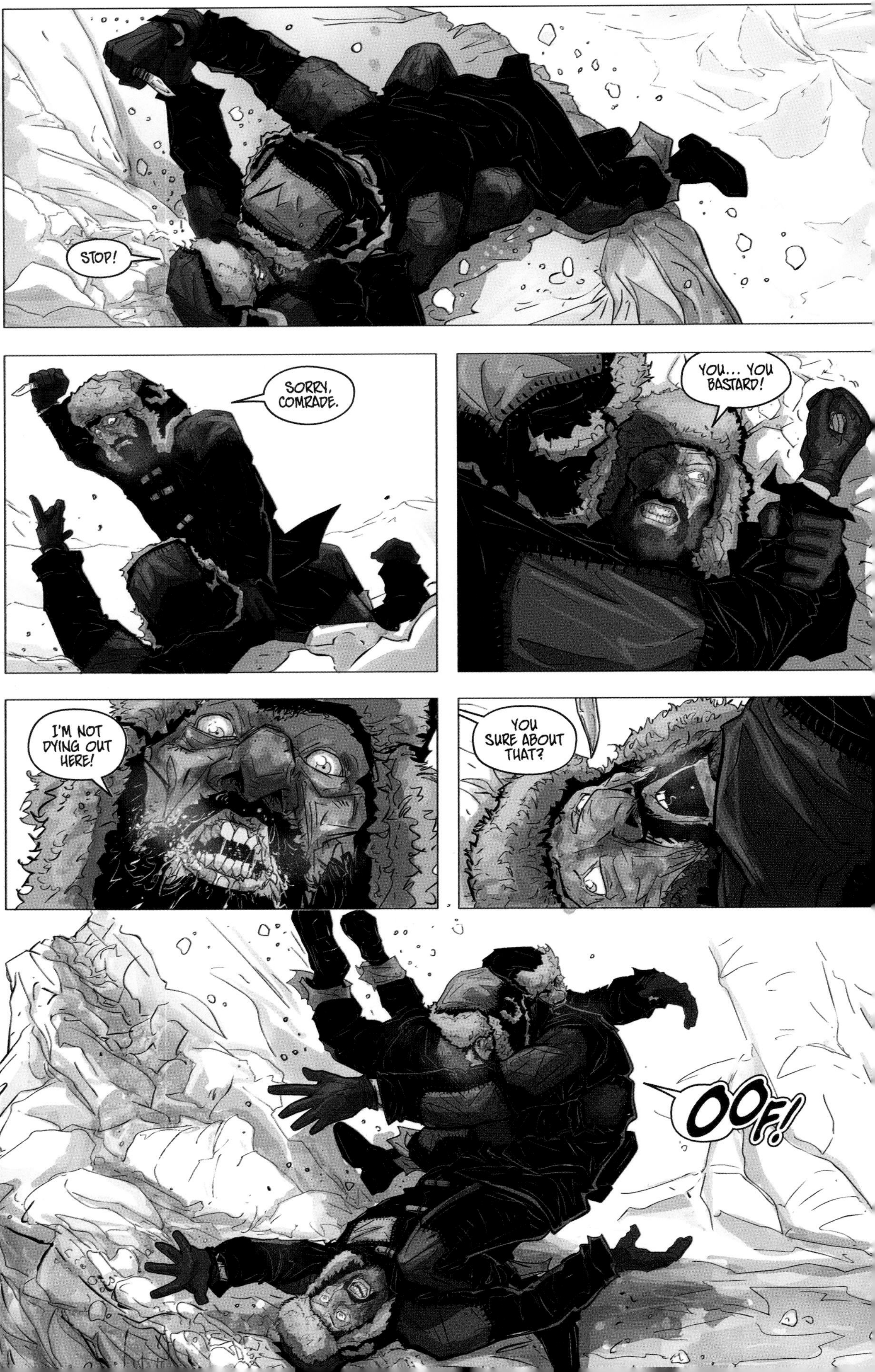
STOP!
SORRY, COMRADE.
YOU... YOU BASTARD!
I'M NOT DYING OUT HERE!
YOU SURE ABOUT THAT?
OOF!

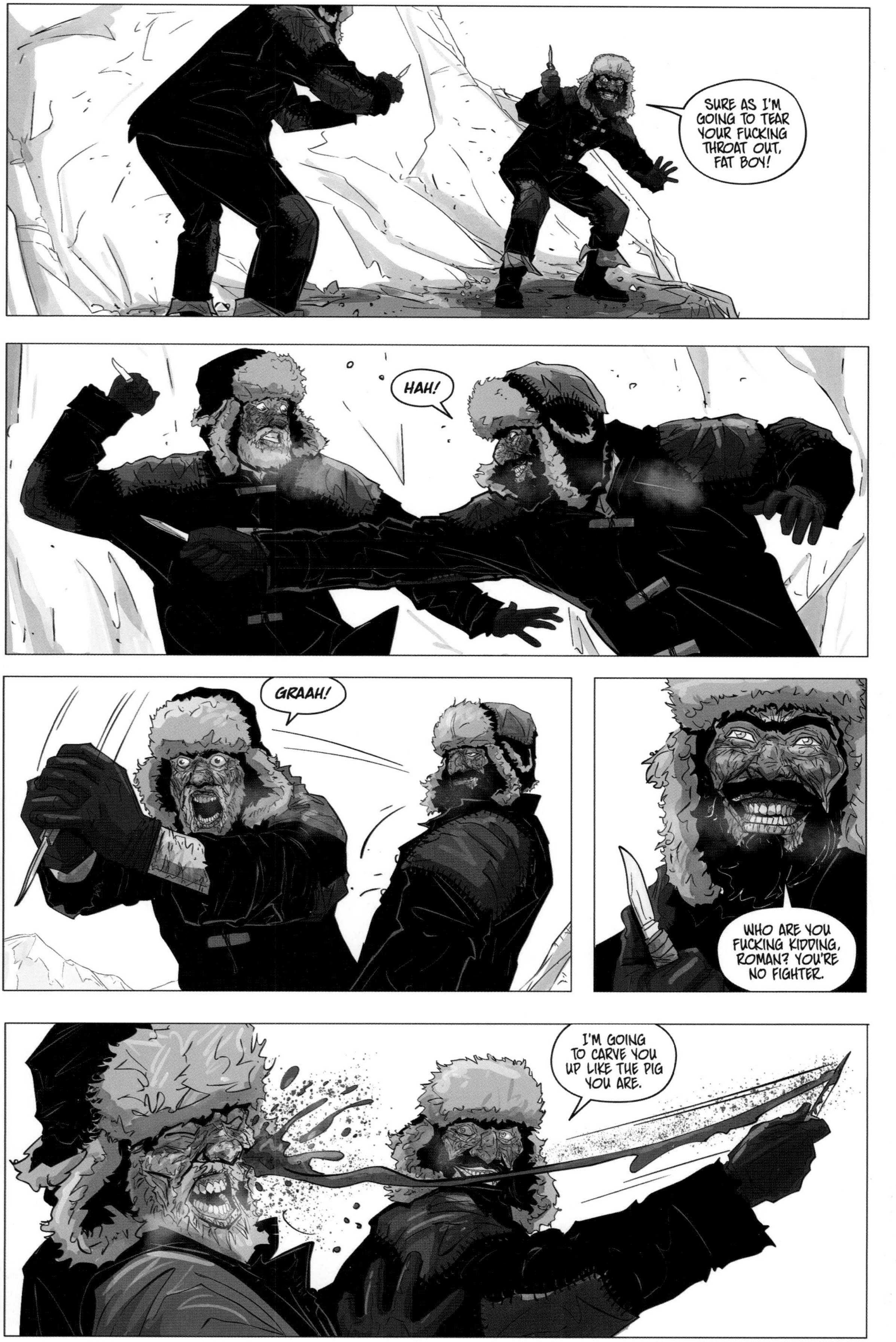
SURE AS I'M GOING TO TEAR YOUR FUCKING THROAT OUT, FAT BOY!
HAH!
GRAAH!
WHO ARE YOU FUCKING KIDDING, ROMAN? YOU'RE NO FIGHTER.
I'M GOING TO CARVE YOU UP LIKE THE PIG YOU ARE.

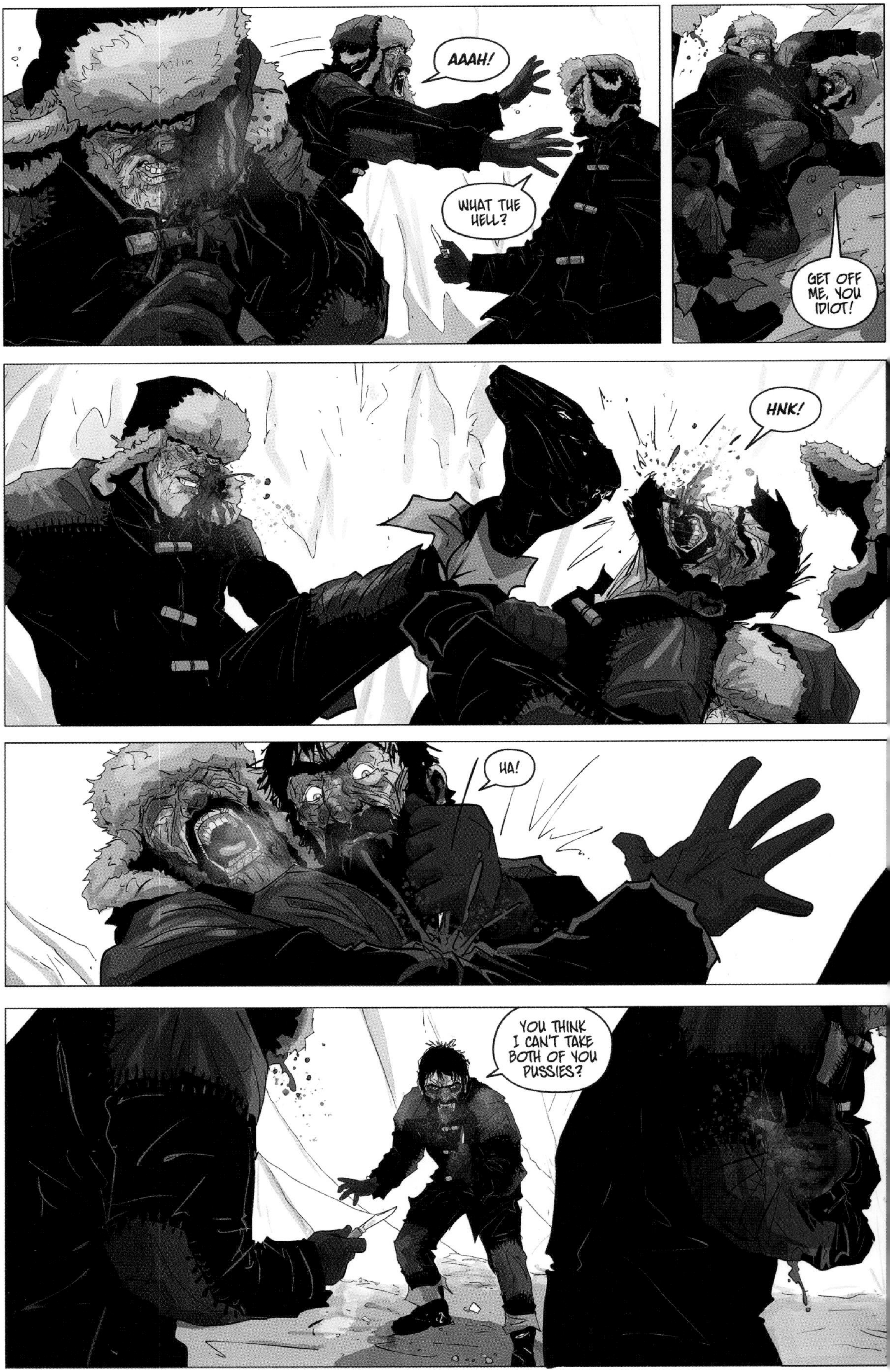
AAAH!
WHAT THE HELL?
GET OFF ME, YOU IDIOT!
HNK!
HA!
YOU THINK I CAN'T TAKE BOTH OF YOU PUSSIES?

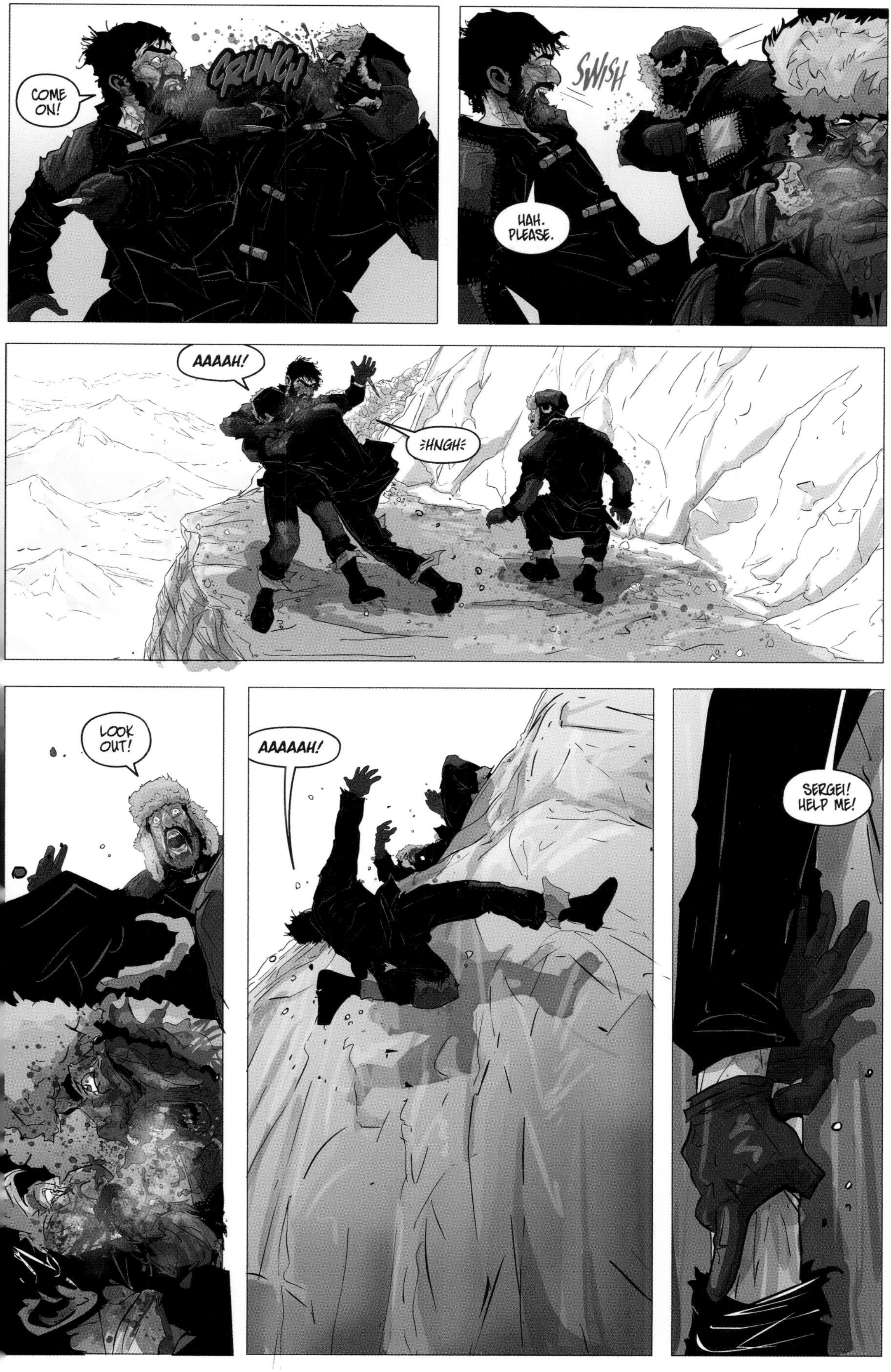
COME ON!
CRUNCH
SWISH
HAH. PLEASE.
AAAAH!
HNGH
LOOK OUT!
AAAAAH!
SERGEI! HELP ME!

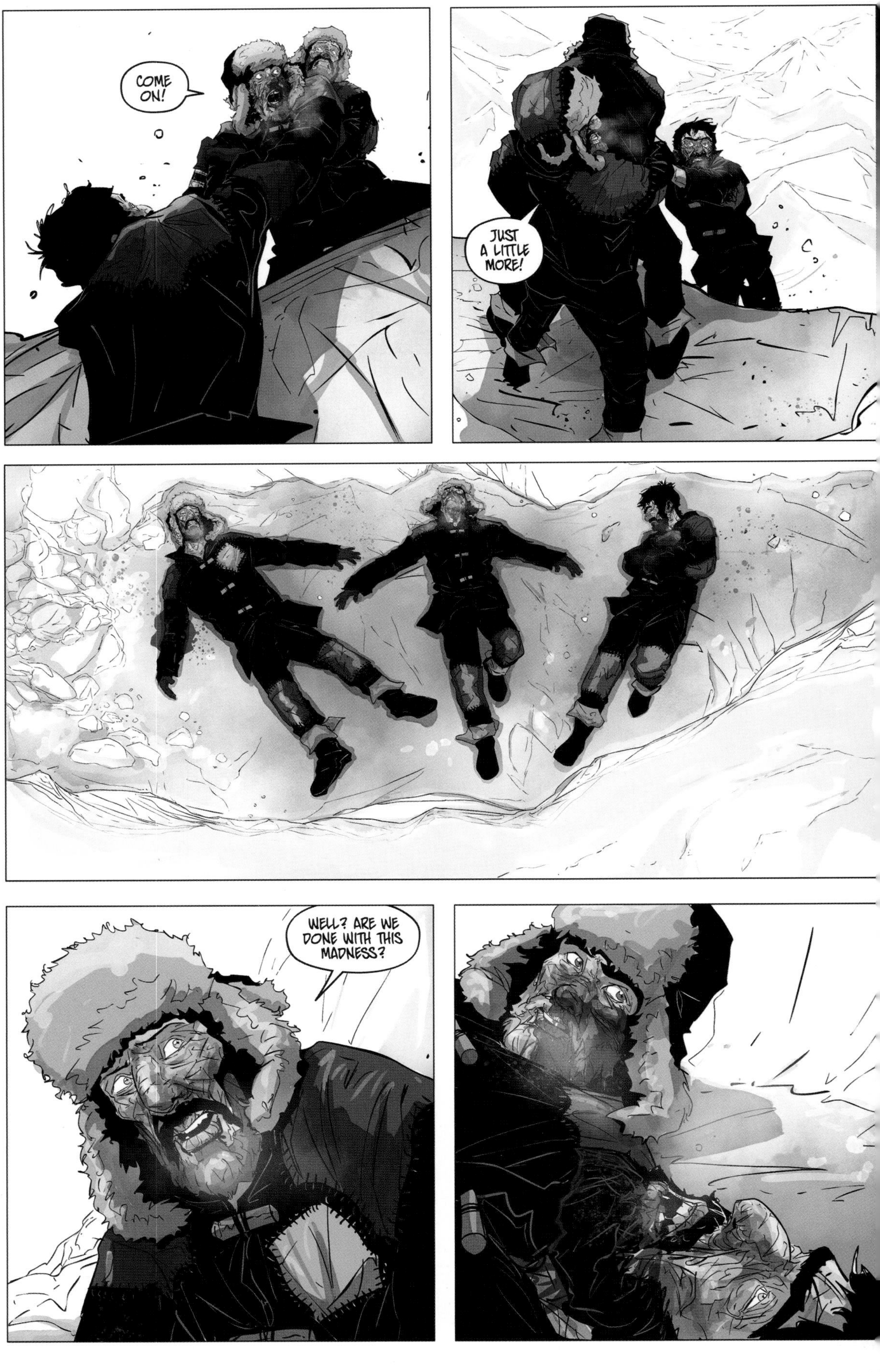
COME ON!
JUST A LITTLE MORE!
WELL? ARE WE DONE WITH THIS MADNESS?

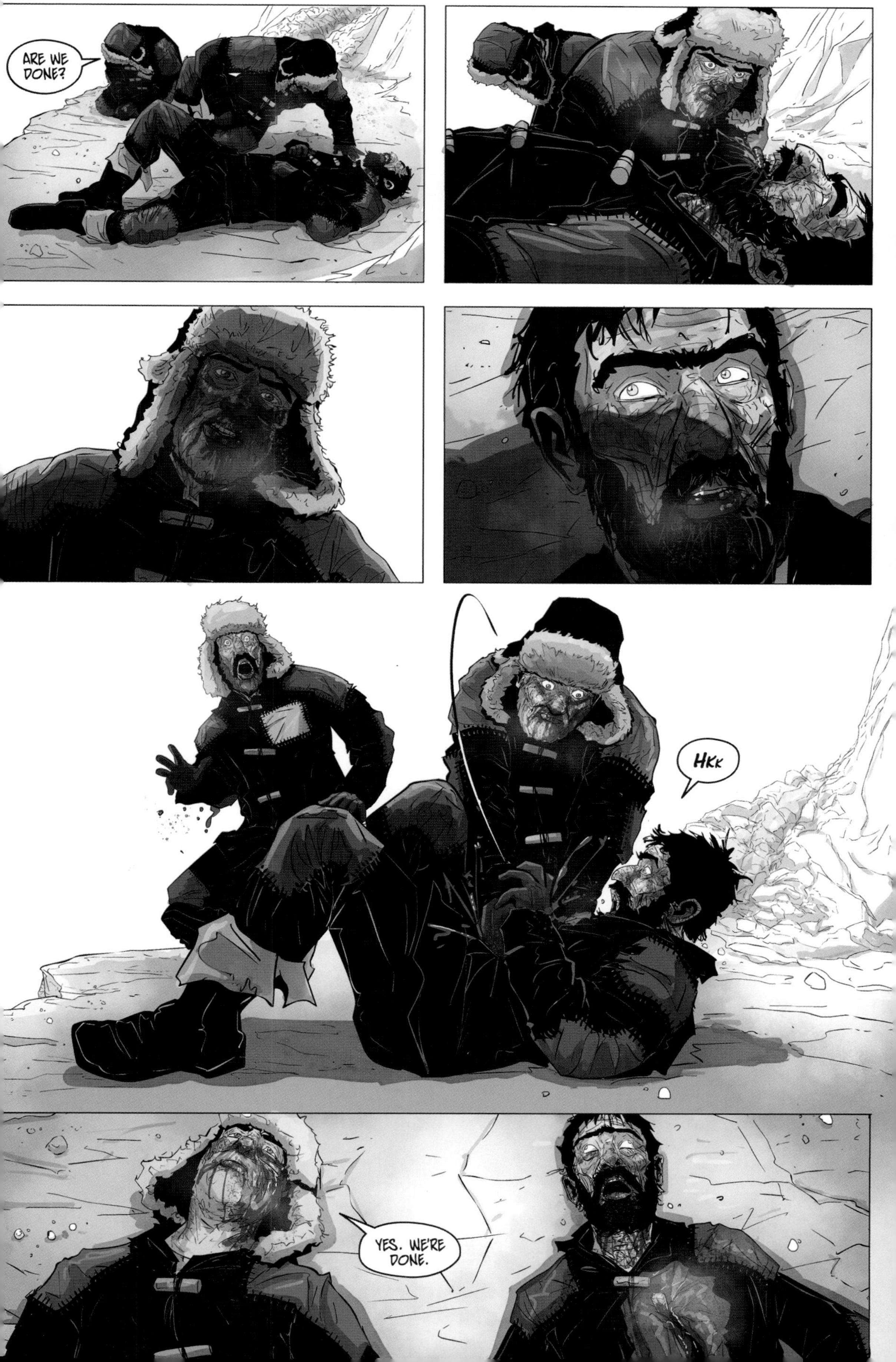
ARE WE DONE?
HKK
YES. WE'RE DONE.

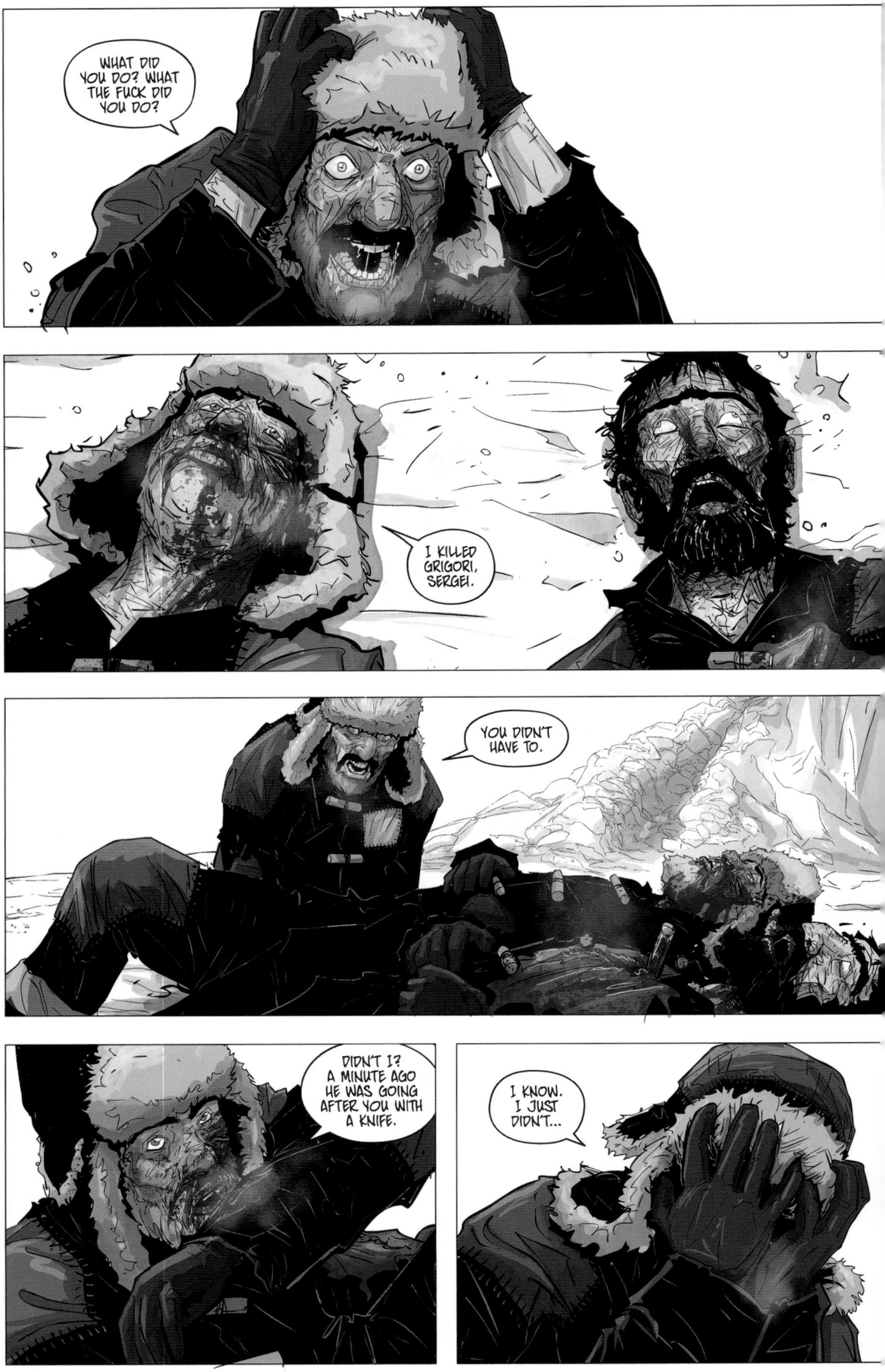
WHAT DID YOU DO? WHAT THE FUCK DID YOU DO?
I KILLED GRIGORI, SERGEI.
YOU DIDN'T HAVE TO.
DIDN'T I? A MINUTE AGO HE WAS GOING AFTER YOU WITH A KNIFE.
I KNOW. I JUST DIDN'T...

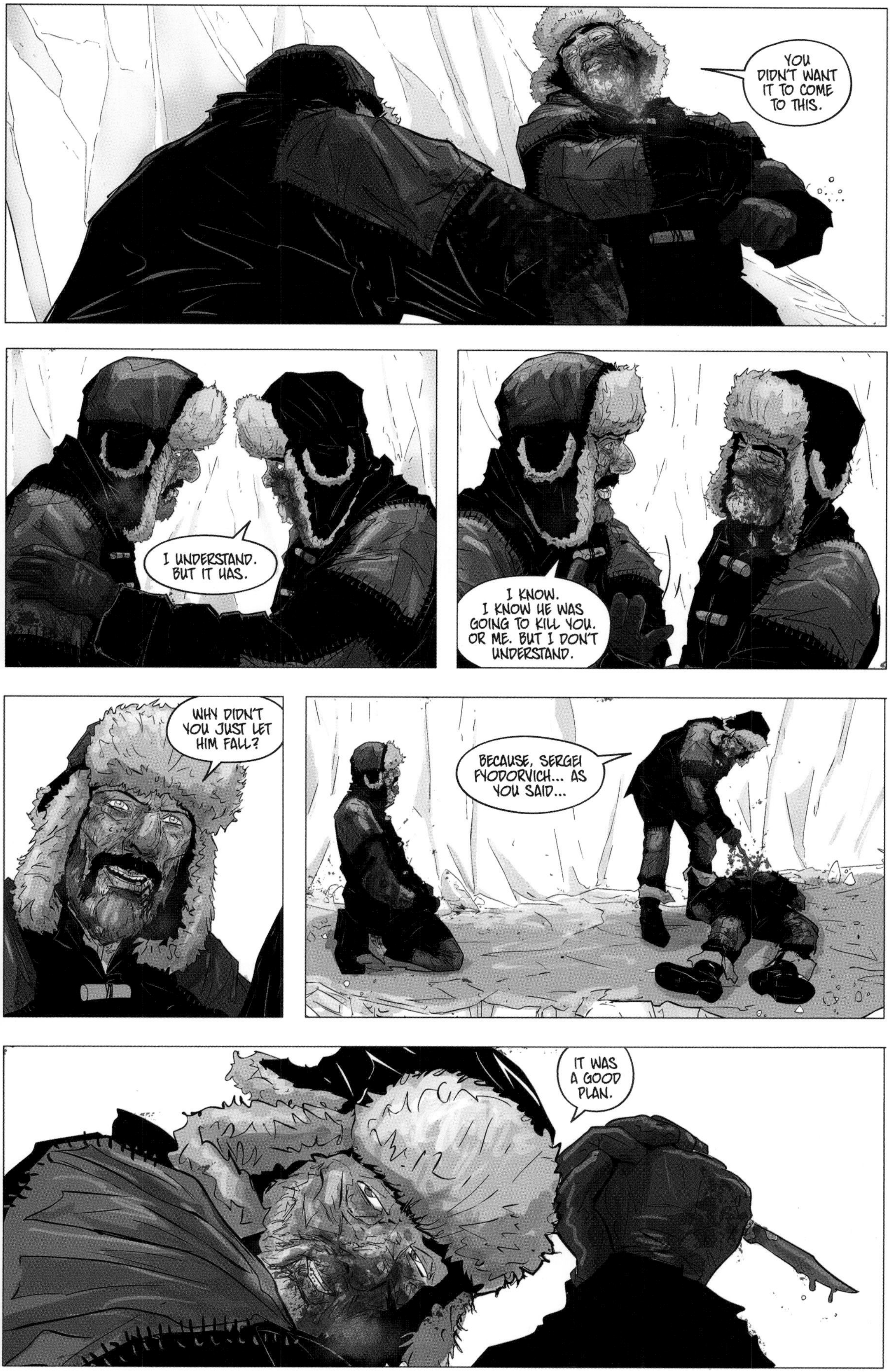
YOU DIDN'T WANT IT TO COME TO THIS.
I UNDERSTAND. BUT IT HAS.
I KNOW. I KNOW HE WAS GOING TO KILL YOU. OR ME. BUT I DON'T UNDERSTAND.
WHY DIDN'T YOU JUST LET HIM FALL?
BECAUSE, SERGEI FYODORVICH... AS YOU SAID...
IT WAS A GOOD PLAN.

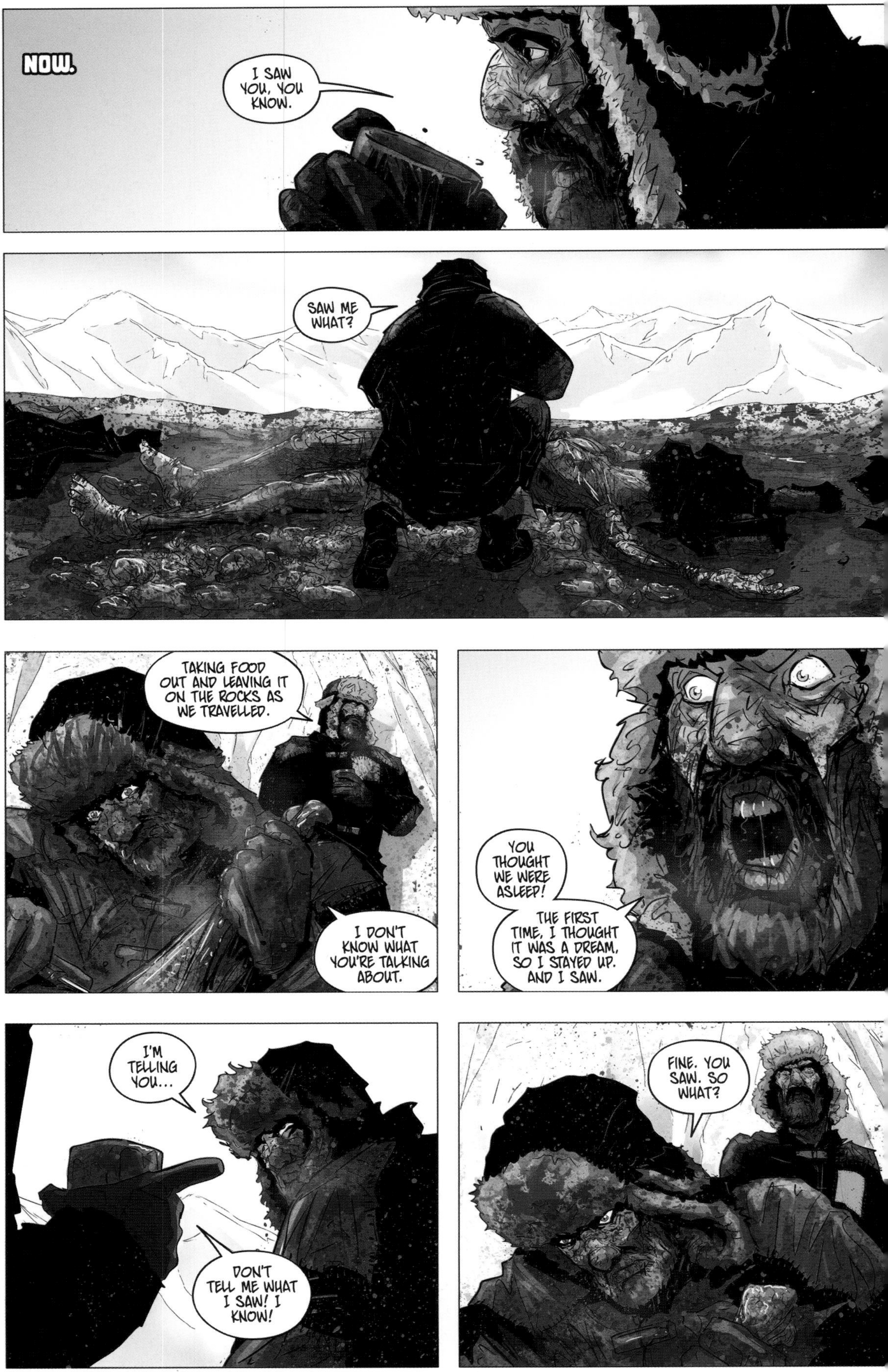
NOW.
I SAW YOU, YOU KNOW.
SAW ME WHAT?
TAKING FOOD OUT AND LEAVING IT ON THE ROCKS AS WE TRAVELLED.
I DON'T KNOW WHAT YOU'RE TALKING ABOUT.
YOU THOUGHT WE WERE ASLEEP!
THE FIRST TIME, I THOUGHT IT WAS A DREAM, SO I STAYED UP. AND I SAW.
I'M TELLING YOU...
DON'T TELL ME WHAT I SAW! I KNOW!
FINE. YOU SAW. SO WHAT?

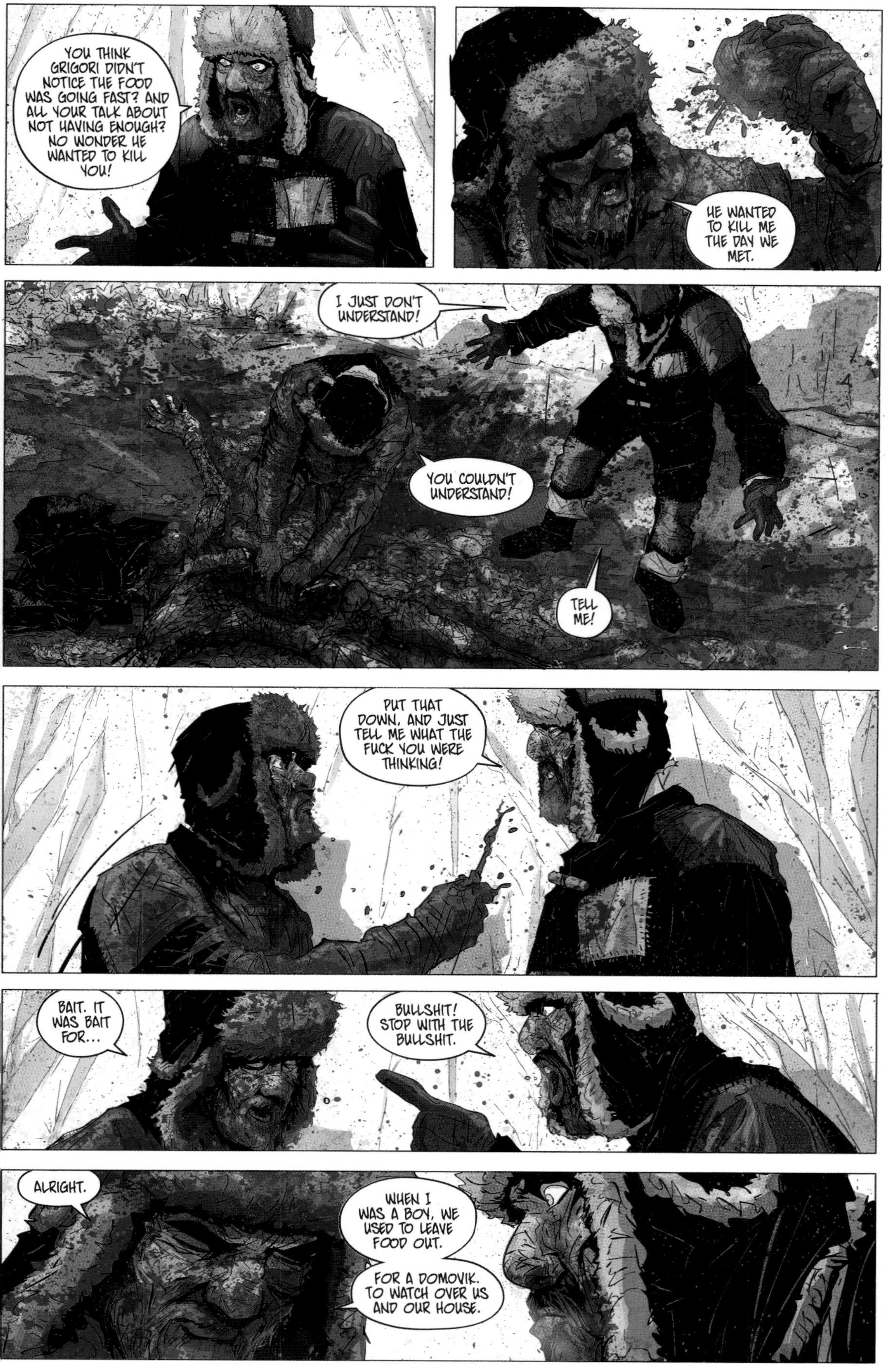
YOU THINK GRIGORI DIDN'T NOTICE THE FOOD WAS GOING FAST? AND ALL YOUR TALK ABOUT NOT HAVING ENOUGH? NO WONDER HE WANTED TO KILL YOU!
HE WANTED TO KILL ME THE DAY WE MET.
I JUST DON'T UNDERSTAND!
YOU COULDN'T UNDERSTAND!
TELL ME!
PUT THAT DOWN, AND JUST TELL ME WHAT THE FUCK YOU WERE THINKING!
BAIT. IT WAS BAIT FOR...
BULLSHIT! STOP WITH THE BULLSHIT.
ALRIGHT.
WHEN I WAS A BOY, WE USED TO LEAVE FOOD OUT.
FOR A DOMOVIK. TO WATCH OVER US AND OUR HOUSE.

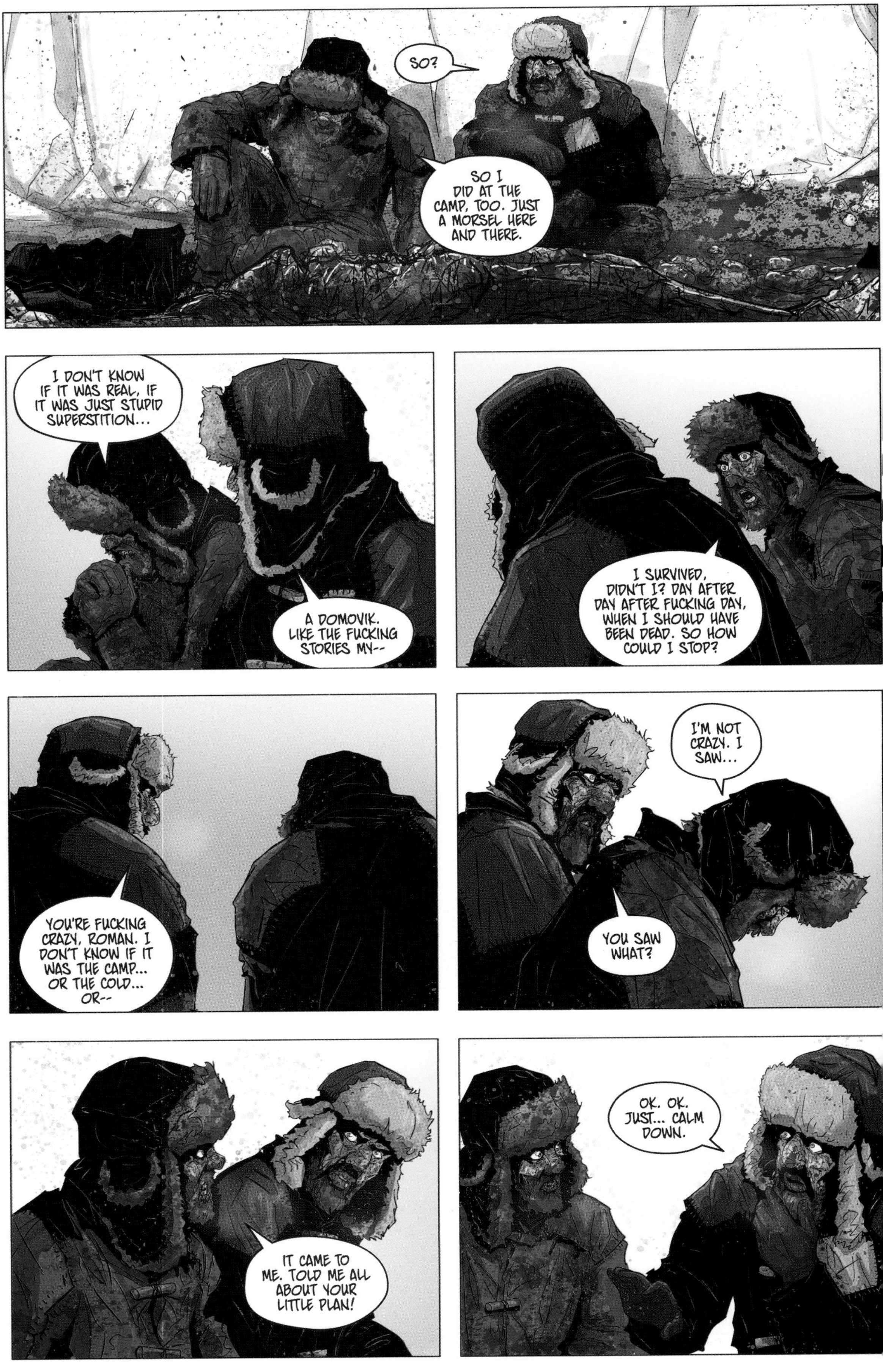
SO?
SO I DID AT THE CAMP, TOO. JUST A MORSEL HERE AND THERE.
I DON'T KNOW IF IT WAS REAL, IF IT WAS JUST STUPID SUPERSTITION...
A DOMOVIK. LIKE THE FUCKING STORIES MY--
I SURVIVED, DIDN'T I? DAY AFTER DAY AFTER FUCKING DAY, WHEN I SHOULD HAVE BEEN DEAD. SO HOW COULD I STOP?
YOU'RE FUCKING CRAZY, ROMAN. I DON'T KNOW IF IT WAS THE CAMP... OR THE COLD... OR--
I'M NOT CRAZY. I SAW...
YOU SAW WHAT?
IT CAME TO ME. TOLD ME ALL ABOUT YOUR LITTLE PLAN!
OK. OK. JUST... CALM DOWN.

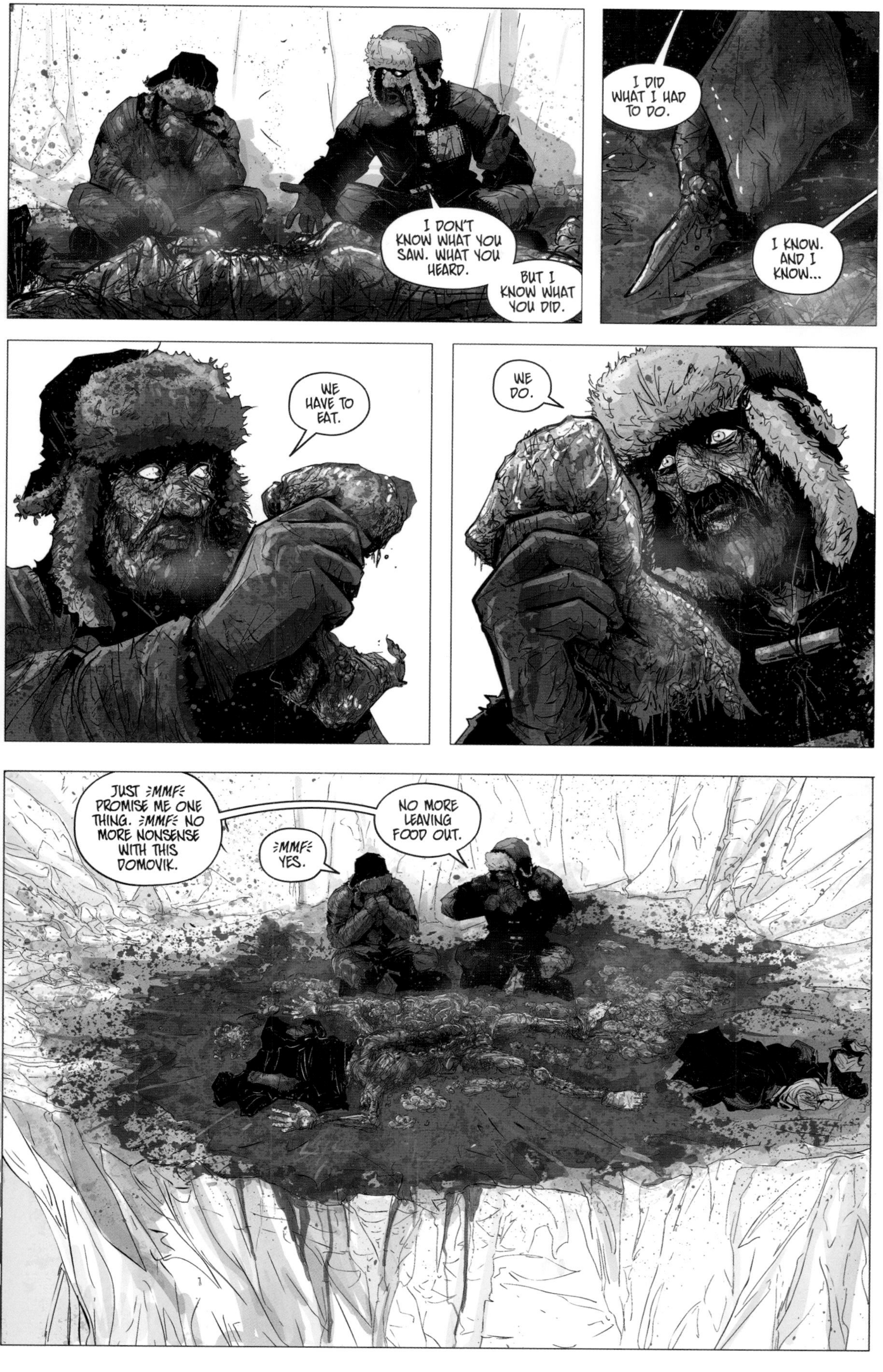
I DON'T KNOW WHAT YOU SAW. WHAT YOU HEARD.
BUT I KNOW WHAT YOU DID.
I DID WHAT I HAD TO DO.
I KNOW. AND I KNOW...
WE HAVE TO EAT.
WE DO.
JUST *MMF* PROMISE ME ONE THING. *MMF* NO MORE NONSENSE WITH THIS DOMOVIK.
NO MORE LEAVING FOOD OUT.
MMF YES.

"I PROMISE, SERGEI."

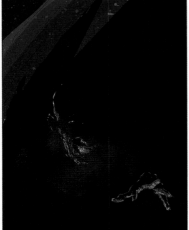

"NO MORE LEAVING FOOD OUT."

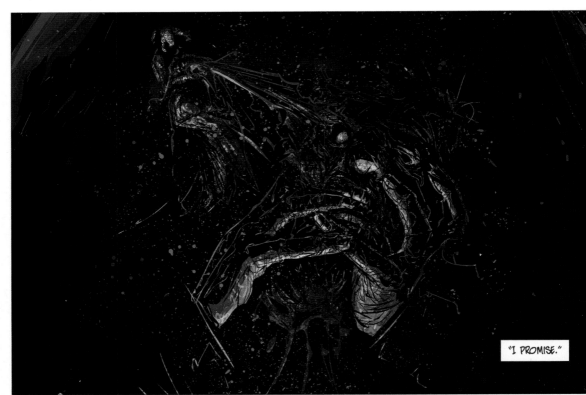

"I PROMISE."

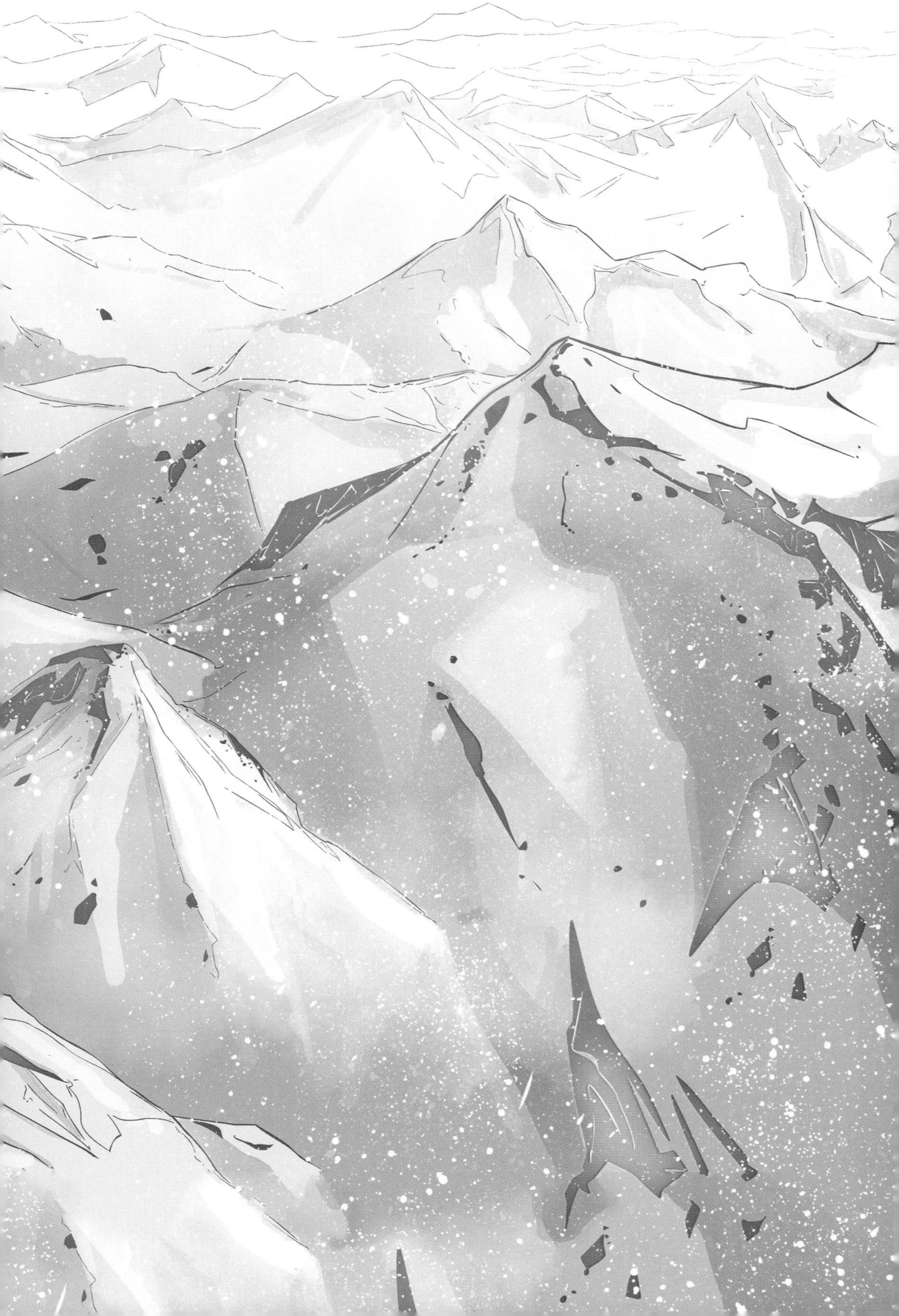

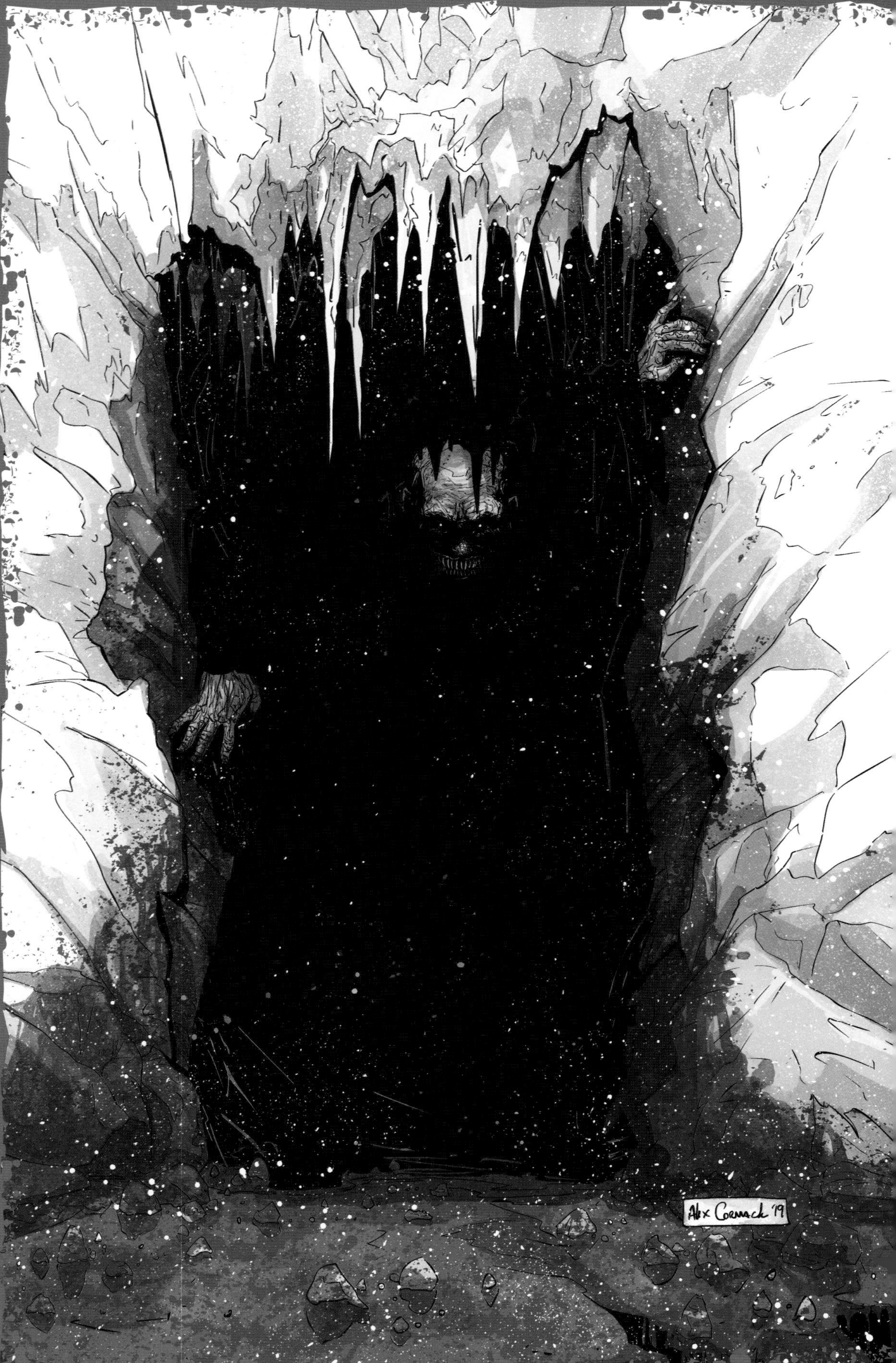
Alex Cormack '19

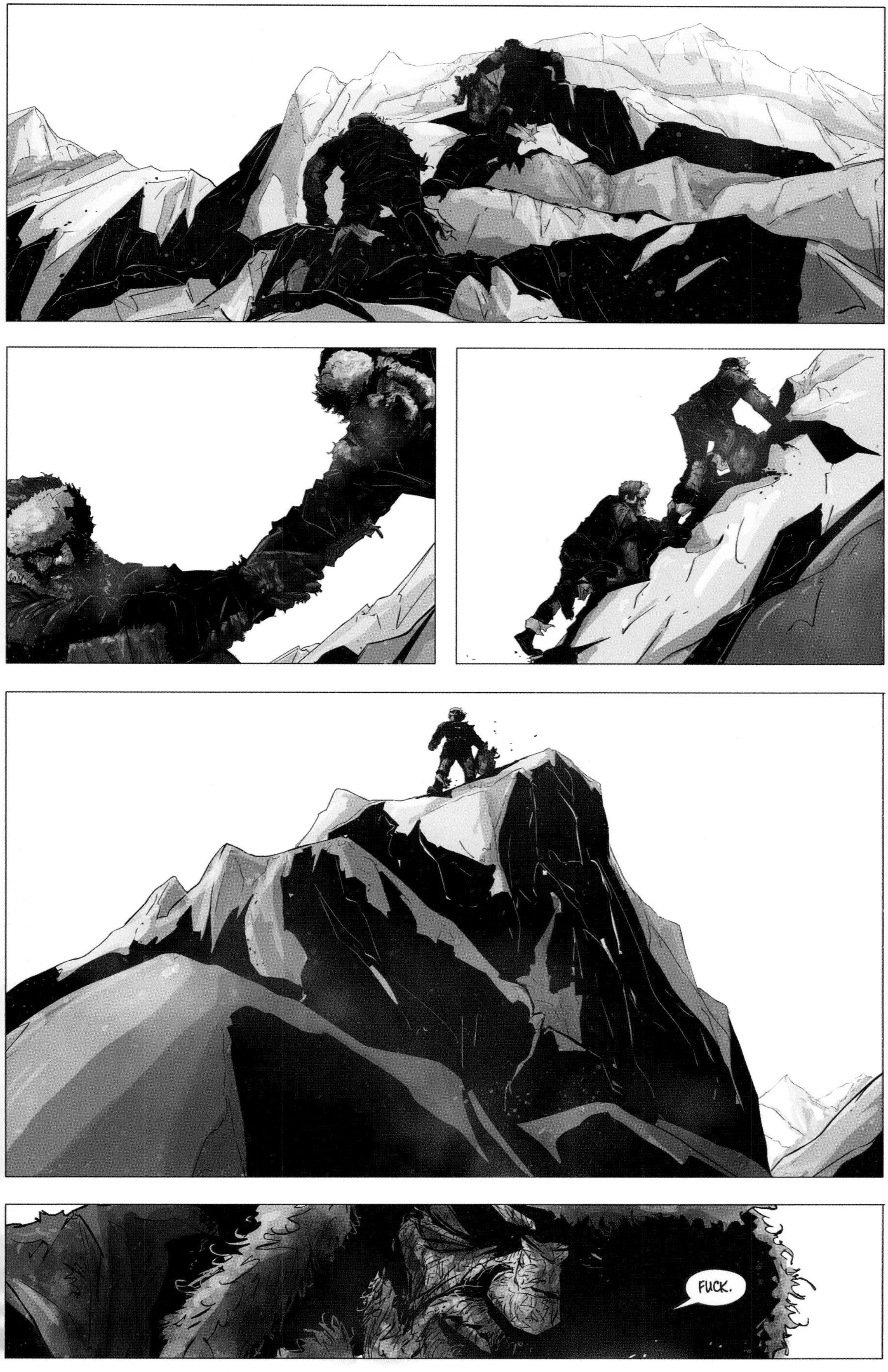
FUCK.

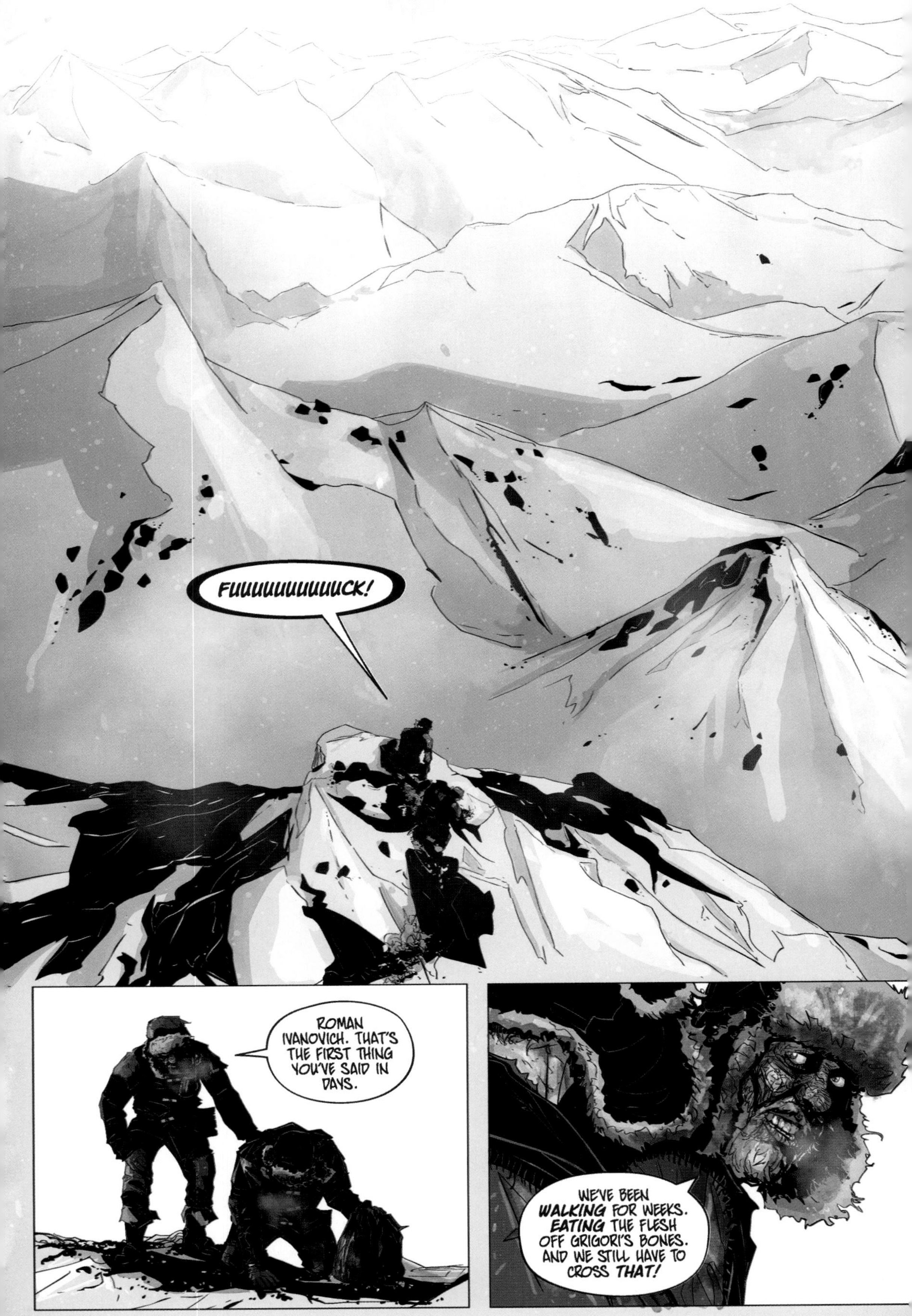
FUUUUUUUUUUCK!
ROMAN IVANOVICH. THAT'S THE FIRST THING YOU'VE SAID IN DAYS.
WE'VE BEEN WALKING FOR WEEKS. EATING THE FLESH OFF GRIGORI'S BONES. AND WE STILL HAVE TO CROSS THAT!

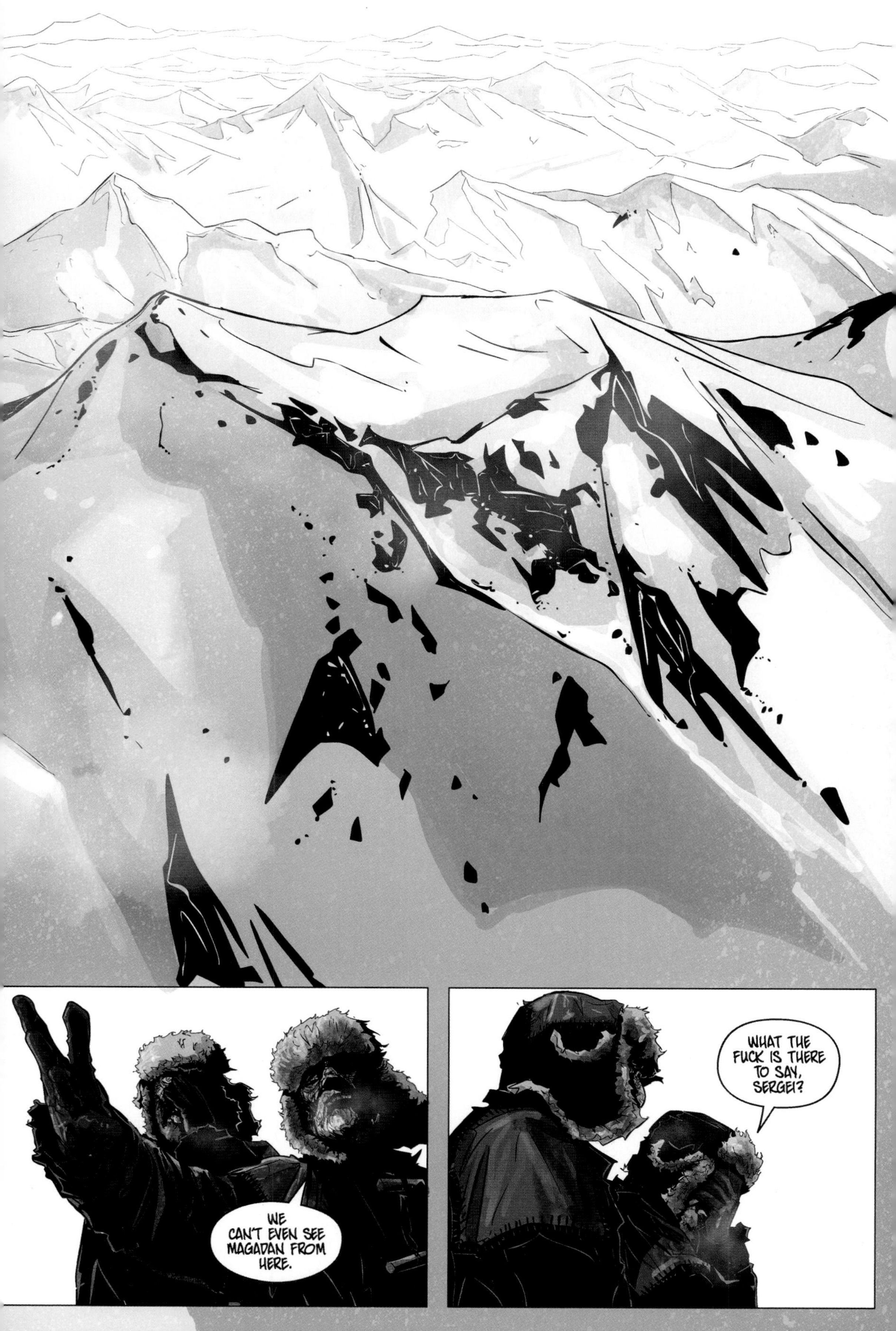
WE CAN'T EVEN SEE MAGADAN FROM HERE.
WHAT THE FUCK IS THERE TO SAY, SERGEI?

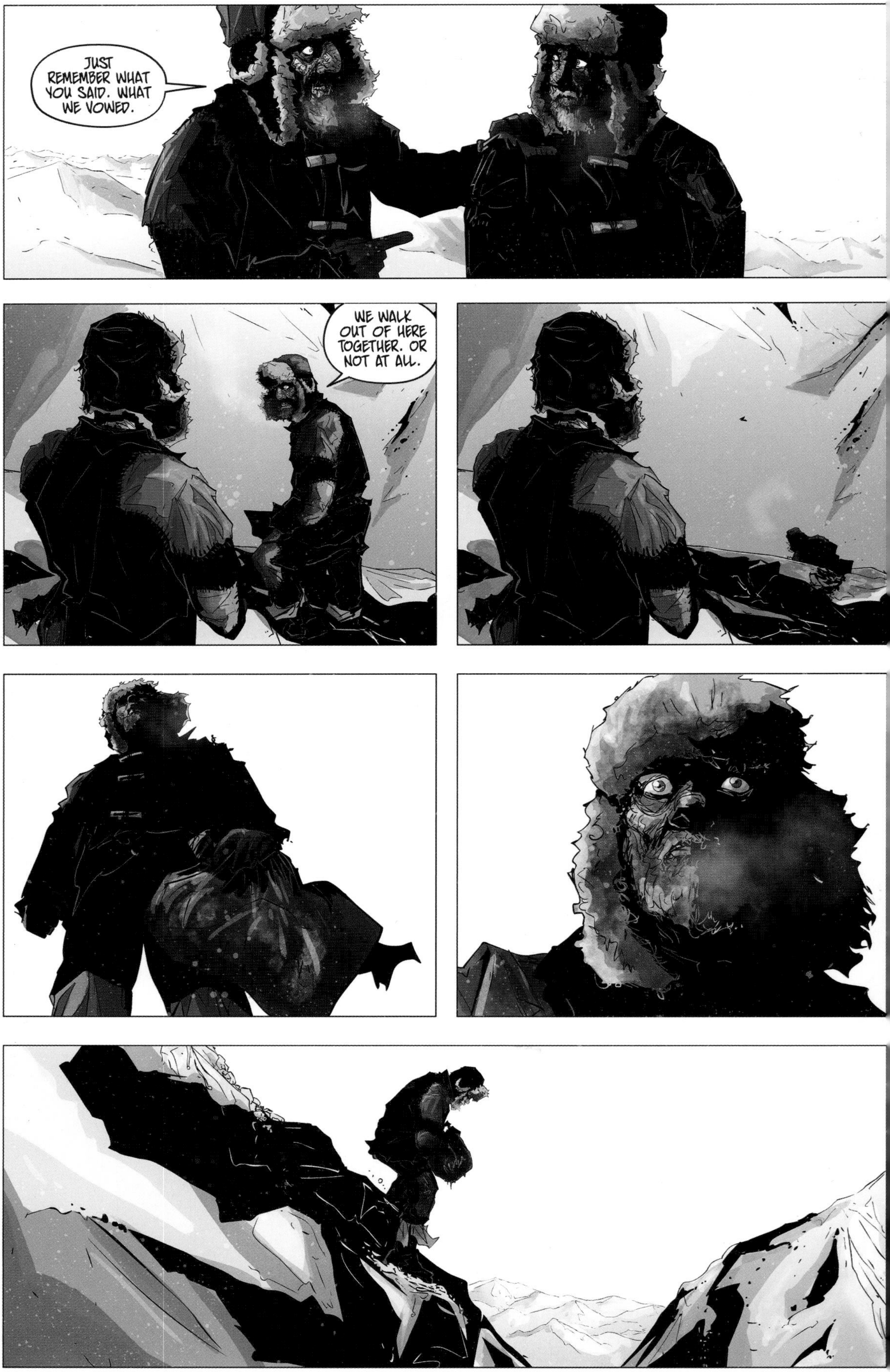
JUST REMEMBER WHAT YOU SAID. WHAT WE VOWED.
WE WALK OUT OF HERE TOGETHER. OR NOT AT ALL.

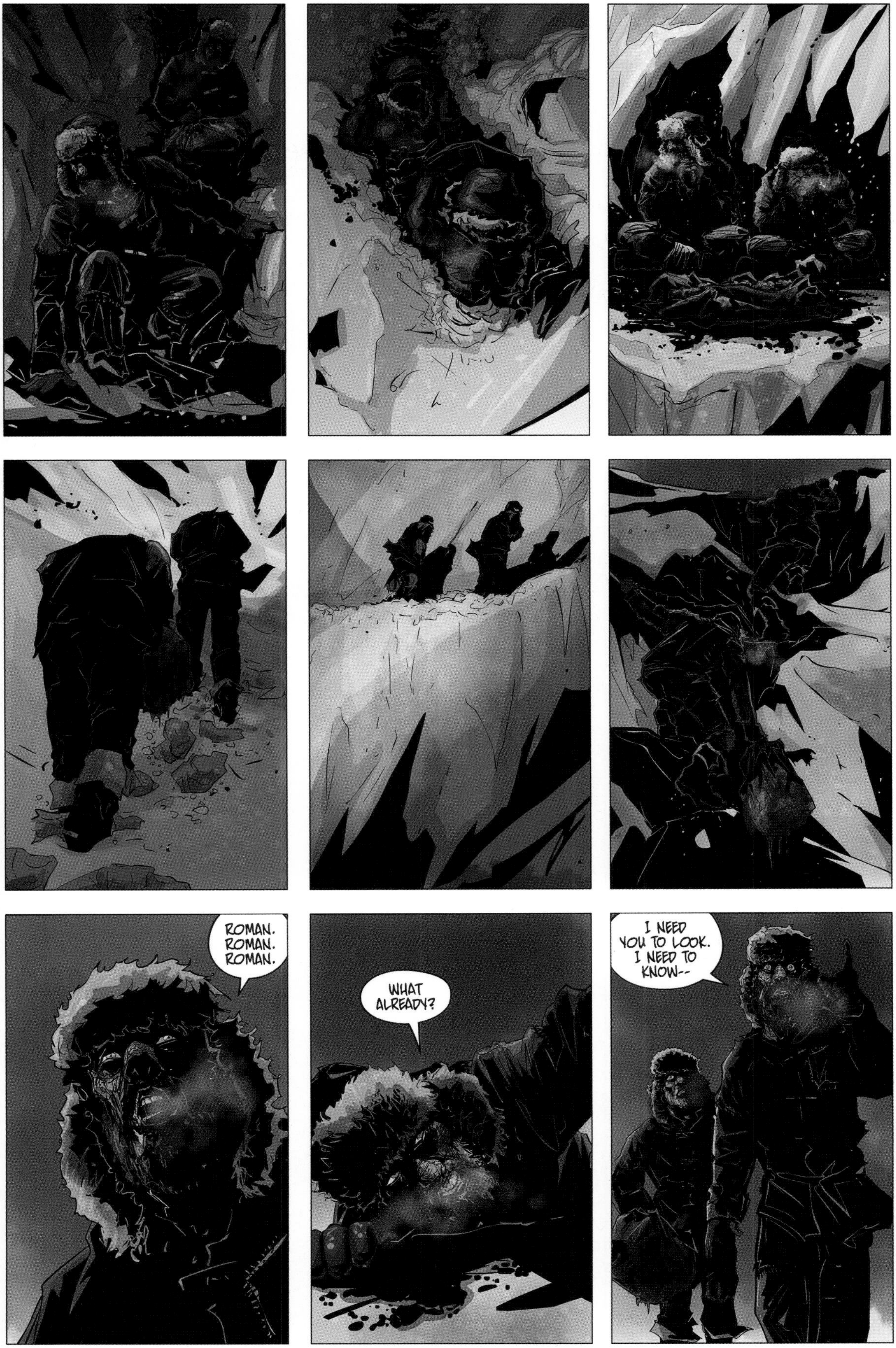
ROMAN. ROMAN. ROMAN.
WHAT ALREADY?
I NEED YOU TO LOOK. I NEED TO KNOW--

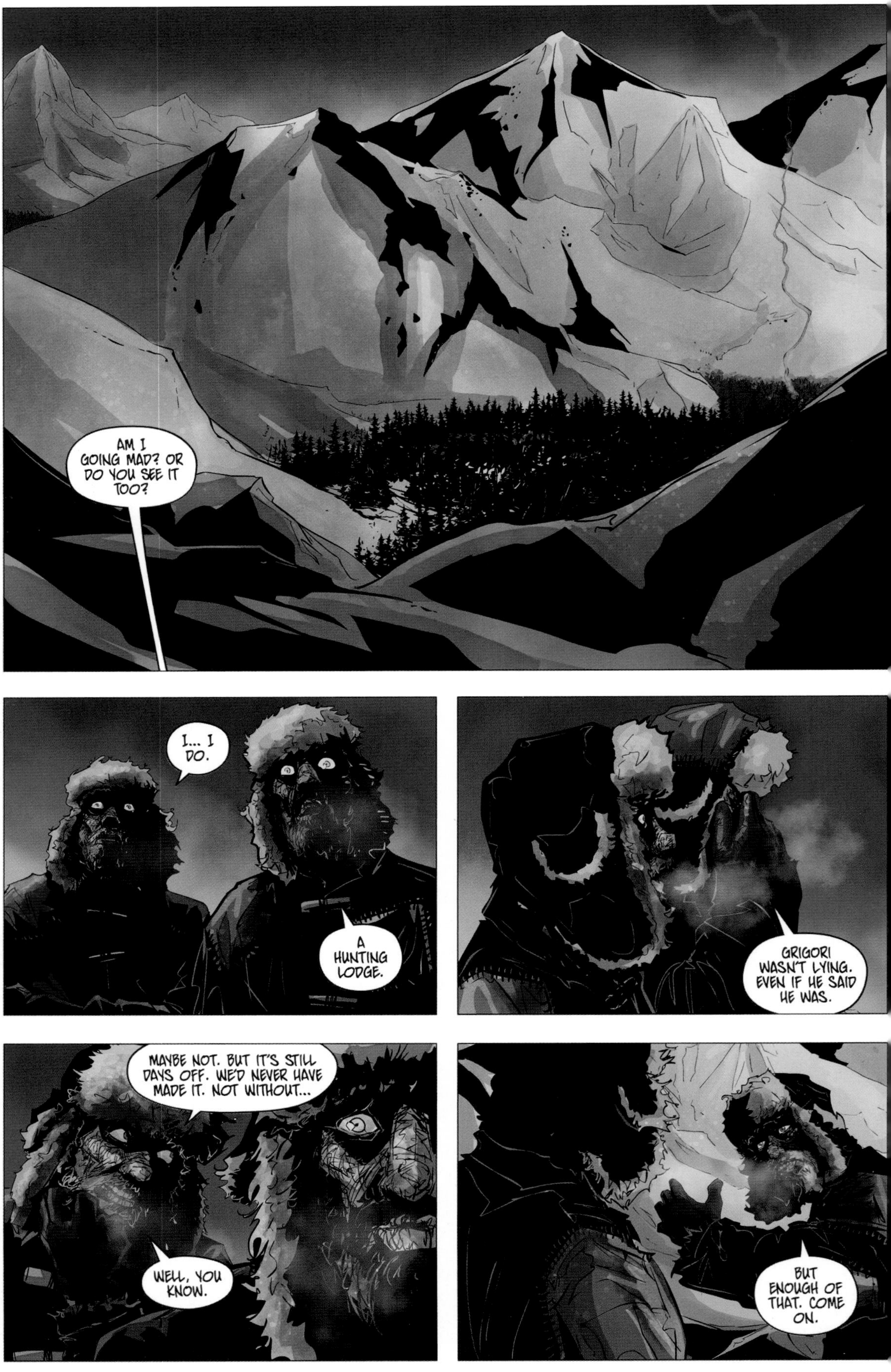
AM I GOING MAD? OR DO YOU SEE IT TOO?
I... I DO.
A HUNTING LODGE.
GRIGORI WASN'T LYING. EVEN IF HE SAID HE WAS.
MAYBE NOT. BUT IT'S STILL DAYS OFF. WE'D NEVER HAVE MADE IT. NOT WITHOUT...
WELL, YOU KNOW.
BUT ENOUGH OF THAT. COME ON.

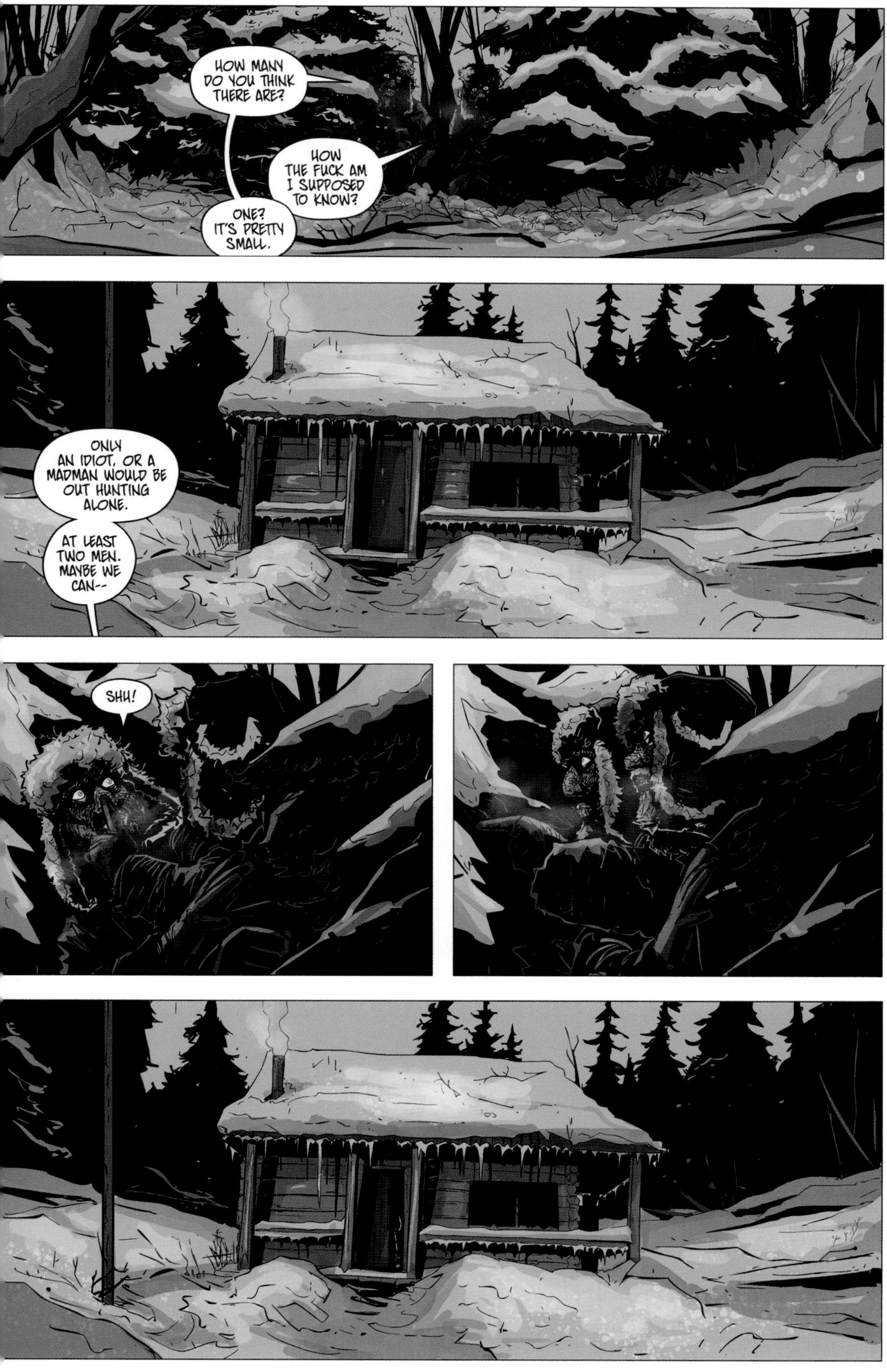
HOW MANY DO YOU THINK THERE ARE?
HOW THE FUCK AM I SUPPOSED TO KNOW?
ONE? IT'S PRETTY SMALL.
ONLY AN IDIOT, OR A MADMAN WOULD BE OUT HUNTING ALONE.
AT LEAST TWO MEN. MAYBE WE CAN--
SHH!

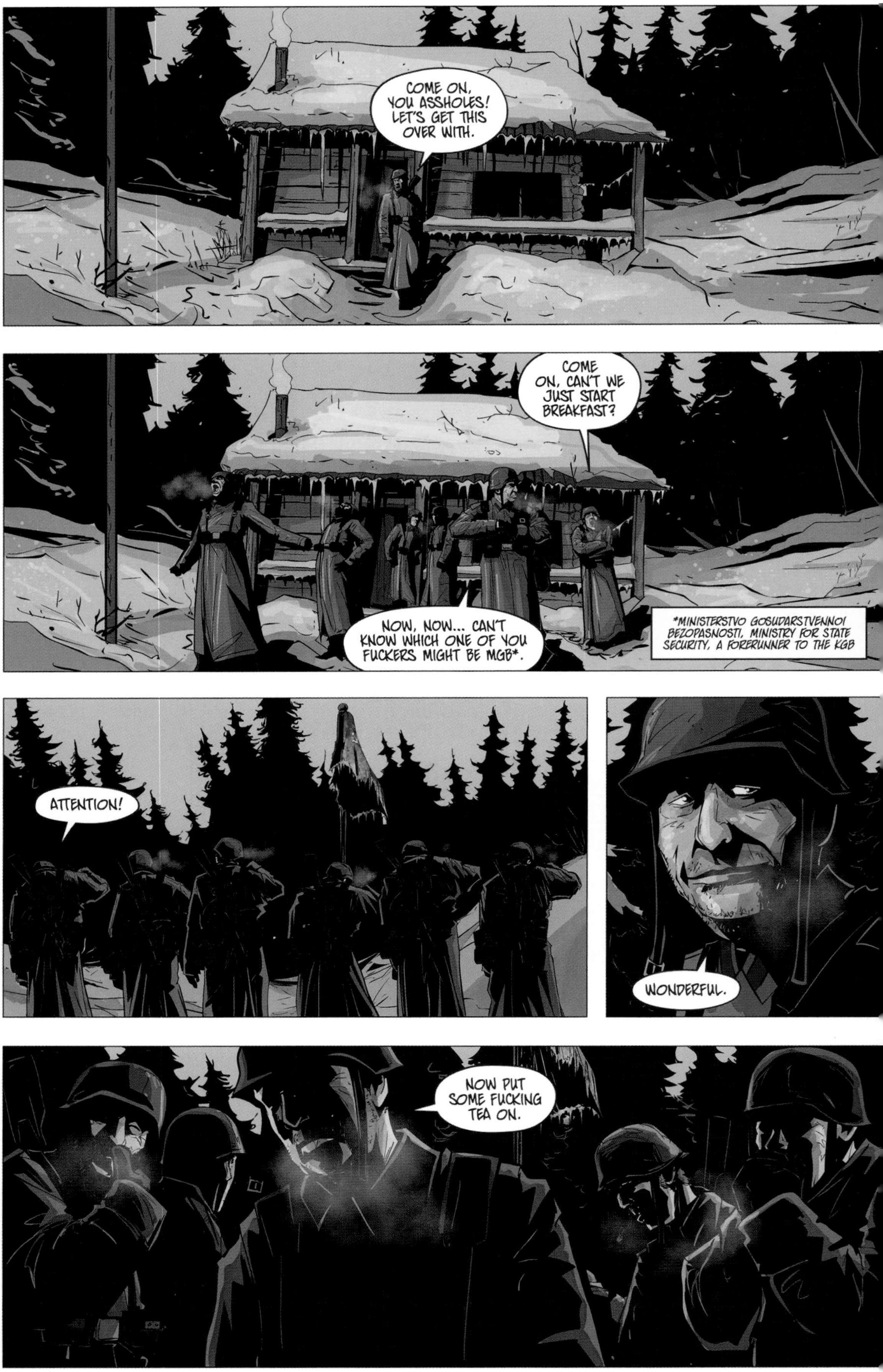
COME ON, YOU ASSHOLES! LET'S GET THIS OVER WITH.
COME ON, CAN'T WE JUST START BREAKFAST?
NOW, NOW... CAN'T KNOW WHICH ONE OF YOU FUCKERS MIGHT BE MGB*.
*MINISTERSTVO GOSUDARSTVENNOI BEZOPASNOSTI, MINISTRY FOR STATE SECURITY, A FORERUNNER TO THE KGB
ATTENTION!
WONDERFUL.
NOW PUT SOME FUCKING TEA ON.

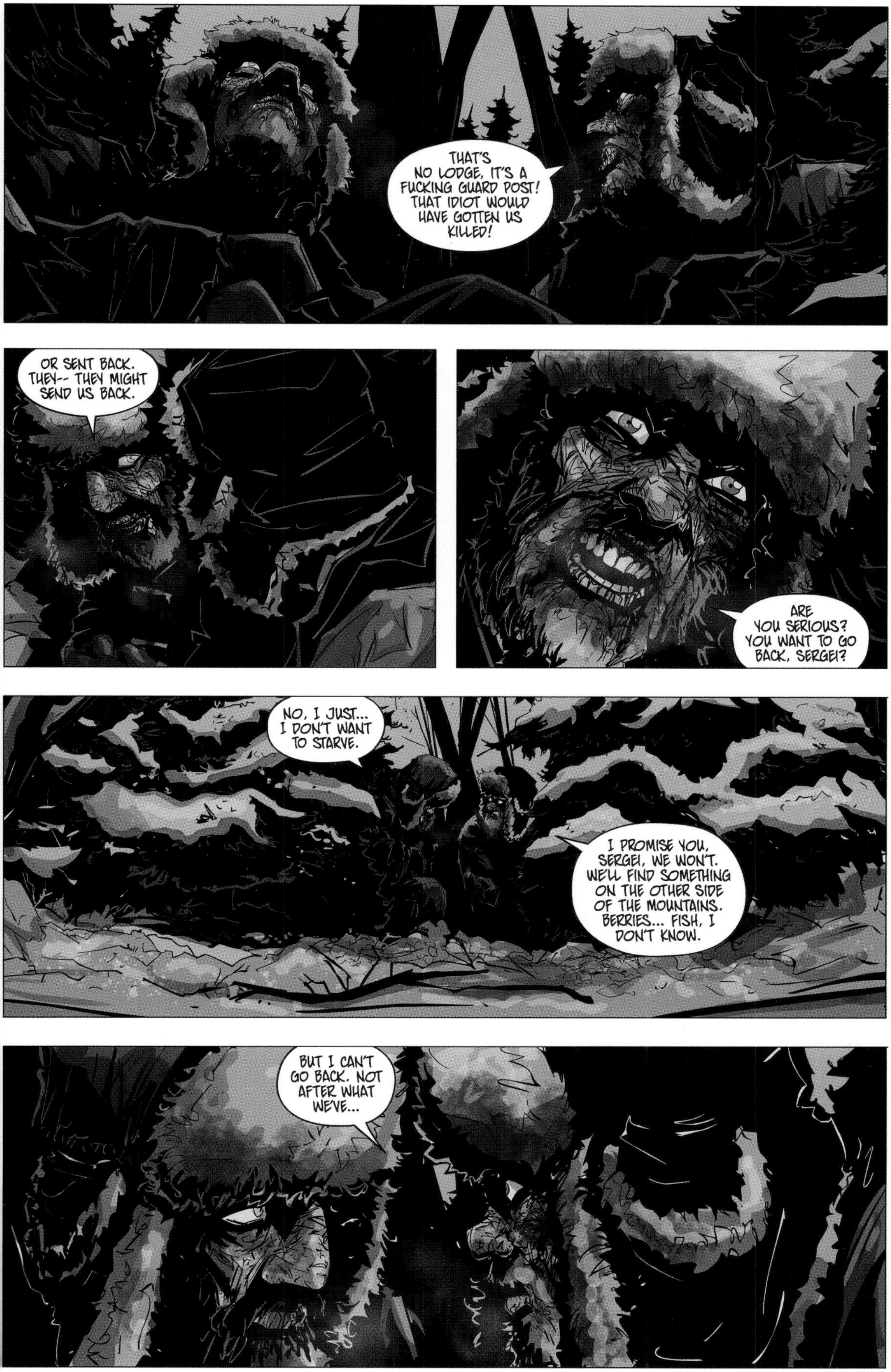
THAT'S NO LODGE, IT'S A FUCKING GUARD POST! THAT IDIOT WOULD HAVE GOTTEN US KILLED!
OR SENT BACK. THEY-- THEY MIGHT SEND US BACK.
ARE YOU SERIOUS? YOU WANT TO GO BACK, SERGEI?
NO, I JUST... I DON'T WANT TO STARVE.
I PROMISE YOU, SERGEI, WE WON'T. WE'LL FIND SOMETHING ON THE OTHER SIDE OF THE MOUNTAINS. BERRIES... FISH, I DON'T KNOW.
BUT I CAN'T GO BACK. NOT AFTER WHAT WE'VE...

WHAT *I'VE* DONE.

I CAN'T HAVE THAT ALL BE FOR NOTHING.

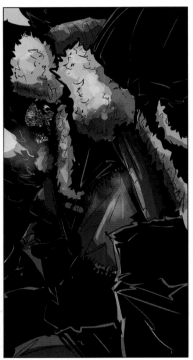

I...

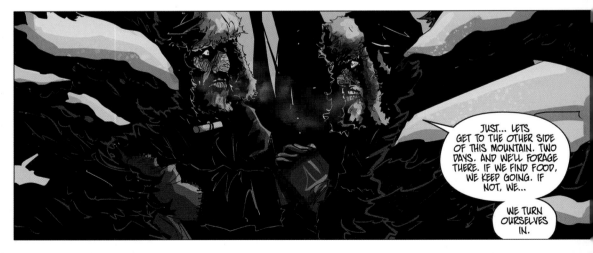

JUST... LETS GET TO THE OTHER SIDE OF THIS MOUNTAIN. TWO DAYS. AND WE'LL FORAGE THERE. IF WE FIND FOOD, WE KEEP GOING. IF NOT, WE...

WE TURN OURSELVES IN.

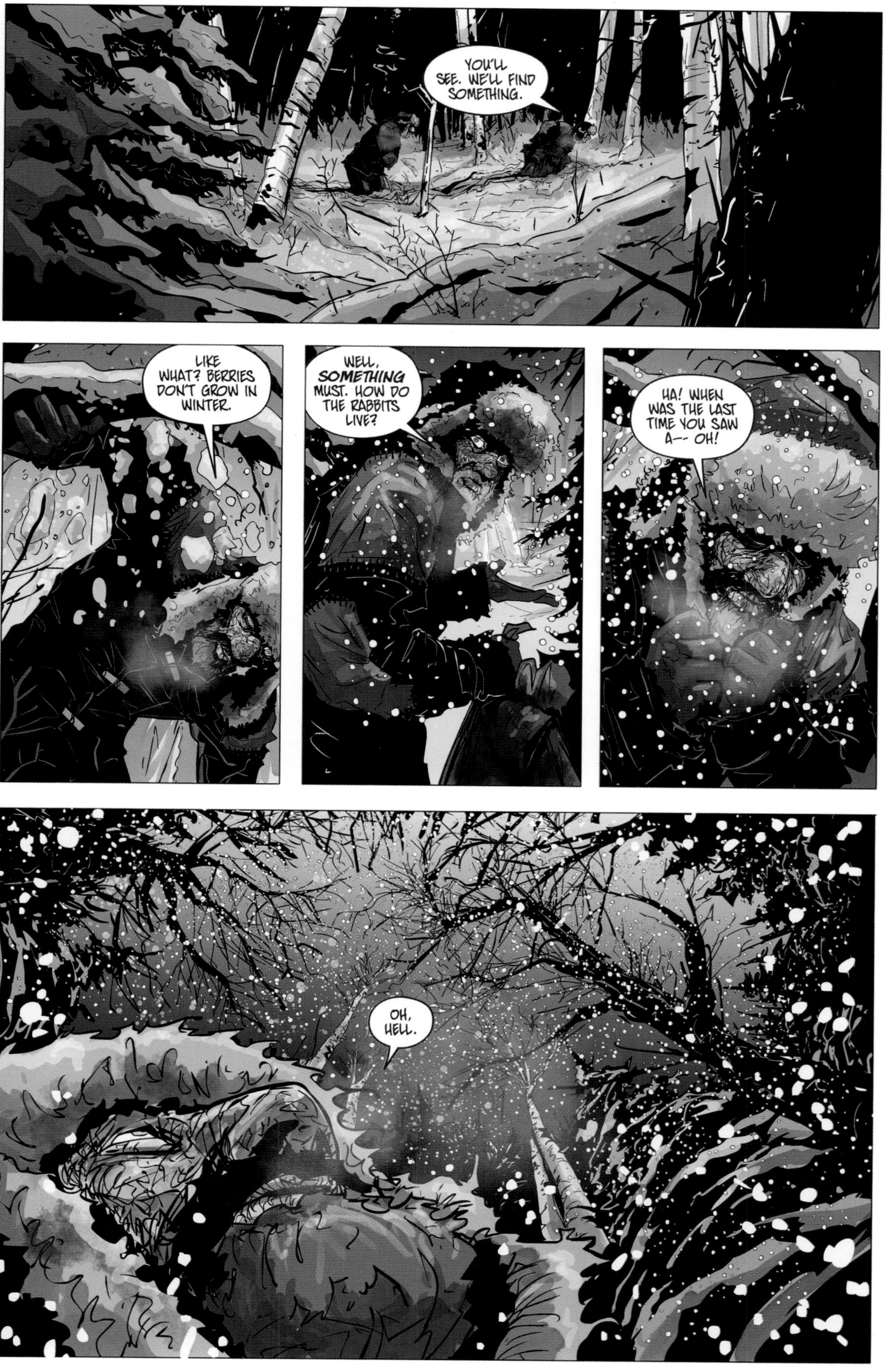
YOU'LL SEE. WE'LL FIND SOMETHING.
LIKE WHAT? BERRIES DON'T GROW IN WINTER.
WELL, SOMETHING MUST. HOW DO THE RABBITS LIVE?
HA! WHEN WAS THE LAST TIME YOU SAW A-- OH!
OH, HELL.

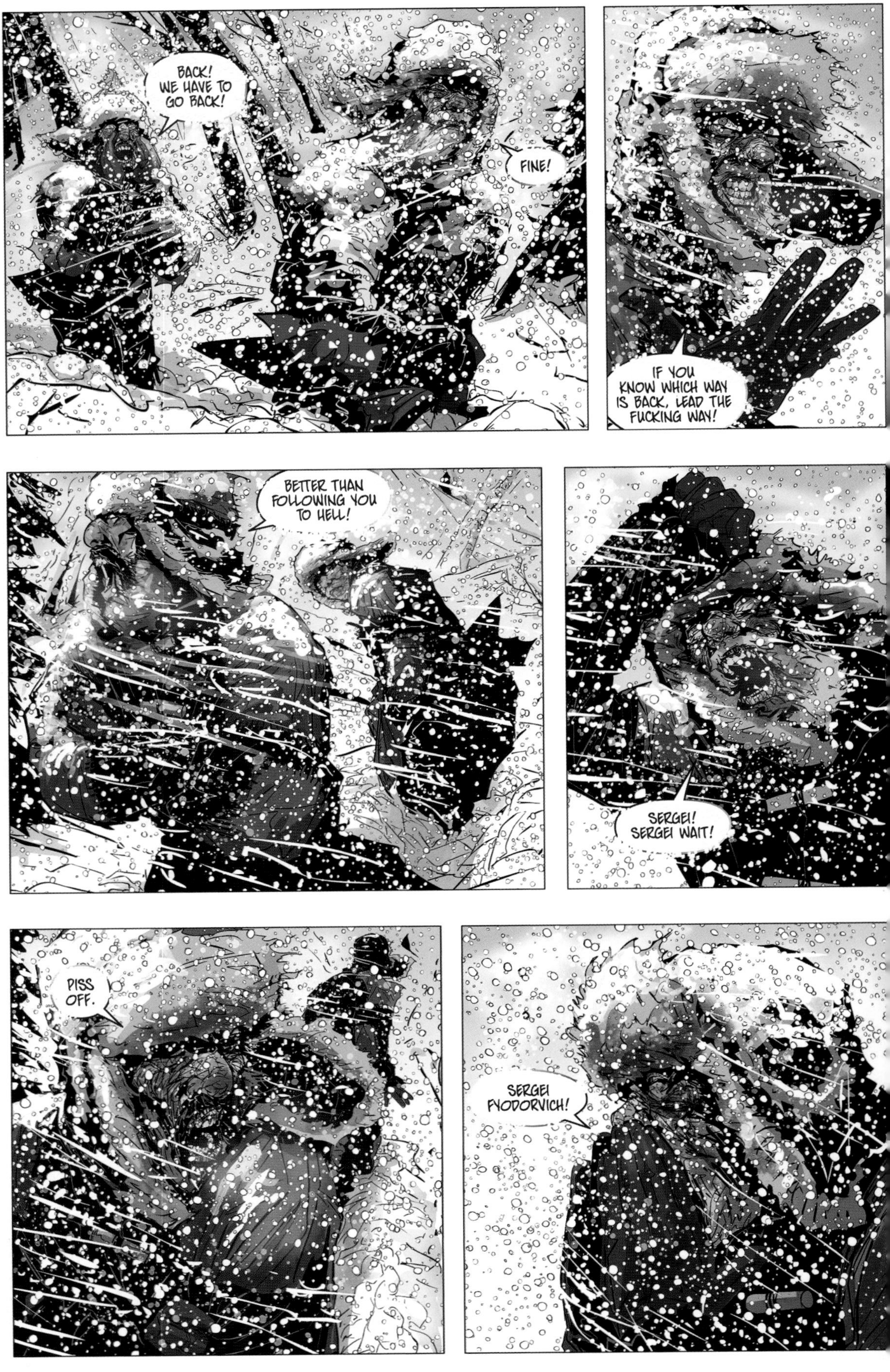
BACK! WE HAVE TO GO BACK!
FINE!
IF YOU KNOW WHICH WAY IS BACK, LEAD THE FUCKING WAY!
BETTER THAN FOLLOWING YOU TO HELL!
SERGEI! SERGEI WAIT!
PISS OFF.
SERGEI FYODORVICH!

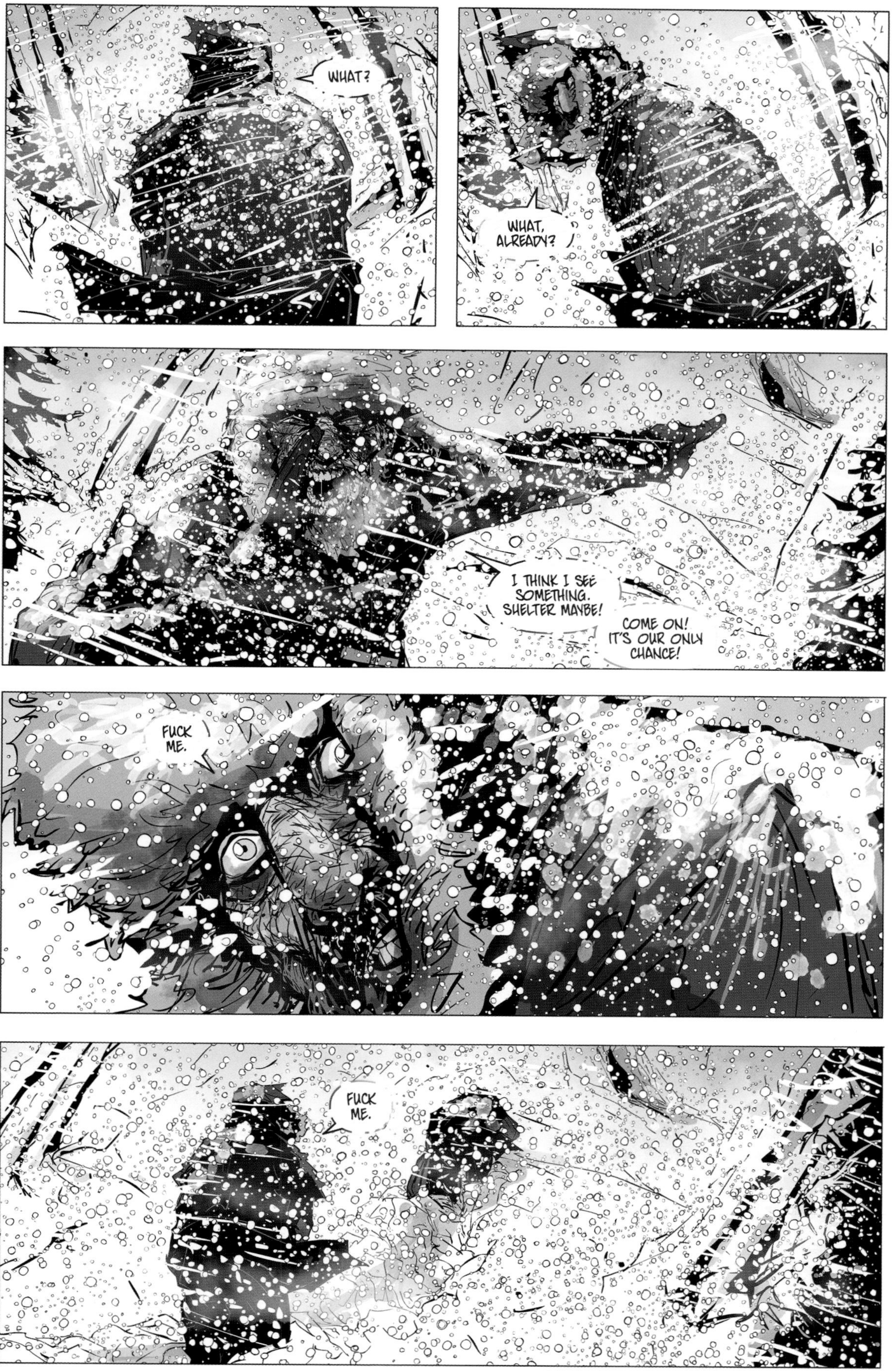
WHAT?
WHAT, ALREADY?
I THINK I SEE SOMETHING. SHELTER MAYBE!
COME ON! IT'S OUR ONLY CHANCE!
FUCK ME.
FUCK ME.

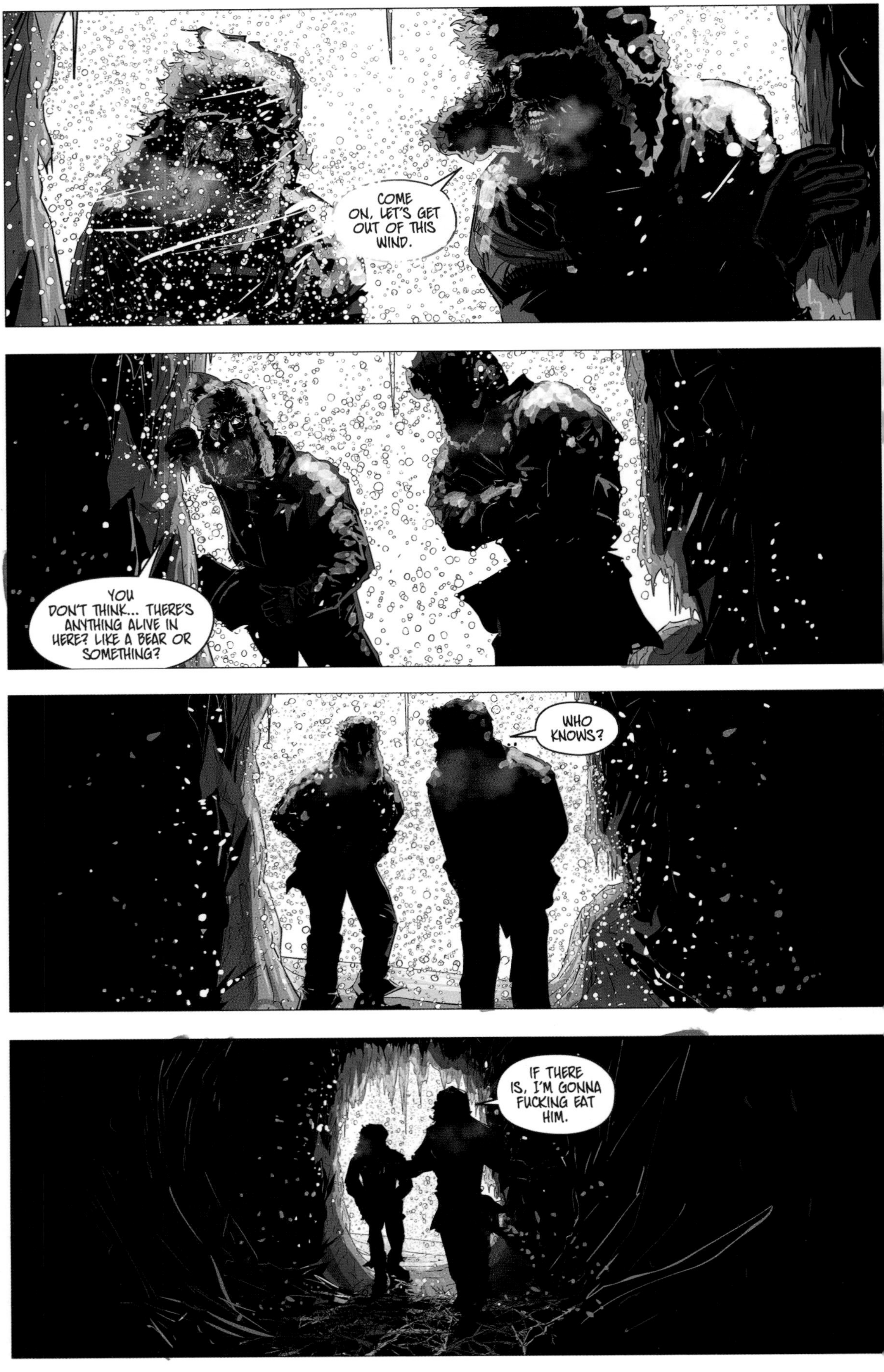
COME ON, LET'S GET OUT OF THIS WIND.
YOU DON'T THINK... THERE'S ANYTHING ALIVE IN HERE? LIKE A BEAR OR SOMETHING?
WHO KNOWS?
IF THERE IS, I'M GONNA FUCKING EAT HIM.

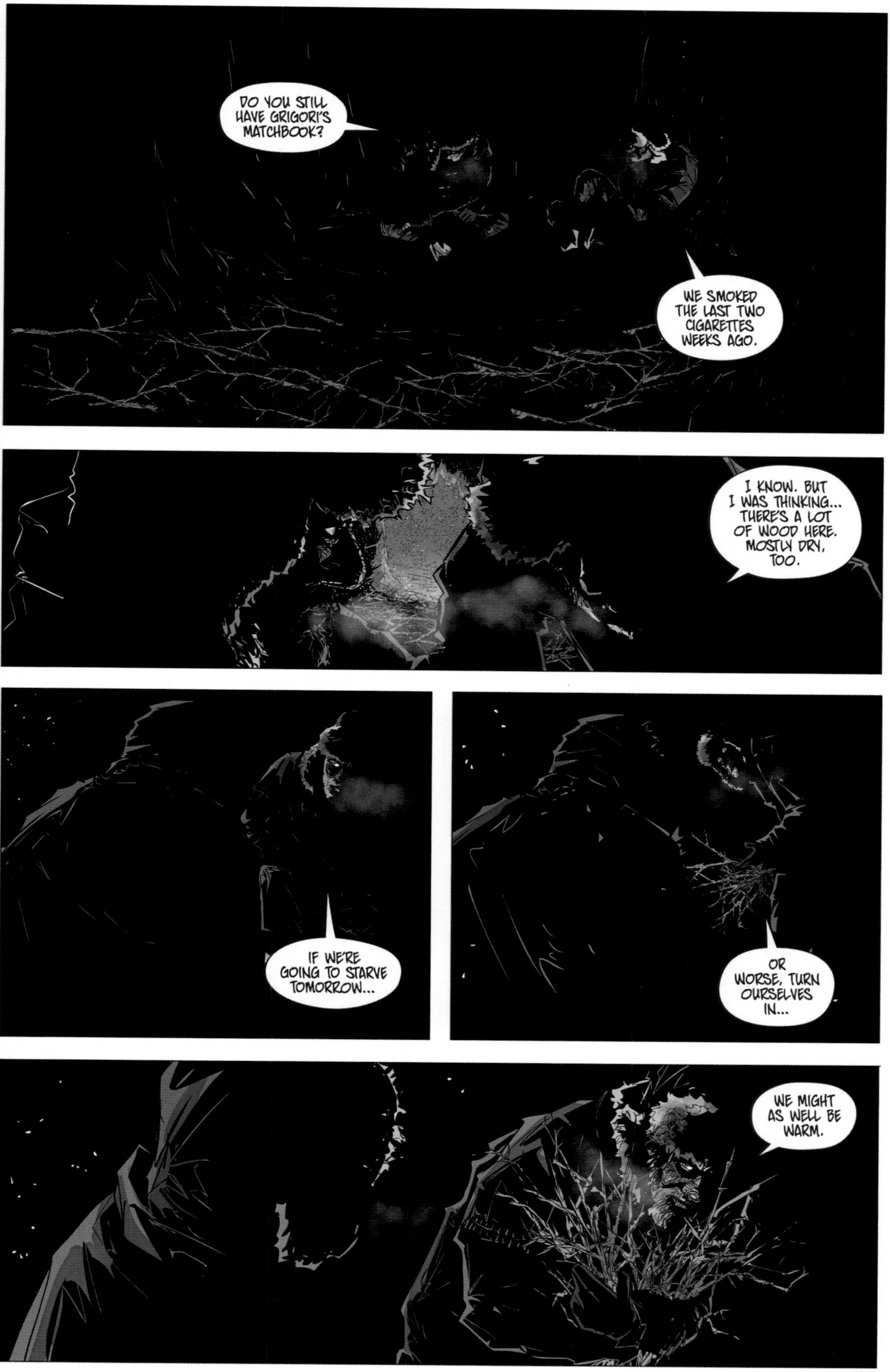
DO YOU STILL HAVE GRIGORI'S MATCHBOOK?
WE SMOKED THE LAST TWO CIGARETTES WEEKS AGO.
I KNOW. BUT I WAS THINKING... THERE'S A LOT OF WOOD HERE. MOSTLY DRY, TOO.
IF WE'RE GOING TO STARVE TOMORROW...
OR WORSE, TURN OURSELVES IN...
WE MIGHT AS WELL BE WARM.

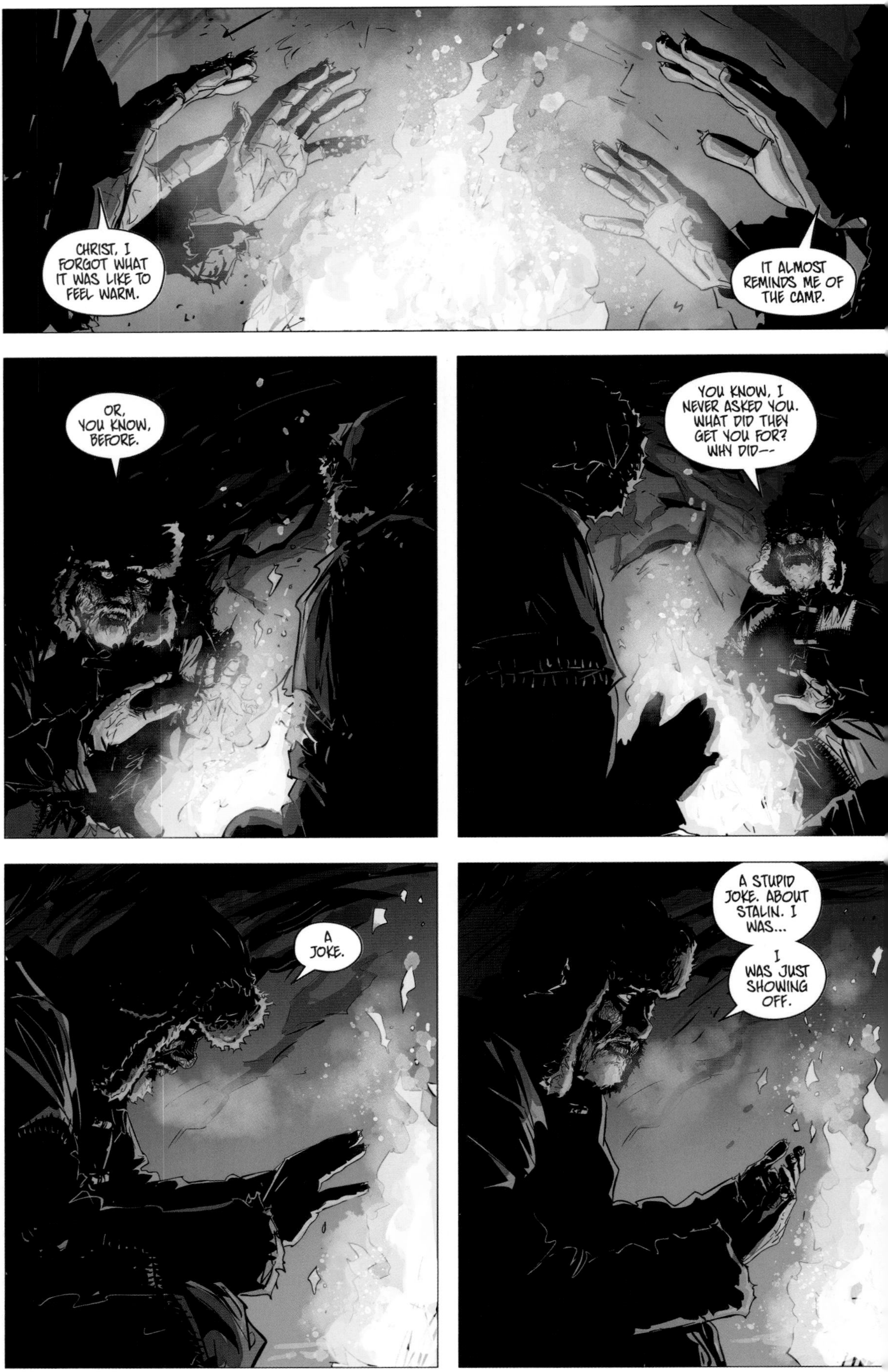
CHRIST, I FORGOT WHAT IT WAS LIKE TO FEEL WARM.
IT ALMOST REMINDS ME OF THE CAMP.
OR, YOU KNOW, BEFORE.
YOU KNOW, I NEVER ASKED YOU. WHAT DID THEY GET YOU FOR? WHY DID--
A JOKE.
A STUPID JOKE. ABOUT STALIN. I WAS...
I WAS JUST SHOWING OFF.

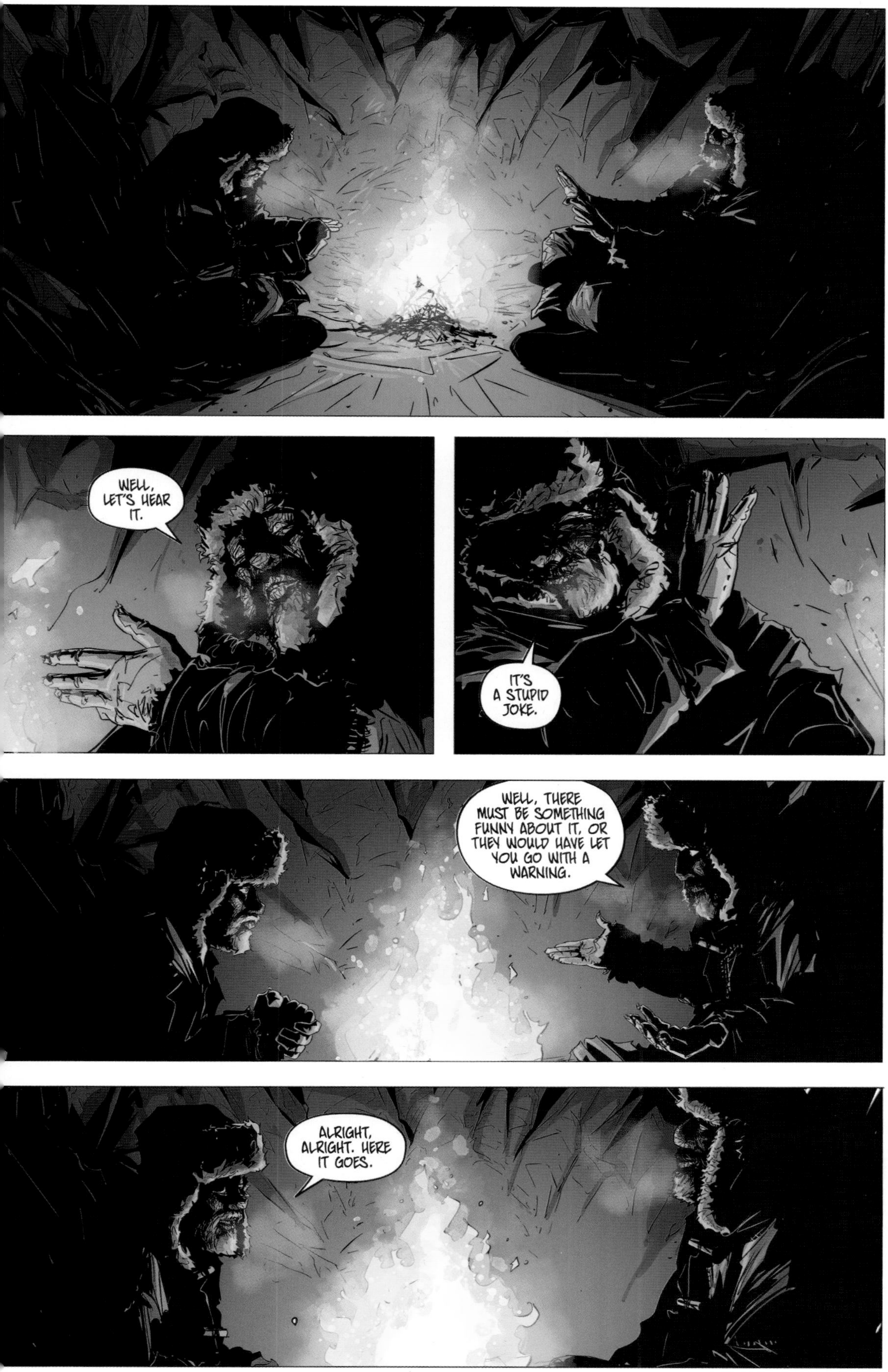
WELL, LET'S HEAR IT.
IT'S A STUPID JOKE.
WELL, THERE MUST BE SOMETHING FUNNY ABOUT IT, OR THEY WOULD HAVE LET YOU GO WITH A WARNING.
ALRIGHT, ALRIGHT. HERE IT GOES.

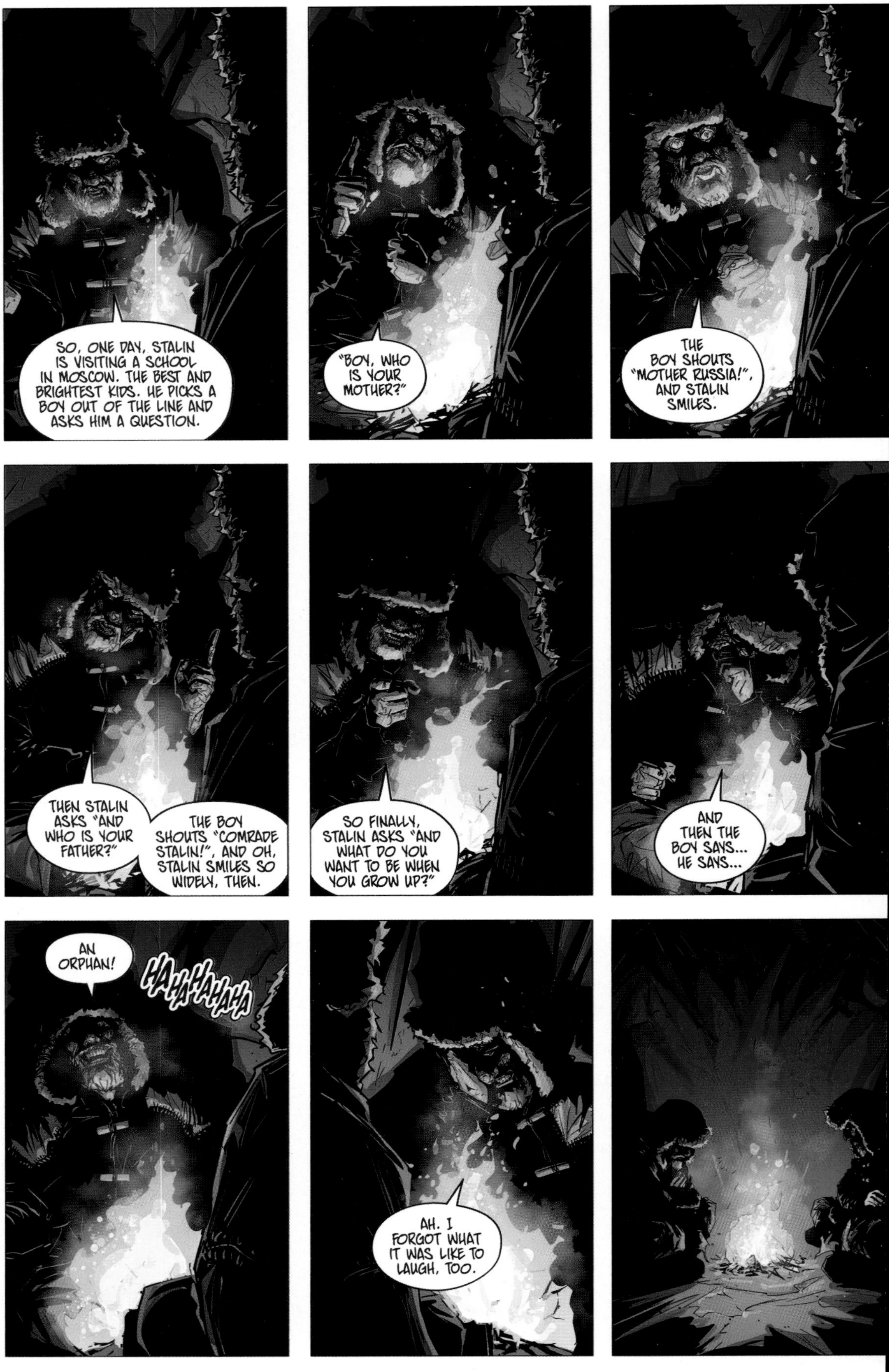
SO, ONE DAY, STALIN IS VISITING A SCHOOL IN MOSCOW. THE BEST AND BRIGHTEST KIDS. HE PICKS A BOY OUT OF THE LINE AND ASKS HIM A QUESTION.
"BOY, WHO IS YOUR MOTHER?"
THE BOY SHOUTS "MOTHER RUSSIA!", AND STALIN SMILES.
THEN STALIN ASKS "AND WHO IS YOUR FATHER?"
THE BOY SHOUTS "COMRADE STALIN!", AND OH, STALIN SMILES SO WIDELY, THEN.
SO FINALLY, STALIN ASKS "AND WHAT DO YOU WANT TO BE WHEN YOU GROW UP?"
AND THEN THE BOY SAYS... HE SAYS...
AN ORPHAN!
HAHAHAHAHA
AH. I FORGOT WHAT IT WAS LIKE TO LAUGH, TOO.

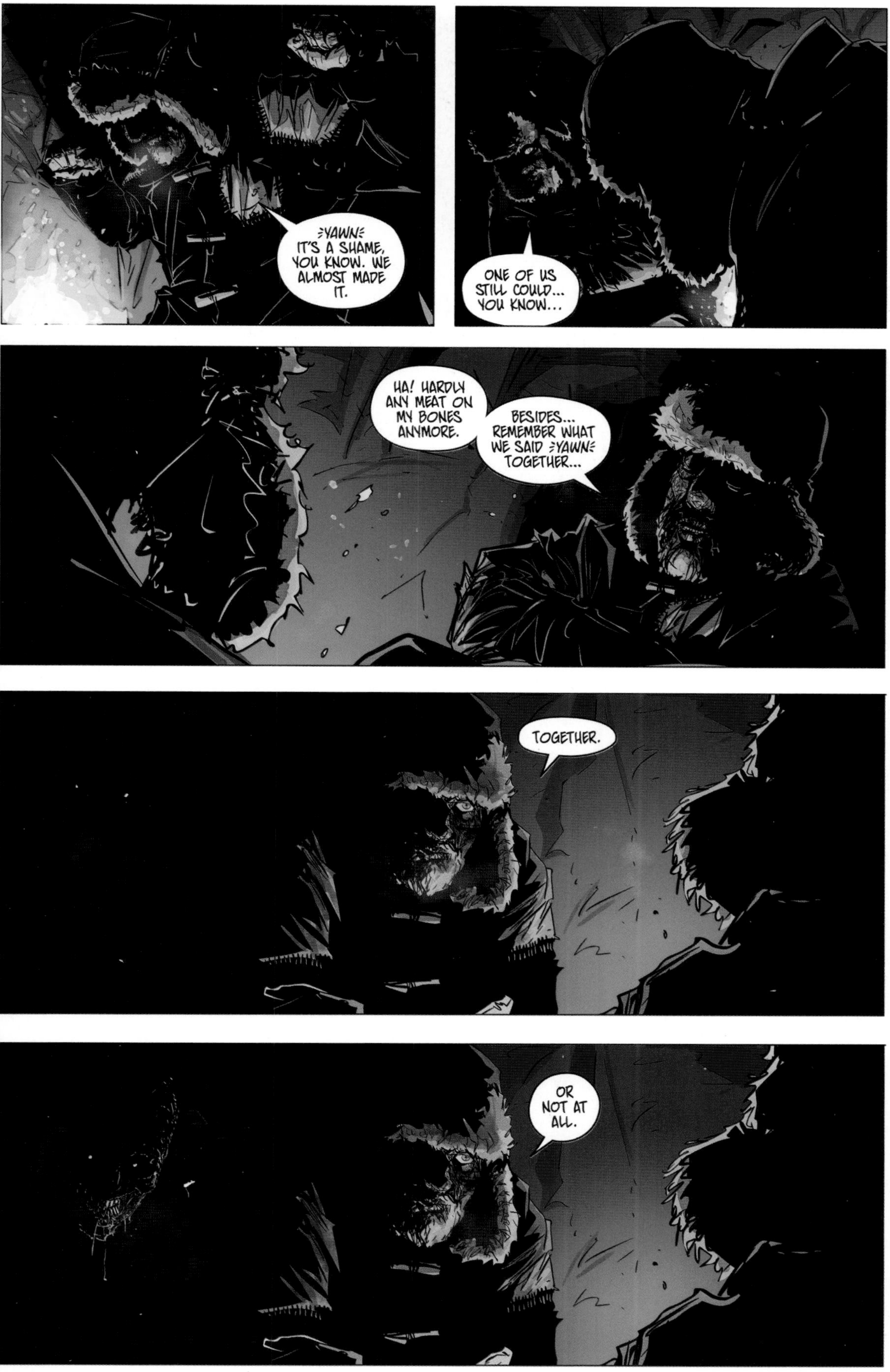
≡YAWN≡ IT'S A SHAME, YOU KNOW. WE ALMOST MADE IT.
ONE OF US STILL COULD... YOU KNOW...
HA! HARDLY ANY MEAT ON MY BONES ANYMORE.
BESIDES... REMEMBER WHAT WE SAID ≡YAWN≡ TOGETHER...
TOGETHER.
OR NOT AT ALL.

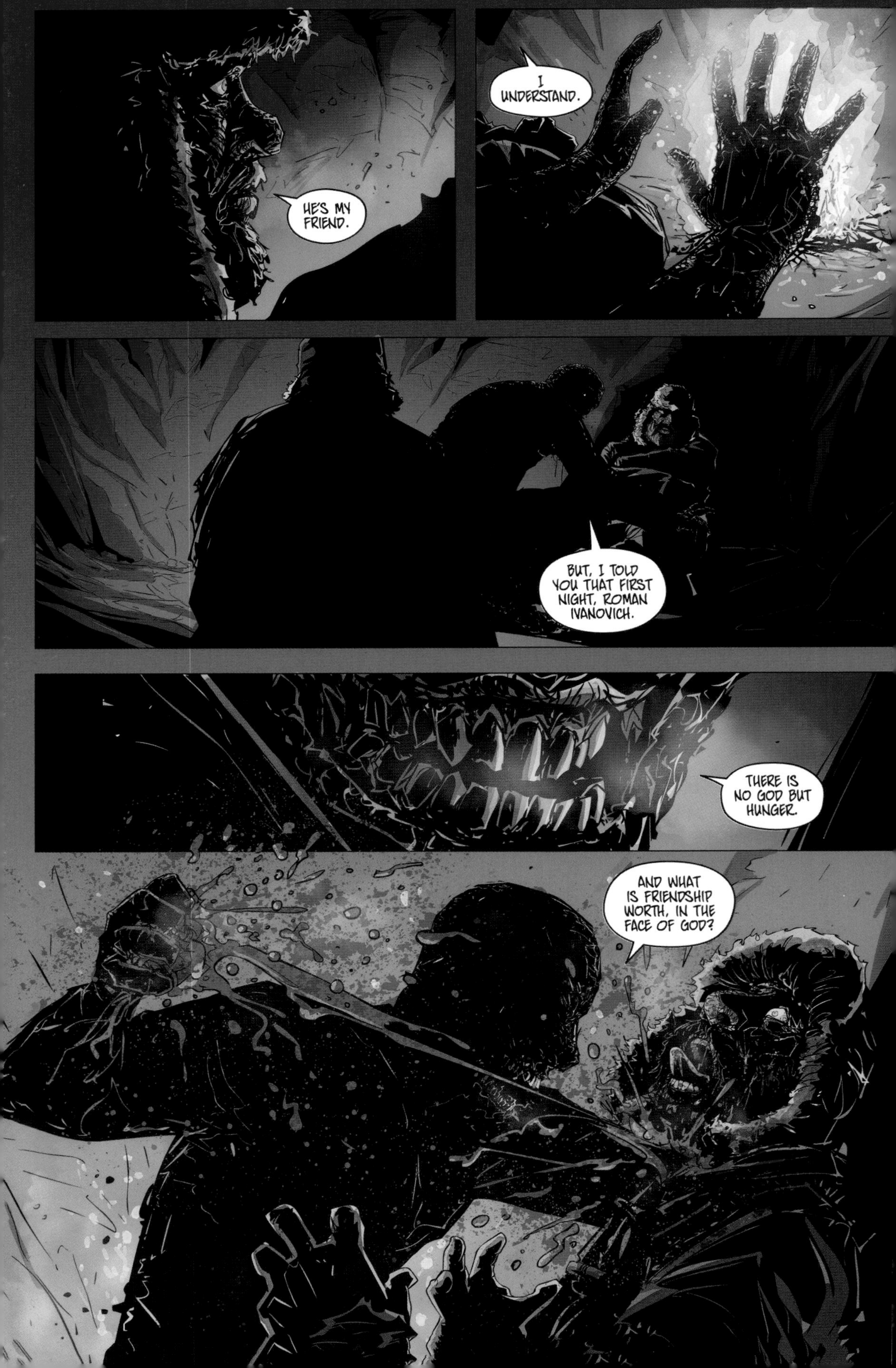
HE'S MY FRIEND.
I UNDERSTAND.
BUT, I TOLD YOU THAT FIRST NIGHT, ROMAN IVANOVICH.
THERE IS NO GOD BUT HUNGER.
AND WHAT IS FRIENDSHIP WORTH, IN THE FACE OF GOD?

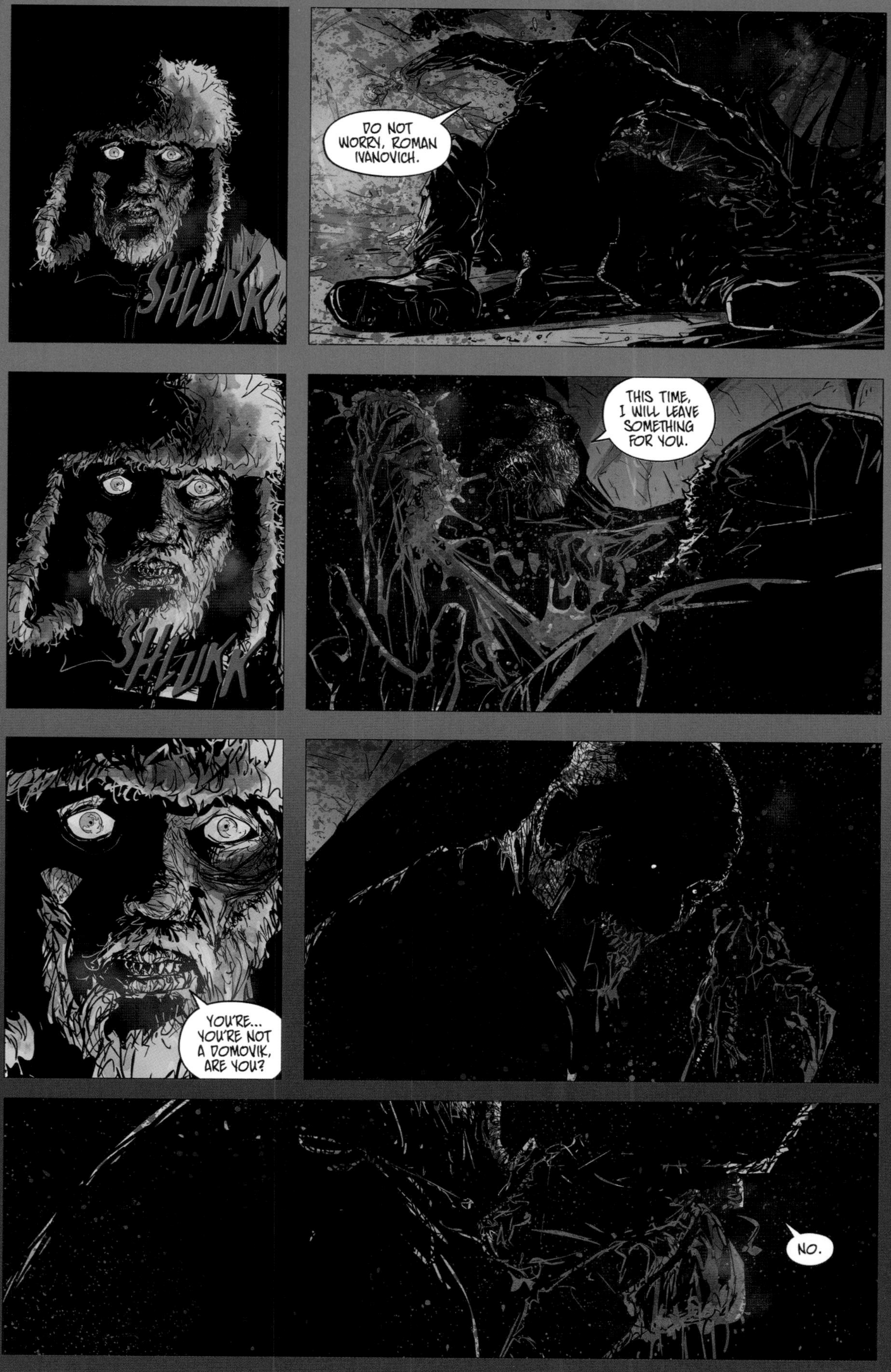

SHLUKK
DO NOT WORRY, ROMAN IVANOVICH.
SHLUKK
THIS TIME, I WILL LEAVE SOMETHING FOR YOU.
YOU'RE... YOU'RE NOT A DOMOVIK, ARE YOU?
NO.

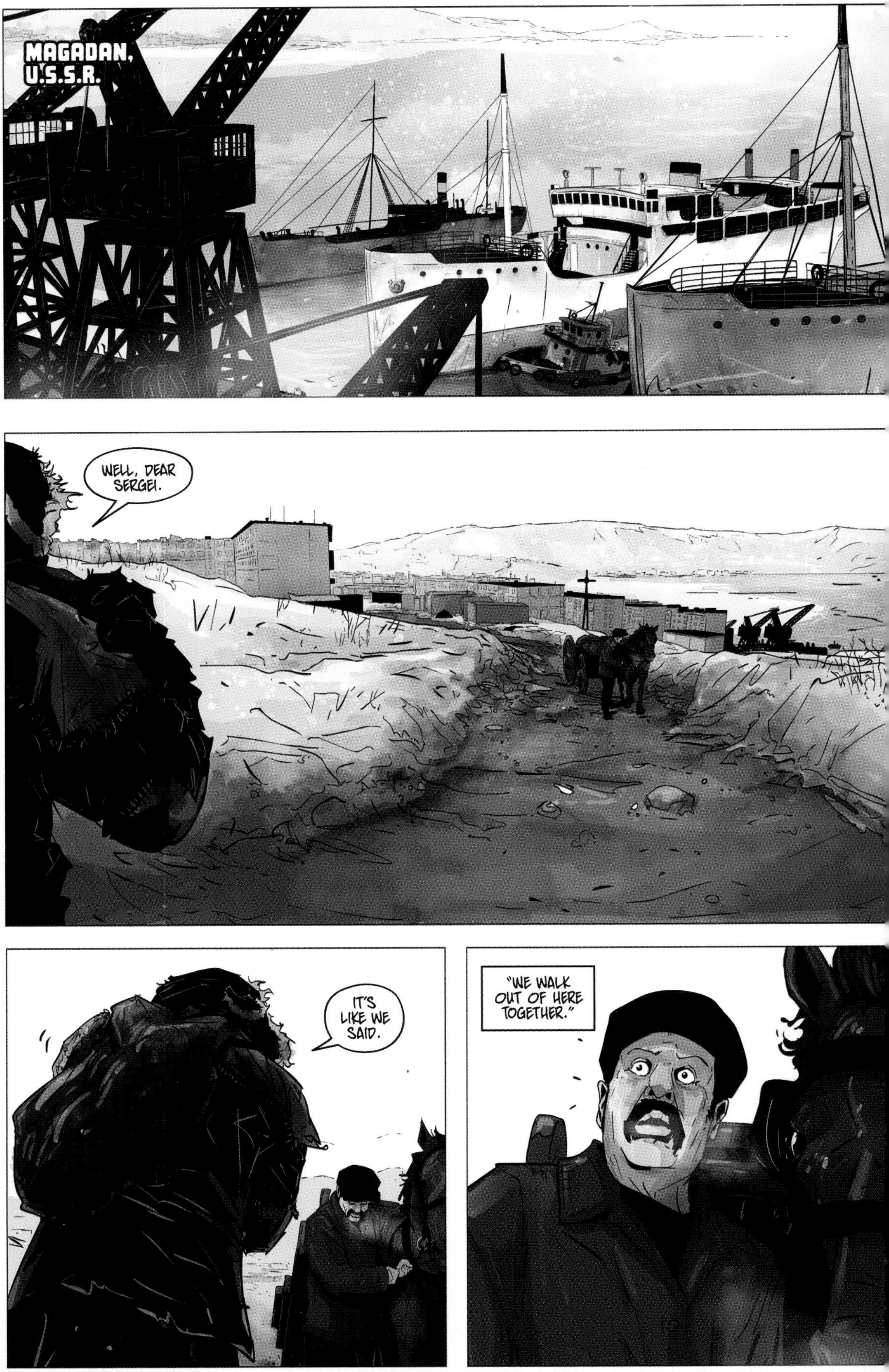
MAGADAN, U.S.S.R.
WELL, DEAR SERGEI.
IT'S LIKE WE SAID.
"WE WALK OUT OF HERE TOGETHER."

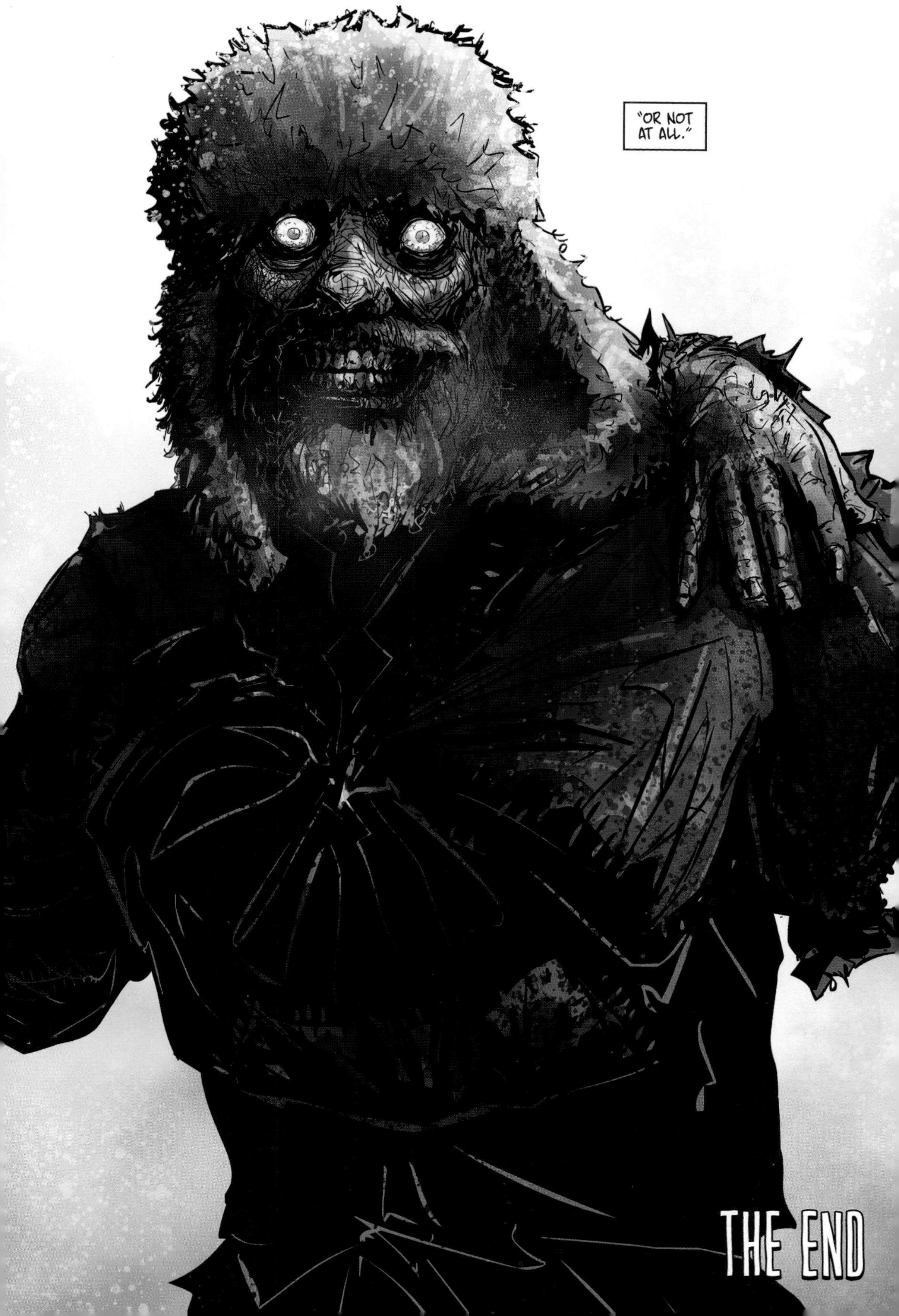
"OR NOT AT ALL."
THE END

I'm half Russian. Well, a quarter—my grandfather was born there, and my grandmother's parents were born close enough to its border with Lithuania that nobody is 100% sure which country their tiny village was actually in. They were lucky enough never to have to endure the horrors of the gulag system, having fled the pogroms decades earlier. So, whatever *Road of Bones* is, it's not the retelling of something that I have a direct connection to. And yet, it's a story that once I started on, wouldn't let me go.

I've said many times in interviews that I think *Road of Bones* will surprise people, and the other day, someone asked me why. Honestly, it's because it surprised me, as I was writing it. If you'd asked me a year ago if I wrote horror, if I even had any more than a passing interest in writing horror, I would have told you no. It's not that I don't enjoy it—I do—it's just that, the picture in my head of what kind of writer I am never really included that. I was a sci-fi guy, a fantasist. I created big, weird worlds, and yes, sometimes those worlds contained horrific things—but horror? Just not me.

Road of Bones changed all of that, and one of the things that's been on my mind as I created it is why—what is it about this story that grabbed me? And what I keep coming back to is that many times, unfortunately, the real world is more horrific and terrible than anything I could possibly conjure out of my own imagination.

Road of Bones is a piece of fiction—but there are many things in it that are based in the horrific reality of the Gulag. Start with the name: The Road of Bones is the colloquial name for the R504 Kolyma Highway, the only road connecting the farthest reaches of the Kolyma region to the rest of Russia. And the reason it has that name is there are people buried in it, literally. You see, when they were digging the road, they built it on permafrost, and it was decided it was more efficient to just bury the bodies of deceased workers under the road rather than dig new holes in the frozen ground—a harsh reality that we open the first few pages with.

Another reality is the situation of our main character, Roman. Here's a man who made an off-color political joke at a party—something I know I've done, and that we all probably have at some point in our lives. The difference is, he was sentenced to 20 years of hard labor for it, which again, I can't stress enough, actually happened to many, many people under Stalin. And keep in mind, he was sentenced to 20 years in a place where the average life expectancy was a little over a year, so it was, in practical terms, a death sentence.

And then there's the cannibalism. There are accounts of it happening both inside the camps and during escapes—for instance, the so-called "Nazino Affair," where guards arrested over 50 prisoners for cannibalism. And stories of prisoners escaping with a comrade they planned to eat were so common there was even a term for it–bringing along a "walking lunch."

What shocked me about it all was how the system seemed to bring out the worst in everyone, from its overseers and guards, to the prisoners themselves, who fought brutally over the scant resources available to them. It was a system that took in men, and churned out monsters—sometimes by design, as when the Soviet regime tacitly supported one prison gang over another; and sometimes by circumstance, as when a prisoner was forced to do the inhuman in order to survive.

And that was where the story took off for me. Survival in a system that is built to grind people into dust. What it would take, what lengths you or I or anyone would go to. And then I started to think about surviving in a place like Siberia. A frigid, harsh environment that, in its own way, seems to do everything it can to crush the life that takes root there.

What do you do when you have no food and no hope of finding any before you starve? We think that facts like "the human body can survive three days without water, and three weeks without food" as common knowledge—but if you haven't had a formal, late-20th-century education, would you know that? Would you even believe it, when the cold wind is blowing, and your stomach is growling like a wolf?

And then, add the fact that you've been a victim of one of the most dehumanizing systems on the planet. That part of you, that is willing to do anything to survive—is it in your nature, or has it been nurtured and honed by the brutality of your fellows?

All of these fears, all of these notions are personified in a monster, the Domovik, but one of the questions running throughout the book is whether it's a real, supernatural monster, or just the personification of something monstrous inside Roman himself.

And, if you still have that question in your head when you turn the last page, that's a good thing, in my eyes. Because I don't know where the evil that could spawn a regime like Stalin's comes from. Whether the monsters stalking the world are born of something else, or out of our own dark hearts.

I didn't write *Road of Bones* to answer that question, but instead, to ask it. Thank you for reading it.

Rich

(Portions of this essay were originally posted on pastemagazine.com, May 22, 2019)

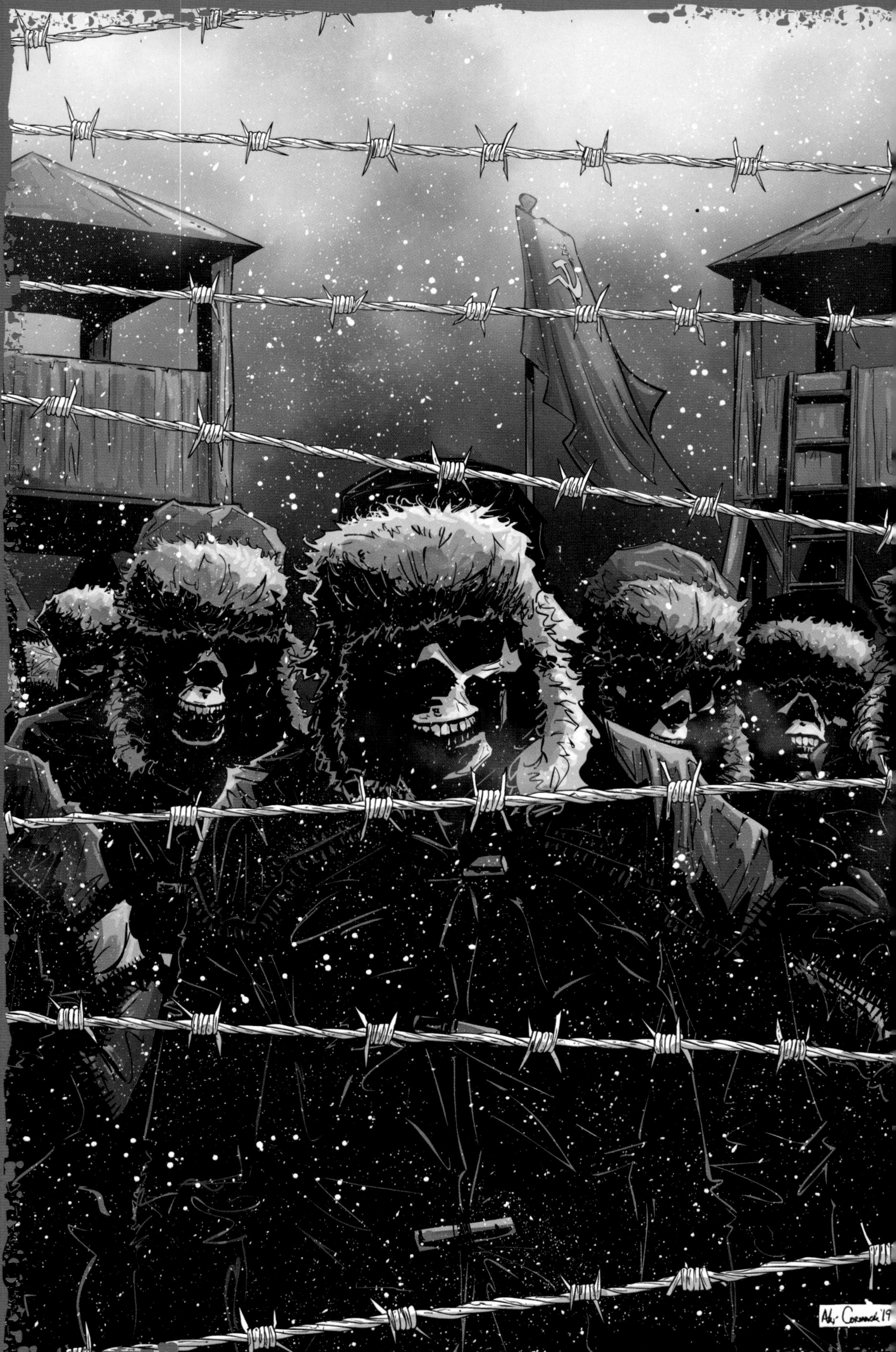
Ali-Cormack '19

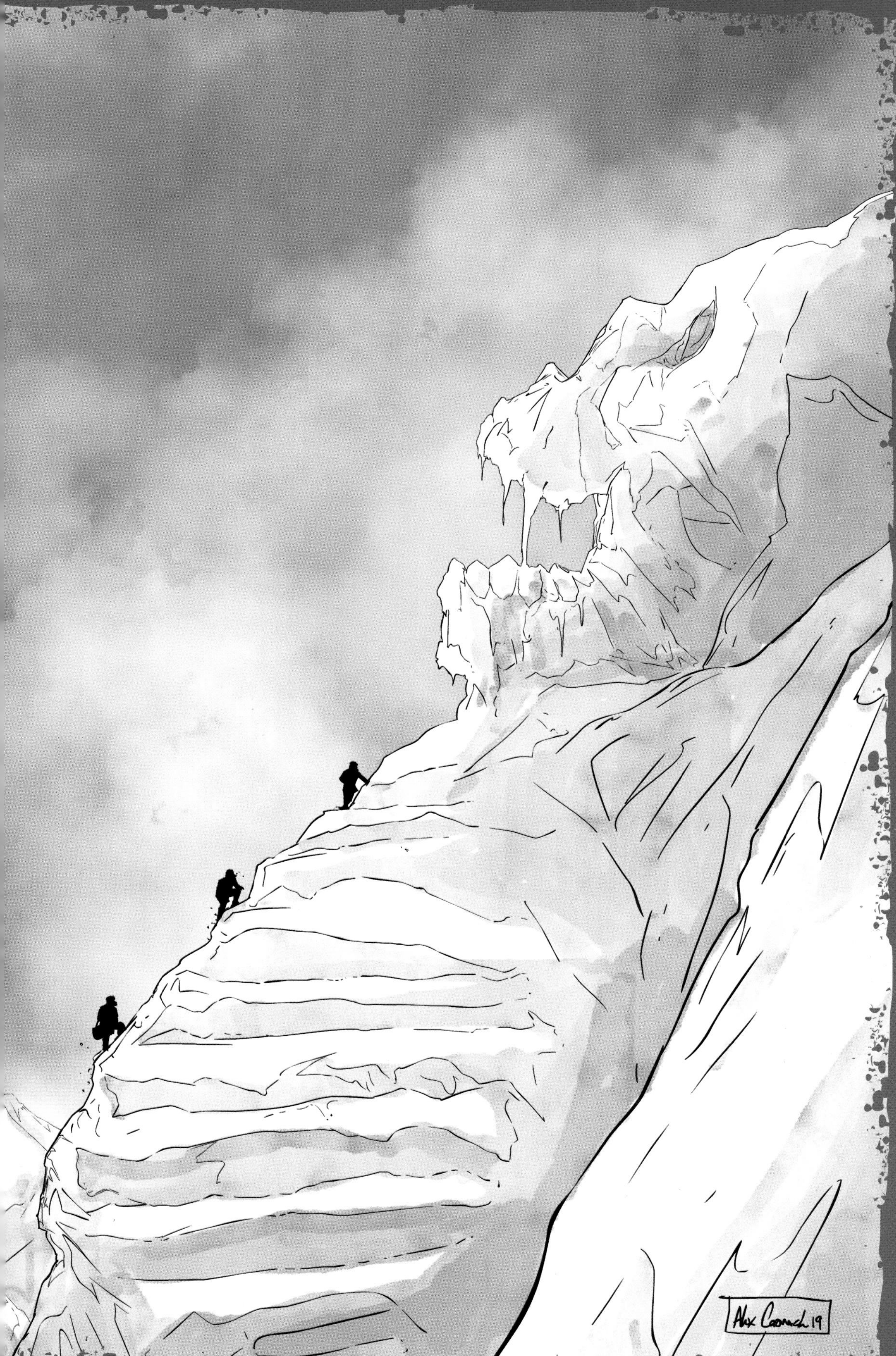
Alex Cormack 19

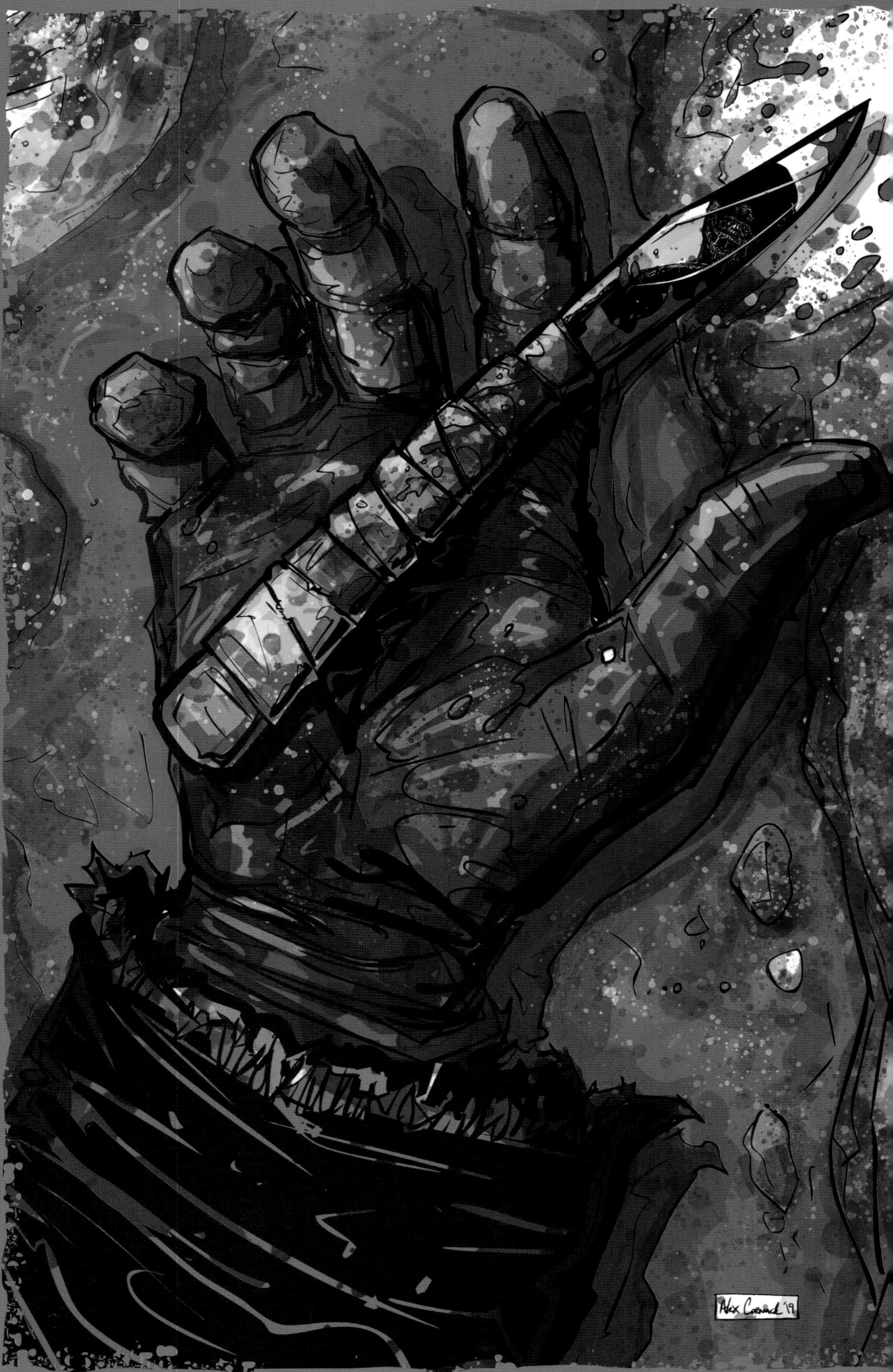
Alex Cormack '19

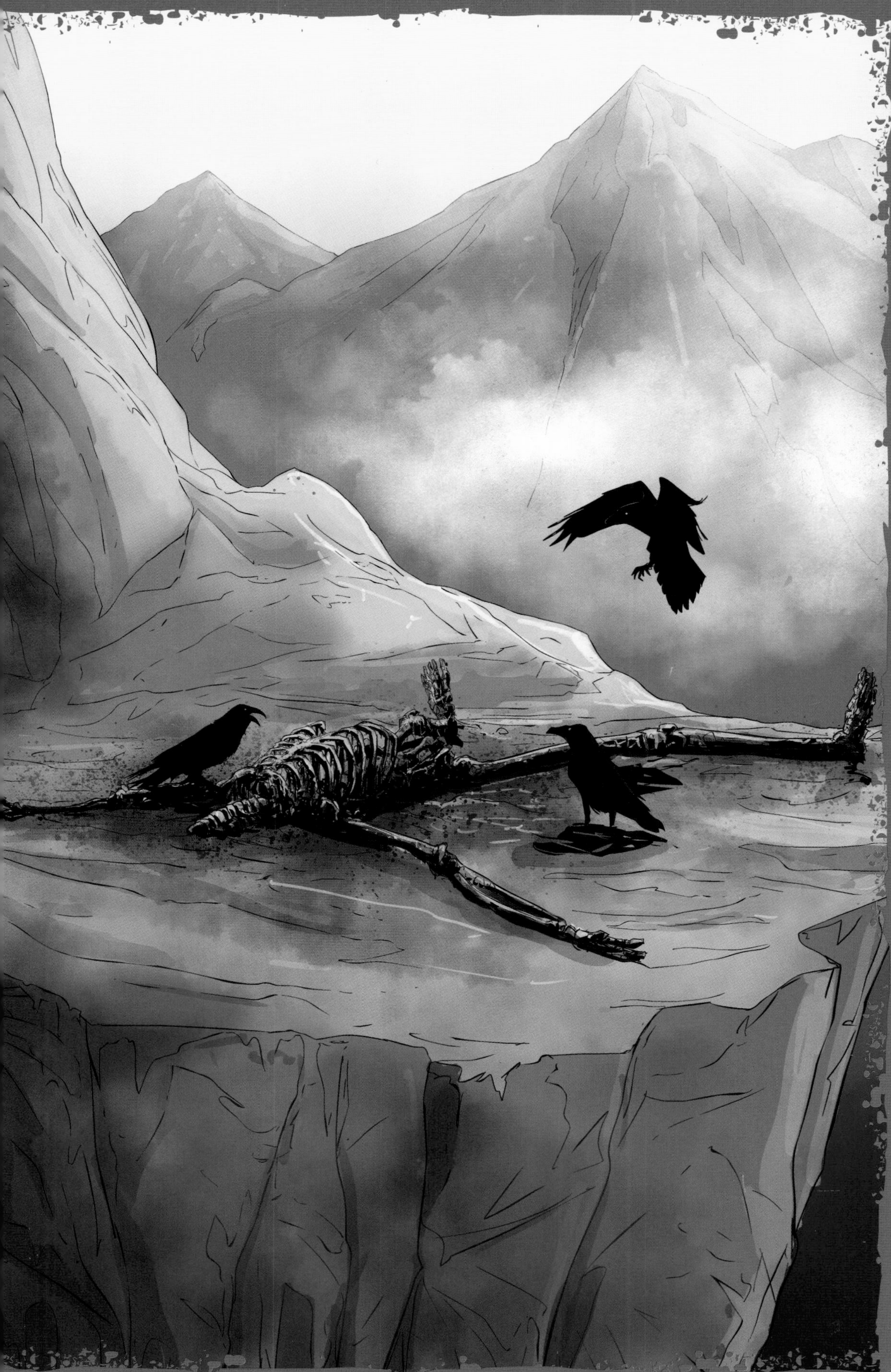

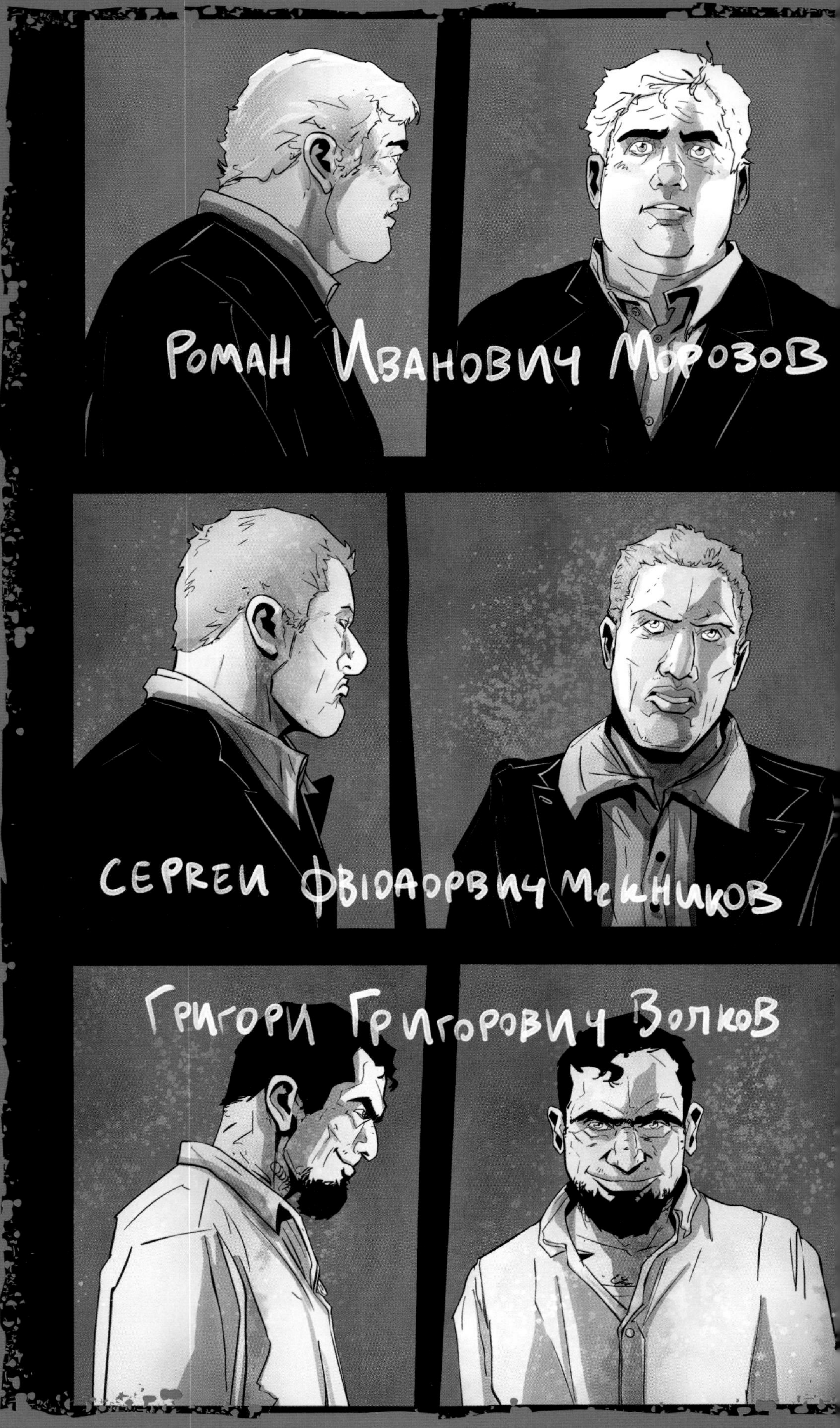

Роман Иванович Морозов
СЕРГЕИ ФВІОАОРВИЧ МсКНИКОВ
Григори Григорович Волков

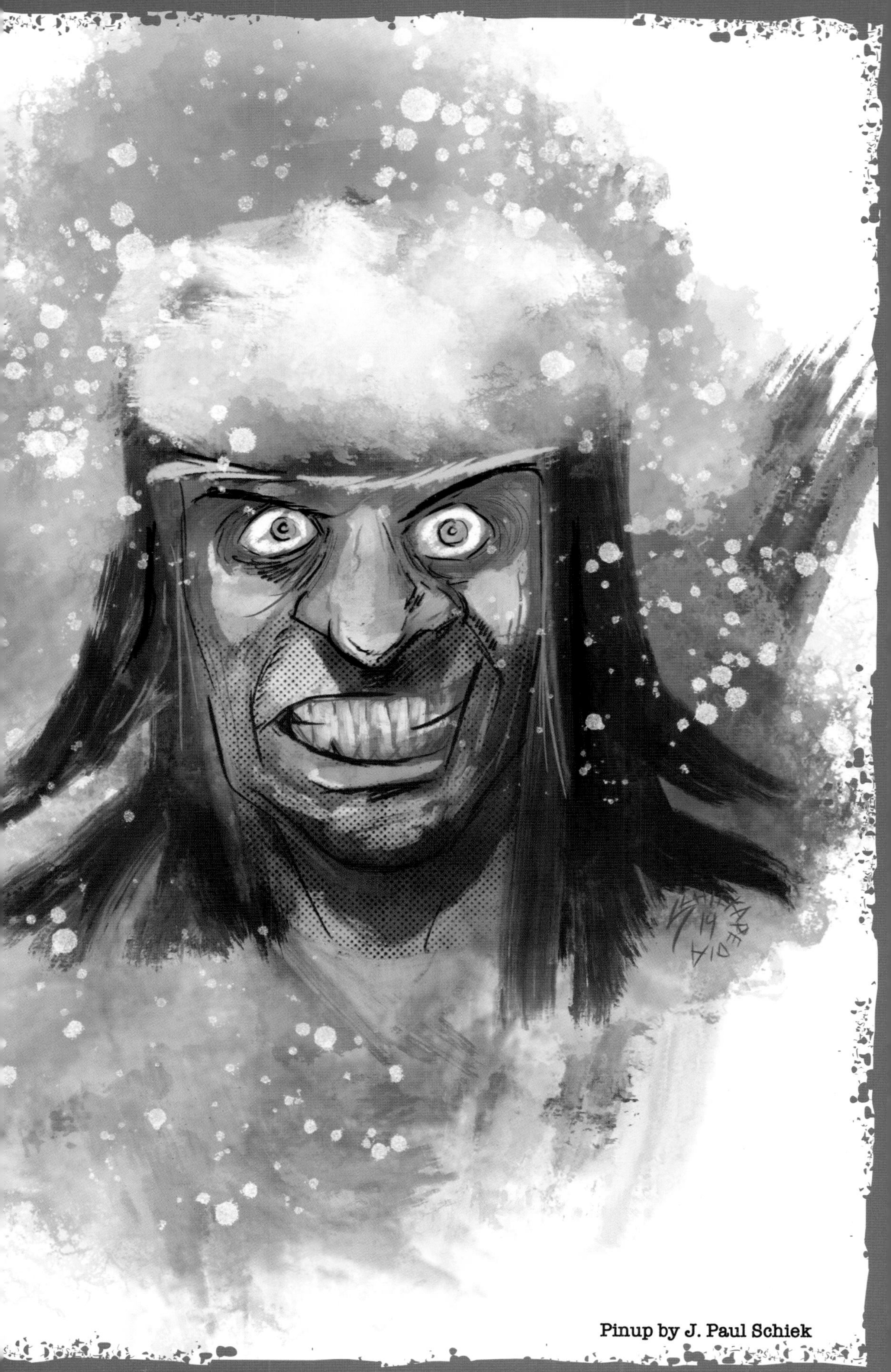

Pinup by J. Paul Schiek

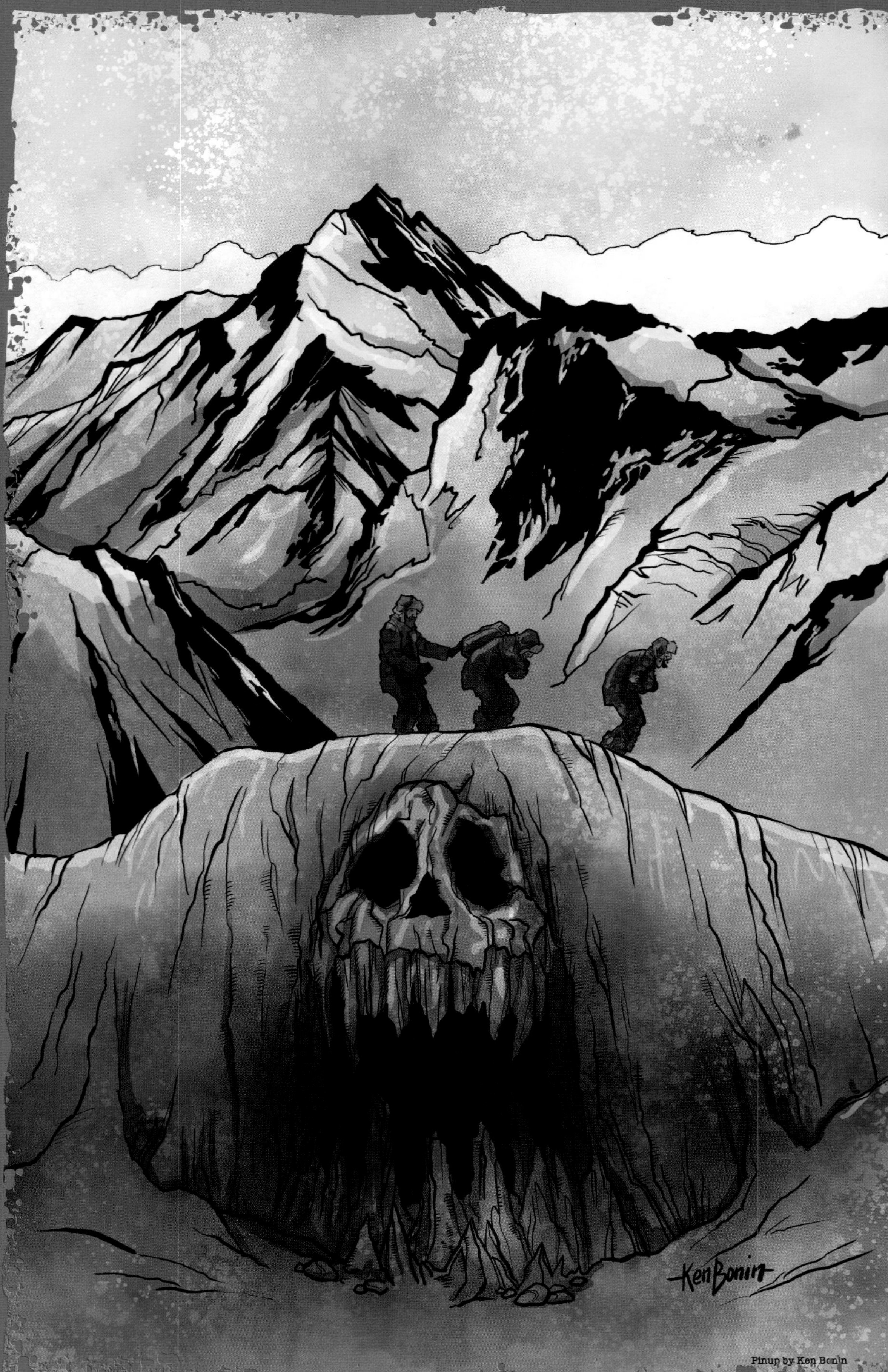
Ken Bonin

Pinup by Ken Bonin

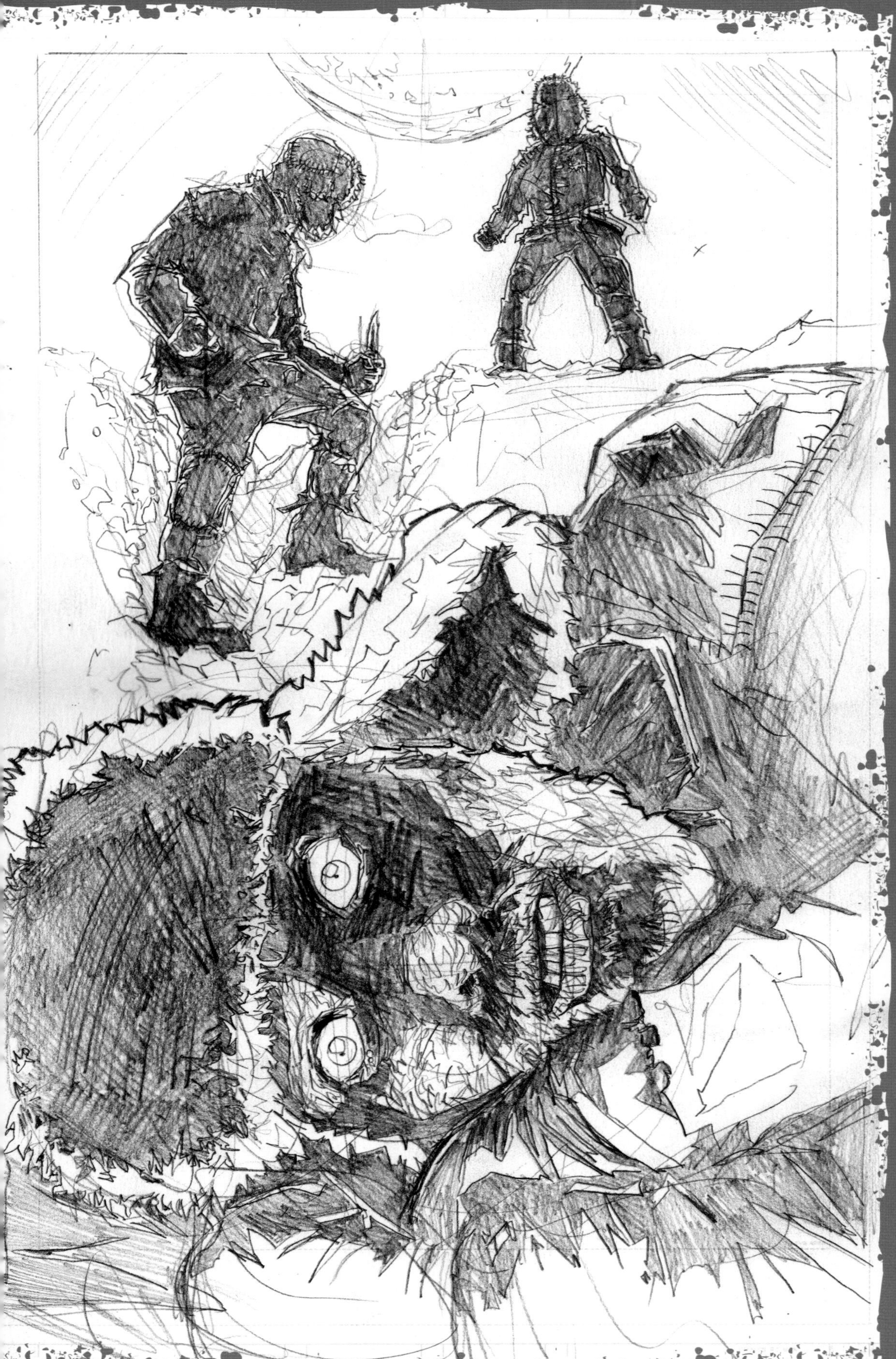

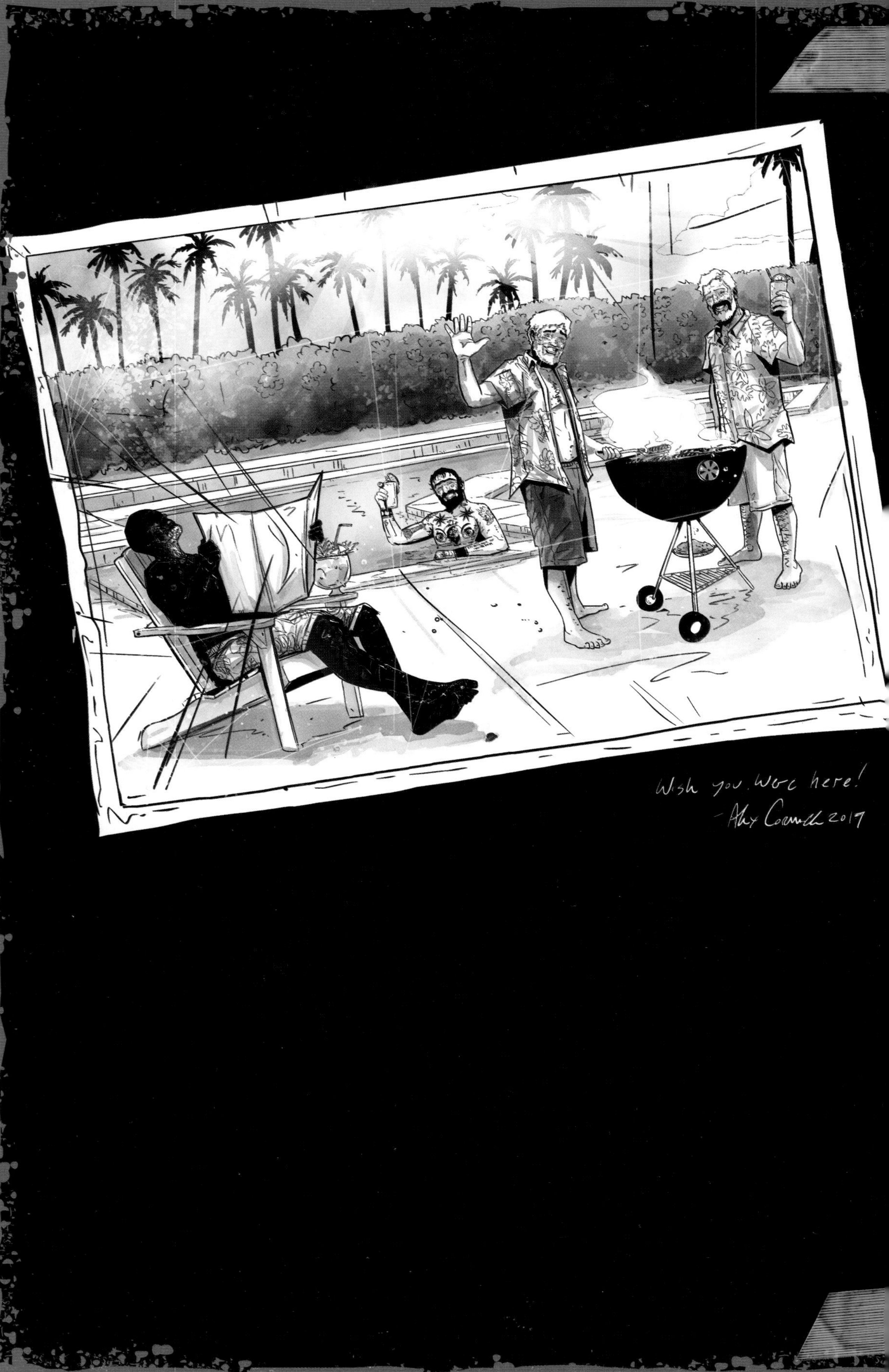
Wish you were here!
-Alex Cormack 2017